上海紧缺人才培训工程教学系列丛书

英语高级口译资格证书考试

总主编　戴炜栋

高级口语教程

第三版

An Advanced Course of Spoken English

Third Edition

严诚忠　戚元方　编著

 上海外语教育出版社

外教社　SHANGHAI FOREIGN LANGUAGE EDUCATION PRESS

图书在版编目（CIP）数据

英语高级口译资格证书考试高级口语教程／
严诚忠，戚元方编著.－3版.
—上海：上海外语教育出版社，2006（2007重印）
（上海紧缺人才培训工程教学系列丛书）
ISBN 978-7-5446-0044-6
Ⅰ.英… Ⅱ.①严… ②戚… Ⅲ.英语－口语－资格
考核－教材 Ⅳ. H319.9

中国版本图书馆CIP数据核字（2007）第012987号

出版发行：上海外语教育出版社
        （上海外国语大学内） 邮编：200083
电　　话：021-65425300（总机）
电子邮箱：bookinfo@sflep.com.cn
网　　址：http://www.sflep.com.cn http://www.sflep.com
责任编辑：刘　璟

印　　刷：江苏句容市排印厂
经　　销：新华书店上海发行所
开　　本：890×1240 1/32 印张10.125 字数290千字
版　　次：2006 年8月第3版 2007年2月第2次印刷
印　　数：20 000 册

书　　号：ISBN 978-7-5446-0044-6 / H · 0012
定　　价：16.80 元

本版图书如有印装质量问题,可向本社调换

总　序

　　由上海市人民政府教育卫生办公室、市成人教育委员会、中共上海市委组织部、市人事局联合组织编写的"九十年代上海紧缺人才培训工程教学系列丛书"将陆续出版。编写出版这套丛书是实施上海市紧缺人才培训工程的基础工作之一，对推动培养和造就适应上海经济建设和社会发展急需的专业技术人才必将起到积极的作用。

　　九十年代是振兴上海、开发浦东关键的十年。上海要成为国际经济、金融、贸易中心之一，成为长江流域经济发展的"龙头"，很大程度上取决于上海能否有效地提高上海人的整体素质，能否培养和造就出一大批坚持为上海经济建设和社会发展服务，既懂经济、懂法律、懂外语，又善于经营管理，擅长国际竞争，适应社会主义市场经济新秩序的多层次专业技术人才。这已越来越成为广大上海人民的共同认识。

　　目前，上海人才的状况不容乐观，与经济建设和社会发展的需求矛盾日趋突出。它集中地表现在：社会主义市场经济的逐步确立，外向型经济的迅速发展，新兴产业的不断崛起，产业产品结构的适时调整，使原来习惯于在计划经济体制下工作的各类专业技术人才进入一个生疏的境地，使原来以面向国内市场为主的各类专业技术人才进入一个同时面向国内外市场并参与国际竞争的新天地，金融、旅游、房地产和许多高新技术产业又急切地呼唤一大批新的专业技术人才，加剧了本市专业人才总量不足、结构不合理的状况。此外，本市的从业人员和市民的外语水平与计算机的应用能力普遍不高。这种情况如不能迅速改变，必将会影响上海的经济走向世界，必将影响上海在国际经济、金融、贸易中的地位，和在长江流域乃至全国经济发展中的作用。紧缺人才培训问题已引起上海市委、市政府的高度重视。

　　"机不可失，时不再来。"我们要大力加强紧缺人才的培训工作和外语、计算机的推广普及工作。鉴于此,及时出版本丛书是当前形势之急需,其意义是深远的。诚然,要全面组织实施九十年代上海紧缺人才培训工程还有待于各有关方面的共同努力。

在"九十年代上海紧缺人才培训工程教学系列丛书"开始出版之际,感触颇多,简述代序。

上海市副市长　谢丽娟

序

　　处于新世纪的中国,改革开放不断深化和发展,对外交流日趋密切和频繁。作为国际大都市的上海与世界各国在经济、金融、贸易、文化、教育等领域的合作越来越多,对外语人才,特别是精通英语、并能熟练进行英汉互译的英语人才的需求也越来越大。为了适应这一需求,早在 1995 年,上海市便启动了"上海市英语高级口译资格证书考试"项目。该项目由上海市委组织部、市人事局、市教育委员会和市成人教育委员会组织和确认,由上海市高校浦东继续教育中心具体负责,为"九十年代上海紧缺人才培训工程"项目之一。十余年来该项目成果斐然:考试规模不断扩大,考生人数、生源范围等不断发展;相关教程、培训等的普及性、社会认可度等不断增强。应该说,这个项目为培养更多高素质、高层次的英语口译工作者,为推动上海经济和文化的发展做出了巨大贡献。

　　一个合格的口译工作者应具备扎实的语言功底,在听、说、读、写、译等方面都达到较高的水平。在该项目进行过程中,英语口译资格证书教材编委会认真规划、精心编写了《高级翻译教程》、《高级听力教程》、《高级口语教程》、《高级口译教程》和《高级阅读教程》,分别供笔译、听力、口语、口译和阅读五门课程教学使用。这套教程因其目的明确、题材广泛、内容丰富、体例科学、新颖实用而广受欢迎。十余年来,为了保持教材的时代性和实用性,编委会已经组织专家学者进行过一次修订。2005 年在广泛征求各方反馈意见的基础上,上海市高校浦东继续教育中心召开考试大纲和教程修订会议,组织相关编者进行第二次修订。各位编者广泛选材,精心编写,反复研讨,认真审核。修订后的教程进一步拓展了选材范围,更加注重内容的新颖性和应用性。如《高级口语教程》不仅包括语言学习、交际技巧、教育政策等内容,还介绍了世博会、奥运精神、和谐社会等国际国内的热点问题。《高级口译教程》不仅涉及到中国改革、外交政策、文化交流等内容,还介绍了外事接待、大会发言、人物访谈等实用交际知识。同时,该套教程适应社会需求,强调理论与实践的有机融合。如《高级听力教程》增加了"英语高级口译资格证书考试笔试听力部分综述",更新了四套模拟试题,以进一步提高学生的理论认识,帮助他们分析听力材料,掌握临战技能。《高级翻译教程》不仅设计了大量的英译汉、汉译英练习,还增加了"英语高级口译资格证书考试笔试翻译部分简介"和六套翻译考试模拟试题。这对于学生熟悉翻译技巧,提高翻译能力不无益处。

多年的培训和考试实践证明,这套教材编排得当、科学实用。学生经过严格的培训,切实熟悉教材内容和掌握相关技能之后,可以进一步提高自己的英语综合水平,适应笔试和口试的形式和要求,顺利通过"上海市英语高级口译资格证书"考试。而这套教材的2006年修订版具有很强的针对性和实用性,不仅对通过参加培训考试以获得"上海市英语高级口译资格证书"的读者十分有用,而且对于提高英语学习者的口译水平、综合能力和整体素质等也大有裨益,值得向广大英语爱好者推荐。该套教材的修订和再版将使"上海市英语高级口译资格证书考试"项目日臻完善,为培养更多的新世纪外语紧缺人才做出贡献。

戴炜栋

上海外语口译资格证书考试委员会顾问

上海外国语大学校长

2005 年 11 月

前 言

作为上海紧缺人才培训工程的一个重要项目，上海英语高级口译资格证书考试自 1995 年开考至今已举办 21 期，参考人数逐年增加，尤其是最近几年，每次参考人数都以两位数的百分比增加。参加 2005 年 9 月考试的人数超过 1.4 万，比 1995 年参加首次考试的 700 多人增加了 20 倍。历年参加上海英语高级口译资格证书考试的人数累计已超过 9 万，其中近 0.8 万多人通过考试并获得了上海英语高级口译资格证书。考点的设置除上海外已扩大至江苏(南京、苏州)、浙江(杭州、宁波)、湖北(武汉)、江西(南昌)、山东(青岛、烟台)、广东(深圳)等地。上海英语高级口译资格证书考试作为考核和遴选紧缺翻译人才的项目经受了时间的考验，引起社会广泛的关注，并得到了领导、专家、学者的高度肯定。

2004 年，原上海市教育委员会主任郑令德教授对上海市高校浦东继续教育中心(以下简称"中心")组织和实施的上海外语口译资格证书培训和考试项目(项目)作了这样的评价：

"十多年来，'中心'走的是一条不断努力超越自我、探索创新之路，走的是着力塑造品牌特色、依靠质量取胜之路，走的是依法依规管理、可持续发展之路。在当前培训市场竞争激烈，国外各种证书纷纷'抢滩'我国继续教育市场的情况下，上海市外语口译资格证书培训与考试项目能得到人才市场的认可，广大学员的青睐，用人单位的欢迎，实属不易，值得庆贺。"

同年，以上海外国语大学校长戴炜栋教授为组长的专家评审组对上海外语口译资格证书培训和考试项目研究报告进行了评审。戴炜栋教授代表评审组作了这样的评价：

"经评审后，专家组一致认为：上海市外语口译资格证书培训和考试项目以市场需求为导向,在考试中突出对'综合应用能力'的评估,不断开拓创新,十年来考生人数持续增加,考试规模不断扩大,市场的认可度提高,该项目已走出上海,向海内外扩展,已成为一项重要的岗位资格证书。"

在项目的成功发展中,英语高级口译资格证书考试系列教程(以下简称"教程")起了重要的作用。这套教程1996年8月由上海外语教育出版社出版发行,2000年经修订后又出版了第二版。教程着眼于为口译资格培训和考试服务,为培养口译人才服务,既强调从事口译工作所必须具备的英语综合运用能力的培养,又突出口译工作的特点和实际需要,目标明确,设计有创意,特点明显,内容新鲜,实用性强,因而受到广泛的欢迎。第二版自2000年发行以来多次重印,截至2005年6月,《高级口译教程》印刷了12次,印数接近21万册,《高级翻译教程》印刷了10次,印数达13万册;《高级听力教程》印刷了6次,印数达11万册;《高级口语教程》印刷了7次,印数近11万册;《高级阅读教程》印刷了8次,印数近10万册。

第二版出版已有5年多,这期间国际和国内形势发生了不少变化,教程部分内容需要更新,读者在使用教程过程中也提出了宝贵的意见和建议。为了使教程更好地为英语高级口译资格证书考试项目服务,作为这个项目的主办单位,上海市高校浦东继续教育中心和上海外语口译资格证书考试委员会于2005年决定修改第二版教程。同时为了在更高层面上实施教程的修改,聘请一直关心和支持外语口译资格证书考试项目的戴炜栋教授担任第三版教程的总主编。戴炜栋教授欣然接受聘任,对教程的修改给予了极大的关注,听取了有关英语高级口译资格证书考试大纲修订和教程修改工作的报告,并提出了重要的意见。他指出,教程用了5年,不少内容过时,必须修改;选材的面应扩展,量应增加;文化知识应作为重点。

在戴炜栋教授指导下,经过英语口译资格证书考试专家组讨论,确定了教程修改工作的基本思路,即:1. 修订英语高级口译资格证书考试大纲,使项目定位更准确,教程的修改向新编大纲靠拢;2. 原有的框架和体例不变;3. 内容需作大幅度调整,选材的面应扩展:一是根据项目近年来的运行情况和口译工作的需要,有针对性地增加一些内容;二是注意时效性,充实近年来国际和国内的热点问题;4. 修改后的教程内容应更广泛、更典型,更好地体现英语高级口译的特点和要求,使用更方便。

为了实现这个目标,参与修改工作的专家殚精竭虑,精益求精。在专家们的努力下,修订后的教程体现了以上四条基本思路。首先,每本教程中课文更新的幅度一般都在1/3以上,《高级听力教程》的课文更换超过1/3,听译部分更换了半数以上的练习材料;《高级翻译教程》新的内容占总量近1/2;《高级口语教程》几乎更新了全部内容。其次,针对从事口译工作可能遇到的情况和需要,增加了一些内容。《高级口译教程》在"口译概论"部分增加了3节,即"口译的模式"、"口译的培训"和"口译的研究";考虑到在贸易领域从事口译的人员很可能需要翻译一些与合同、协议书有关的内容,《高级翻译教程》的编者在中译英部分增加了"对外经济合同的一般条款",与英译中部分的类似内容相呼应,引导参加培训和考试的学员注意和培养在商务和法律范围内进行翻译的能力。第三,鉴于口译工作的特点是接触到的永远是最新的语言表述形式,修改后的教程无论是题材还是语言对这一点体现得很充分。通过学习教程,学员可以接触到近年来国际和国内的热点问题及有关的背景知识,认识并掌握一些相应的语言表述形式。

教程的第一和第二版主编孙万彪和教程的编者周国强教授、梅德明教授、严诚忠教授、戚元方和陈德民教授齐心协力为教程的开发和发展做出了重要贡献。第三版教程仍由原编者担纲编写,其中听力、口译、口语教程还配有录音磁带,可以说第三版教程是在前两版基础上的提升和发扬光大。

对第三版教程的出版,上海外语教育出版社给予了全力支持,社长庄智象教授亲自过问和安排编辑出版事宜,各责任编辑为教程的出版不辞辛苦,认真负责,对他们高效率的工作,我们表示由衷的感谢。

上海外语口译资格证书考试委员会办公室的工作人员为教程的编写和出版做了大量不可或缺的事务性工作,有效保证了教程的修改得以顺利进行。

希望第三版教程的发行出版能进一步推动英语高级口译资格证书考试的发展，能为有志于从事口译工作的人们提供他们所需要的帮助和指导。对于教程中存在的问题和不足之处，欢迎专家、学者、使用教程的教师、学员和读者提出意见和批评，以便编者及时改进。

张永彪　编审

上海外语口译资格证书考试委员会副主任

2005 年 12 月

编 者 的 话

　　作为上海英语口译资格证书考试高级口译项目应试培训指定教材之一，《高级口语教程》已经过两度修改与优化。我们所一贯坚持的编写宗旨在于帮助具有一定英语基础的成人学员提高交际会话中的表达能力和技巧。考虑到学习对象以通过上海英语高级口译资格证书考试为目的，并希望通过强化训练切实提高口语水平，以胜任一般的陪同接待、业务洽谈和英汉口译工作要求，本书 2006 年重新修订改编的指导思想定位于：遵循成人外语学习规律，选择多方面的语言题材，注重时效性、口语化和实用性。在培训过程中，通过指导和组织学员进行有效的演练，以期在短期内取得显著成效。

　　近年来，由于全社会英语学习效果与水平的提高，面临淡出和淘汰的各类英语口语教材大多以很具体的情景会话为内容，偏重于引导学生进行"固化"的机械性操练，而相对忽视学生的主动表达能力，致使学生（由于心理上和习惯上的原因）在学习中局限于跟读和背诵，虽能说几句英语，却很难体现较高的口头交流能力，更别说在实践运用中继续提高了。根据高级口译人员口语技能的要求，在本书的编写中，我们注重培养系统性专题表述的技能，希望探索通过有意识地进行"朗读理解——操练运用——自主表达"三位一体有机循环的实践操练，把学员业已掌握的英语知识和技能"盘活"、"变现"，以流畅的口语沟通效果实现"学以致用"的最终目标。这也是一名英语口译人员所必备的基本素质。本书内容编排上以一学期为限，设计了 16 个单元。各单元语言教材的选题涉及语言学习、交际原理、日常生活、科学技术、旅游观光、社会热点、教育政策、环境保护、经济贸易等方面的内容，为口语表达实践提供话题、表达方式、思路和操练等方面的参照性材料。每一单元都采用相似的体例，包括："核心课文（The Core Text）"、"访谈范例（Sample

Interview)"、"知识性阅读材料与小组讨论（Information Input and Group Discussion)"，以及"演讲范例与表达练习（Sample Speech and Oral Practice)"四方面具有一定内在联系的内容。

使用本书作为口语训练教材，始终应该强调的有两个要素。一是教师的语言素质条件和启发、组织能力。实践证明，学生学好口语，好教材的作用远不如好教师。教师能否组织动员学生、相互配合、营造良好的语言环境气氛是有效发挥本教材特点的关键和保证。二是学生的自觉程度和学习能力。语音、语调和基础水平固然重要，但在课堂教学中，全班学生基础参差不齐是普遍的现象。因此，在大量朗读兼顾背诵的前提下，增强"开口讲话"的内在动力、克服"多讲多错"的心态、抓紧讨论和演讲的实践环节，以及强化语言的组织和表达能力则是取得口语学习效果的最根本要素。光凭"弄懂、弄通书本"是远远不够的。教师在处理教材时可视具体情况作适当调整、取舍或有所侧重。帮助学生正音并传授一些语音、语调方面的知识技巧是很必要的，但不宜做过多的理论性讲解。学生则应充分重视课前、课中、课后的实践性训练，认识"自主、自觉和自为"理念在语言学习中的关键性作用。

在教材修编中，我们坚持尽量少地用汉语注释，因为语言学习本质上是一个自主认知的过程，感性认识的作用尤为重要，由于采用的词汇和语句都十分浅近、常用，而且口语化，估计学生在学习理解上不会有大的困难。当然，作为服务于应试培训的教材，本书按考纲要求编写，对考试的形式和内容有较强的针对性。但是，提高英语口语能力绝非仅仅为了应付某次考试。我们的信念是：口语能力的提高有赖于在不同的客观情景和主观条件状态下对语言的实践运用，只有多练，方可"熟而生巧"。而教材的功能无非在于提供教学上的参考性依据和相关语言材料而已。相信新版教材是完全能起到这一作用的。因此，本书也可作为大专院校英语专业口语教材，或供高层次自学者选用。

限于编者的水平，该修订版中疏漏和缺陷在所难免，希望得到各方面专家学者的指正和批评，以便改进。本书的修订改编、资料重组和校勘仍由东华大学严诚忠和华东理工大学咸元方两位教授合作主持，孙丽君参与了编写。在 PCEC 有关领导和张永彪教授的指导下，我们在坚持语言的实践性和应用性,把握考试委员会所确定的《考纲》精神和要求方面取得了新的共识。蒙本丛书主编戴炜栋教授及其他各位编委和专家组成员的指点,使本书新版在原有的基础上得到了提高。谨此致谢。

严诚忠　戚元方
乙酉年秋于沪上

使 用 说 明

  这本 2006 年修订本《高级口语教程》的编写宗旨是为具有一定基础的、有志参加上海英语高级口译资格证书考试者提供英语口语训练的语言材料。它以强化口头表述能力为核心,通过多种形式和不同题材,综合地训练和提高使用本教材的学员运用英语作为口头交际(oral communication)手段的能力。在现代社会生活中,一个人的交际技能,特别是外语交际技能的提高,其价值和意义远远超过任何一次考试本身。鉴于我国外语学习的历史和现状,如能促使越来越多的学习者切实地完成从理解到运用的跨越,以提高沟通效果为导向,造就一批高素质的口译人才将大有益于在新世纪新形势下推进我国的对外经济文化交流。

  在过去五年多使用本教材第二版的实践中,很多学员获得了口头表达能力的切实提高,证明了教与学两方面的相互配合和主观能动性的充分发挥是使口语训练达到其既定目标的关键。口语学习重在训练,而这种训练又是一个以自我表达为核心的认知与实践的过程。它受到学员的语言条件、思维方式、心理素质、环境氛围等多方面因素的制约,只有通过点滴进步的积累和不断的创造性的运用,才能突破各种不利因素的束缚而取得期望的成绩。学习的效果只能通过在实际运用中的交际沟通水平的提高来检验。

  基于以上认识,编者在坚持一贯宗旨的基础上对使用新版教材提出几点教学建议,仅供教与学两方面参考。

  一、对本教程的结构和系统有一个整体的理解。《高级口语教程》的基本体例为 16 个单元的课文主体,每个单元又分为"核心课文"、"访谈范例"、"知识性阅读材料与小组讨论",以及"演讲范例与表达练习"等四方面内容。

二、关于课堂教学。在以 220 至 240 学时为基准的应试培训时段内,用于口语教程的时间是十分有限的,教师不可能按常规"精读"的教法实施口语的教学。因此,教师可选择本书部分单元或各个单元中的部分内容进行重点指导或练习,或指导学员有重点地利用课外时间进行个别单元内容的学习。在每单元的教学过程中,根据编者的经验,应首先强调句子正确与流畅的表达(造句)。在此基础上,建立合理的思路则是连贯表达的实质,以及口语训练的目的所在。同时,通过以段落为单位的言语操练,有助于学员在短期内掌握"有长度的英语口头表达(to talk at length)"的机理。本教材中,每一单元的核心课文大多取材于原版英文短文或新闻报道材料,经过筛选与改写,使之更加口语化,在篇幅容量上也同口语考试大致匹配。学生可被要求背诵课文和阅读材料中的相关段落,一则从朗读中形成正确的语音、语调,二则记忆若干有用的句型和表达方式。访谈范例提供了不同情景和话题下的人际交流实例,作为学习如何"有效对话"的参考资料。学生可按需要将其用于对话操练或由学生进行合理的"改编",做到消化吸收,为我所用。知识性阅读材料有长有短,着重提供更多的专题性表达的示范,也有助于学生直接引用其中的句型或现成的表达方式。每一单元的练习主要提供话题和基本思路,让学员自我拓展与发挥,训练其运用语言的能力。有条件的班级应该选择适当的话题,尽量开展不同规模的课堂讨论(classroom discussion)和公开演讲(public speaking),让学员经受有一定环境压力的表达训练,克服心理紧张情绪。实践证明,这是非常有效的教学措施。总之,教师在口语训练中的主导作用是不言而喻的。

三、关于预习和复习。本教材的编纂意图立足于要求学员通过预习和复习养成自我认知和自我训练的习惯。口语训练光靠有限的课堂教学时间显然是不够的。对核心课文和知识性阅读材料内容的理解、培养针对口译实践要求迅速建立思路和组织表达的能力、不间断地朗读操练,以及为课堂上的表达练习做准备等都需要大量的课余时间。做好这方面的动员和组织工作,辅之以有效的检查和组织口头陈述是非常必要的。在此,编者再次提醒教师和学员:应该重视课外学习内容和时间的搭配!在口语训练中,这本《高级口语教程》不仅仅是传统意义上的教科书和读本，要弄懂弄通，它还应起到在整个教学过程中的"指导和参谋"作用。请汲取教学方法论的格言：提高口语能力的根本在于——不断地观摩别人的表述和积极的自我实践！

　　在突破我国传统英语教学的旧模式、培训英语高级口译人才的全过程中，口语训练是其中的"基础技术课"，也是全套系列教材和全部教学内容的有机组成部分。很难设想一个不具备良好的口语功底者，能够胜任各种不同场合的译员工作。"任重而道远"，每位学员只有通过时间和精力的合理、优化配置，充分发挥现有基础的潜力和学习的主动性，才有可能在较短的时间内，通过教师的有效指导，迅速提高英语口译所需要的综合能力和素质，为国际化人才的培养探索出一条更为有效的路子来。

编　者

乙酉年秋于沪上

目 录

Unit *One*

Unit *Two*

Unit *Three*

Unit *Four*

Unit *Five*

Unit *Six*

Unit Seven

Unit Eight

Unit *Nine*

Unit *Ten*

Unit *Eleven*

Unit *Twelve*

Unit Fifteen

Unit Sixteen

Unit One

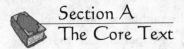

Section A
The Core Text

Secrets of Powerful Speaking

Public speaking, just the thought of it, sends shivers down the spines of so many. In fact, when people are asked to identify their greatest fear, public speaking is typically the number one response.

If you think I'm going to tell you that public speaking is simple and that anyone can become an accomplished speaker overnight, guess again. It's not that easy. But at the same time, I'm not here to discourage you. The truth is you can become an effective speaker, no matter what you think of your current speaking ability — or lack of it! Naturally, it will take some effort and preparation. But developing your public speaking skills is well worth your while. Here's why.

Organizations are always looking for effective communicators, so when you demonstrate that you can speak persuasively in public you'll advance more quickly in your career. You'll also build confidence and self-esteem, which will carry over into everything you do. You'll be more influential in your interactions, both personally and professionally. You'll be able to contribute to the lives of others by informing them, entertaining them and inspiring them.

After nearly 20 years as a speaker, I've come to the conclusion that you need two things to lay the **groundwork** for an effective presentation. You must be knowledgeable about the subject matter and you must be passionate about the topic. Everything else can be learned, but if you don't have these two things, you won't be very effective.

First, let's talk about knowledge. You don't have to know everything on the subject. However, the audience should feel that you've done research and/or have personal experience in that area. In short, you should know what you're talking about. That said, knowledge alone is not enough. You can be extremely knowledgeable, but if you aren't enthused about the subject, the audience will feel it and tune you out. Great speakers have a passion for what they're expressing.

At this point, I know many of you are still thinking, "I'm just too afraid to speak to groups of people." You may find this hard to believe, but fear has nothing to do with your ability to speak effectively. Unless you're paralyzed to the extent that you can't even open your mouth, fear is irrelevant. It's okay to be afraid. It's okay if your voice is shaking a bit. You can still be a tremendous speaker.

I know many professional speakers who are terrified before they go out and speak. You'd never know it, and they do a **fabulous** job each time. I have some nervousness before I speak, but it doesn't get in the way of my presentation. On the other hand, I know many speakers who are perfectly relaxed every time they speak. Here again, they captivate the audience consistently. The point is that fear is not what separates good speakers from bad speakers. And fear is not what's preventing you from being a good speaker.

The only thing standing in your way is technique. There are

several techniques that great speakers use to be effective communicators; ineffective speakers seldom use these methods. Here are the keys to success for delivering effective presentations of five minutes or longer.

Speak from notes — not from a verbatim script. There's nothing wrong with having notes to remind you of the main points you want to include. On the other hand, when you read from a prepared script, you "disconnect" from the audience and people get bored. You should know the topic well enough to speak from notes. At the beginning, you'll be nervous and you may need to look at your notes a lot. That's fine. As you speak more often, you'll rely on your notes less and less.

Keep it conversational — Most people think they have to use big words or alter their normal speaking style when they speak in public. Not true. Use simple words and convey them just as you would if you were sitting with friends in your den. You'll come across as "real" and establish **rapport** with the audience. It's okay to pause or to be less than perfectly articulate. After all, isn't that the way you speak at home? Of course, if you say "um" or "like" consistently, that's something you have to work on. But don't feel that you need to be absolutely perfect.

Use stories to illustrate your points — People love stories and they remember stories years later. So, if you want people to pay attention and to remember your presentation, tell stories that support your points. You may think that you can just **spout** lots of substantive material and facts without using **anecdotes**. You can — but you won't be as effective.

Where do you get your stories? Your most effective stories come from your own personal experiences. Think about something that happened to you, a co-worker, or a member of your family. Think about funny habits or traits that you have. There's no shortage of material. Of course, your story should be relevant to the point you're making.

Sprinkle humor throughout your presentation — There's a well-known saying among professional speakers that "you only have to use humor if you want to be paid!" Humor keeps people interested, gets them laughing and builds rapport. Here again, the humor should be relevant to the point you're making.

Use **props** and involve the audience — Variety creates interest. Take a break from simply being a "talking head" and introduce a prop or an audience participation exercise now and then. Most speakers think they need to use multimedia graphics or hi-tech gadgets to hold the audience's attention.

Prepare a powerful closing. An effective closing usually has two components — First you briefly summarize the points you made in your presentation. For instance, "This afternoon, we covered three strategies for effective networking." You then quickly state those principles again. Second, you want to leave the audience with a "call to action" — that is, you want to inspire or challenge them to use the material you've just given them.

Finally, please don't worry about whether these techniques will work for you. The truth is, they work for everyone. Put in the effort to apply these principles in your next presentation and I promise you that you're going to get an audience response like none you've ever gotten before!

Notes to the Text:

groundwork	基础，根基
fabulous	寓言般的，神话般的；惊人的，难以置信的
rapport	和谐，亲善

spout	滔滔不绝地讲
anecdote	轶事,奇闻
sprinkle	洒,喷洒;点缀
prop	小道具

⊙ Understanding the Text:

1. According to the author, what makes an effective speaker?

2. What are the possible advantages of being a good communicator in public?

3. How should we lay the groundwork for an effective presentation?

4. How many strategies or skills are mentioned in the passage? What are they?

5. Why does humor play a critical role in delivering an effective speech to your audience?

6. What are the two important components of a powerful closing in a speech?

Section B
Sample Interview

Strategies for Public Speaking

News Reporter: What led you to write *Working the Room*?

Morgan: Two things: first of all, in 17 years of coaching people, I've seen the same issues come up repeatedly and I wanted to put some of the stories down on record. And, I wanted to express the ideas I developed working with clients.

News Reporter: What are some of those issues you've seen over and

6

over again?

Morgan: Many speeches, especially in the business world, are important for the speaker but end up boring the audience. So one issue is how does the speaker break through that mediocrity of connection and take full advantage of a speaking opportunity? Another issue, of course, is just fear. Everybody has nervousness associated with public speaking. Traditional speech coaching involves tricks like physical relaxation and visual imaging, and there's nothing wrong with those techniques. If you have powerful abilities to visualize, that's one of the best ways to get over the fear. But what I have found is that when you have great content, a lot of the nervousness goes away. What we tend to think of as a performance question really has more to do with the preparation you do beforehand.

News Reporter: Part of that preparation is to figure out what audiences really want when they listen to a speech. So what do audiences want?

Morgan: Well, the wonderful thing about audiences is that they want to be enthralled and moved. They come in with a positive attitude in spite of the fact that they have been disappointed so many times. Audiences want you to succeed. That support is yours to squander. If you fail to connect, midway through your speech the audience will no longer be on your side — they will be looking for the exit. Keep in mind that audiences vote with their feet when they come to listen to you. They give you provisional authority over them for an hour or 90 minutes, and they want you to do something for them.

News Reporter: How do you know when you have made that connection to the audience?

Morgan: A successful speech takes your audience on a journey from why to how. Audiences come in asking why — Why am I here? Why is this important to me? They want the answer to be that this is going to be good for them in some way. If you succeed, by the end of your speech they will be asking how — How do I do what you are talking about? How do I get to work on this? That's when you know you have gotten your message across.

News Reporter: So how do you go about preparing a speech that accomplishes that?

Morgan: It always begins with the audience. You need to sit down and think, not about yourself and the information you want to convey, but about the audience. Who are they? What do they care about? What do they fear? What is going to move that audience? Then there are the practical questions — What time of the day is the speech going to be? How many people will be in the room? After you have thought through all that, then you can start to think about how the information you have will connect with the audience. I can always tell watching a speech the difference between somebody who has thought about the audience and somebody who hasn't. And it's more than just saying,

"Anybody here from Dubuque?" A lot of professional speakers are adept at putting in little touches that give the appearance of connecting with audiences. But there is a difference between that and truly understanding what makes an audience tick and why you are the right person at the right moment for that audience.

News Reporter: For many business speakers, stories are a lead-in or an afterthought. Do you think stories have a legitimate part to play in a good speech?

Morgan: Stories are essential for the simple reason that the mind works in stories. Neurological research has shown how we construct the world from the time we are babies. Take this scenario: a baby in a highchair spills a glass of milk. A parent comes running, cleans it up and makes all kinds of noises. That's pretty exciting. What you have there is an agent, the baby, an action, pushing over the milk, and an object or result, the milk goes on the floor — a little story. At the simplest level that's what stories are: agents, actions and objects. That's how our minds work and how we absorb information. Too many speeches just dump facts on the audience. We don't retain things that way. Stories help us retain information because they respect the way the mind works.

News Reporter: Is there a risk that your speech might fall flat if you end up the hero of a quest or journey story?

Morgan: Yes, that has to be handled carefully. But people do love underdog stories. For example, the classic tale of a person who came from the school of hard knocks had to overcome many obstacles and is now a success. That genre of story can be powerful for an audience if it is told with genuine humility and honest attention to the mistakes made along the way. The audience members have to see enough of themselves in the story that they think they could do that too. The humanity of the speaker has to come across for that kind of story to work. It leaves you cold when it's all about glorifying the speaker. Then it's repellant because the speaker leaves the audience out of the circle of glory.

News Reporter: Thanks for some great tips.

Section C
Information Input and Group Discussion

Directions: *Read the passages and discuss the questions with your classmates. You may base your discussion on the information given in the passage or on your own ideas.*

1. The Art of Oral Presentation

Oral presentations, like written presentations, can enhance a person's reputation within an organization. Therefore, consider every speaking opportunity an opportunity to sell not only your ideas but also your competence, your value to the organization. Being an effective speaker requires you to:

- understand the context of your presentation;
- analyze your audience;
- choose and shape your presentation's content;
- organize your presentation;
- choose an appropriate speaking style.

Understand the Context of Your Presentation

In order to design an effective oral presentation, you should understand the situation or context of your presentation. For example, delivering a presentation at a meeting of project directors is different from briefing other people in your team about what you've been doing. Making a presentation at a company picnic is different from delivering a presentation at the annual meeting of a professional society. Knowing the situation is as important as knowing your audience and your purpose. In many cases, situation will be inextricably bound up with questions of audience attitude and the way you shape your purpose. Audience attitude frequently results from situational problems or current issues within the organization, and what you can or should say in your presentation, your purpose and the content you choose to present may be dictated by the context surrounding your presentation and the perspective that your audience brings.

Questions for Discussion:
1. Why is it important to understand the context of your presentation?
2. What is the broader concern underlying the need for a presentation?
3. How does your presentation fit into the organizational situation?
4. How does your talk relate to other participants' actions?
5. What is the context of your presentation when you sit for the advanced oral test?

Analyze Your Audience

Analyzing your situation is often difficult to separate from analyzing your audience; in fact, audience is one facet of the larger situation.

Just as readers determine the success of written communication, audiences determine the success of oral presentations. Writing or speaking is successful if the reader or listener responds the way you desire: the reader or listener is informed, persuaded, or instructed as you intend and then responds the way you want with goodwill throughout.

Just as writing effectively depends on you understanding your readers as thoroughly as possible, effective speaking depends on you understanding your listeners. You cannot speak or write effectively to people without first understanding their perspective. You must know how your audience will likely respond based on its members' educational and cultural backgrounds, knowledge of the subject, technical expertise, and positions in the organization.

When you analyze your audience, focus on its members' professional as well as personal attributes. Your audience members will pay attention to some things because they belong to a specific department or class; they'll react to other things because of their likes, dislikes, and uncertainties. You have to keep both profiles in mind. Your analysis will suggest what you should say or write, what you should not say, and the tone you should use.

These are particularly crucial ones, since you need to know, before you begin planning your presentation, whether your audience will consider you trustworthy and credible. To be an effective speaker, you must know your audience, establish a relationship by being sincere and knowledgeable about the subject, and then

12

conform to their expectations about dress, demeanor, choice of language, and attitude toward them and the topic.

Questions for Discussion:

1. Why is it significant for you to know about your audience?
2. To what extent do they play a critical role?
3. Is it vital for you to know how much they know about the subject you are going to talk about?
4. In what ways can you get to know about their interests, expectations and attitudes towards your talk?
5. Shall we know about their educational/cultural/ethnic backgrounds?
6. Who will be your audience members when you sit for the oral test? Do you know about them?

Choose and Shape Your Presentation's Content

Preparing an oral presentation often requires the same kind of research needed for a written report.

You will need to determine what information you will need. In selecting content, consider a variety of information types: statistics, testimony, cases, illustrations, history, and particularly narratives that help convey the goal you have for your presentation. You will also want to choose information that will appeal to your audience — particularly their attitudes, interests, biases, and prejudices about the topic. Because listening is more difficult than reading, narratives can be particularly effective in retaining the attention of your listeners. While statistics and data are often necessary in building your argument, narratives interspersed with data provide an important change of pace needed to keep your listeners attentive.

Audiences generally do not enjoy long presentations. Listening is difficult, and audiences will tire even when a presentation is utterly smashing. For that reason, as you design your presentation and select content, look for ways to keep your message as concise as possible. Don't omit information your audience needs, but look for ways to eliminate non-essential material. Again, without carefully analyzing your audience's attitude toward the subject, and their backgrounds, knowledge of the topic, and perspective toward you, you cannot begin to make accurate decisions regarding the content of your presentation.

Questions for Discussion:

1. What is important for you to do while designing the presentation's content?
2. How many types of information will you consider while selecting the content?
3. What can be particularly effective in retaining the attention of your audience?
4. What can you do to appeal to your examiner as far as the content is concerned?

Organize Your Presentation

The structure of an oral presentation is crucial for one main reason: once you have spoken, the audience cannot "rehear" what you have said. In reading, when you do not understand a sentence or paragraph, you can stop and reread the passage as many times as necessary. When you are speaking, however, the audience must be able to follow your meaning and understand it without having to stop and consider a particular point you have made, thereby missing later statements. To help your audience follow what you say easily, you must design your presentation with your audience, particularly their listening limitations, in mind.

14

Helping your audience follow your message easily requires that you build into your structure a certain amount of redundancy. That means that you reiterate main points. When you divide your presentation into an introduction, the main body, and the conclusion, you are building in this necessary redundancy.

The introduction should clearly tell the audience what the presentation will cover so that the audience is prepared for what is to come. The body should develop each point previewed in the introduction. In the introduction, you state the main issues or topics you plan to present. Thus, in designing the body of the presentation, you develop what you want to say about each of these main points or ideas. The conclusion should reiterate the ideas presented and reinforce the purpose of the presentation. It usually answers the question: "So what?"

Questions for Discussion:

1. Why is the structure of an oral presentation crucial?
2. What is the most important for the introduction part of your speech?
3. How can you come to a sound conclusion at the end of your presentation?
4. Based on your purpose and the audience's expectations, in what order will you present your ideas?

Choose an Appropriate Speaking Style

How you sound when you speak is crucial to the success of your presentation. You may have effective content, excellent ideas, and accurate supporting statistics. However, if the style you use in speaking is inappropriate to the occasion, to the audience (as individuals and as members of an organization), or to the purpose you are trying to achieve, your content will more than likely be ineffective.

In general, you want to sound respectful, confident, courteous, and sincere. However, the precise tone and degree of formality will be dictated by your organizational role and your relationship to your audience.

Style in writing refers basically to your choice of words, the length and structure of your sentences, and the tone, or attitude you express toward your audience. Style in delivering oral presentations is also defined by these same characteristics plus many nonverbal cues that can either enhance or detract from your presentation. While the style you use will vary with the audience, topic, and context, always consider the following guidelines that can enhance your delivery style:

Avoid long, cumbersome sentences. Use phrases, and use a variety of sentence lengths. Avoid excessively long, complex sentences, as listeners may have difficulty following your ideas.

Avoid overuse of abstract, polysyllabic words. Instead, use concrete language that your audience can visualize.

Avoid overuse of jargon, unless you are sure that your audience will be readily familiar with all specialized terms.

Use sentences that follow natural speech patterns.

Use short, active voice sentences.

Avoid memorizing the presentation verbatim — doing so will likely result in a presentation that sounds as though you are reading rather than talking to the audience.

The most effective style is usually a conversational style: short sentences, concrete language, speech that suggests to your audience that you are really talking to them. If you concentrate on getting your point across by having a conversation with the audience, you will likely use a natural, conversational style.

Questions for Discussion:

1. Based on the information above, what is the most effective style?
2. What does an appropriate speaking style stand for?
3. In order to make your speech more persuasive, what should be done and what should be avoided?
4. What techniques or skills do you usually use while giving a presentation?
5. According to your personal experience, which technique or skill is the most effective while delivering a speech?

2. Body Language Speaks Louder than Words

Directions: *Read the following short passages about **body language** and discuss them with your partner by giving your own opinions.*

- Eye contact is the most obvious way you communicate. When you are looking at the other person, you show interest. When you fail to make eye contact, you give the impression that the other person is of no importance. Maintain eye contact about 60% of the time in order to look interested, but not aggressive.
- Facial expression is another form of nonverbal communication. A smile sends a positive message and is appropriate in all but a life-and-death situation. Smiling adds warmth and an aura of confidence. Others will be more receptive if you remember to check your expression.
- Your mouth gives clues, too, and not just when you are speaking. Mouth movements, such as pursing your lips or twisting them to one side, can indicate that you are thinking about what you are

hearing or that you are holding something back.

- The position of your head speaks to people. Keeping your head straight, which is not the same as keeping your head on straight, will make you appear self-assured and authoritative. People will take you seriously. Tilt your head to one side if you want to come across as friendly and open.

- How receptive you are is suggested by where you place your arms. Arms crossed or folded over your chest say that you have shut other people out and have no interest in them or what they are saying. This position can also say, "I don't agree with you." You might just be cold, but unless you shiver at the same time, the person in front of you may get the wrong message.

- The angle of your body gives an indication to others about what's going through your head. Leaning in says, "Tell me more." Leaning away signals you've heard enough. Adding a nod of your head is another way to affirm that you are listening.

- Posture is just as important as your grandmother always said it was. Sit or stand erect if you want to be seen as alert and enthusiastic. When you slump in your chair or lean on the wall, you look tired. No one wants to do business with someone who has no energy.

- Control your hands by paying attention to where they are. In the business world, particularly when you deal with people from other cultures, your hands need to be seen. That would mean you should keep them out of your pockets and you should resist the urge to put them under the table or behind your back. Having your hands anywhere above the neck, fidgeting with your hair or rubbing your face, is unprofessional.

- Legs talk, too. A lot of movement indicates nervousness. How and where you cross them tells others how you feel. The preferred positions for the polished professional are feet flat on the floor or legs crossed at the ankles. The least professional and most offensive position is resting one leg or ankle on top of your other knee. Some people call this the "Figure Four." It can make you look arrogant.

- The distance you keep from others is crucial if you want to establish good rapport. Standing too close or "in someone's face" will mark you as pushy. Positioning yourself too far away will make you seem standoffish. Neither is what you want, so find the happy medium. Most importantly, do what makes the other person feel comfortable. If the person with whom you are speaking keeps backing away from you, stop. Either that person needs space or you need a breath mint.

Section D
Sample Speech and Oral Practice

Part A Sample Speech

How to Make a Good Presentation

Many oral presentations of individuals are 10 to 20 minutes long with 15 minutes being the most common. It is very difficult to get and then keep your audience's attention long enough for them to get and then be convinced of your point. Your presentation has to be very clear and concise with a few very well selected, absolutely clear visual aids. Unless you happen to be the first speaker, your audience is already fatigued from hearing other talks and the competition from extraneous sounds and the slow pace of talking vs. thinking has probably left much of the audience daydreaming about more interesting topics. You will lose your audience after just one moment of droning on semi-intelligibly about numbers in front of an unreadable slide covered with unintelligible lines or a table stuffed with even more numbers. Some pointers include:

When you speak, make sure that your topic is obviously relevant to the audience's clinical interests or they won't begin to listen.

Decide just what message you want to get across, and then plan your talk and slides based on how you are going to do it.

Tell the audience what you are going to tell them, tell it to them, and tell them what you told them — then ask for questions.

People have a lot of trouble following oral presentations because they can't flip back a page or two to pick up a point they missed so you need to be very well organized and leave out all information which doesn't lead directly to your goal.

Your slides need to be very clear. Nobody can follow a graph with more than a few lines, and tables with more than three columns and rows (or so) are hopeless because of size and complexity. Having the main points of the talk on successive slides presented as you go is a big help, but keep the verbiage down to a few lines per slide. Get rid of any slides the audience doesn't need to follow your talk. They are simply distractions. Slides full of text can't be read at the same time you talk, so people miss both.

Your key slides are the title of your talk, a simplified diagram of the study design, a summary of the key results, and a few slides on the conclusions.

Practice your talk so you get the length right. Assume that you will go slower on stage. While practicing, get some emotion into your voice (other than terror) and learn to give the talk from an outline. People that read their talks well are incredibly rare. Usually they present in rushed, boring monotones which few people follow.

If you keep these in mind and practice frequently in your daily life, you are sure to get a good result.

Part B Presentation Practice

Directions: *Talk on each of the following topics for at least five minutes. Be sure to make your points clear and logical with adequate supporting details.*

Topic 1: A good speaker is made not born.
Questions for reference:
1. How do you understand the statement that a good speaker is made not born?
2. Is there any in-born ability such as eloquence (for example, some can speak fluently without great efforts while others can't)?
3. Do you believe that the seemingly effortless talks given by experienced speakers are in most cases the result of hours of thinking, painstaking preparation, and practice?
4. According to your personal experience, what makes a good speaker?

Topic 2: Body language speaks louder than words.
Questions for reference:
1. Do you agree or disagree with the statement that body language speaks louder than words?
2. Can you mention some expressions of the body language you have often used while talking with others?
3. What are the possible advantages and disadvantages of using body language?

Topic 3: Is English a passport to a better life?

Questions for reference:

1. English is getting increasingly popular in our country. Why are so many Chinese people enthusiastic about English learning?
2. What English levels are required of Chinese people in their different careers and jobs? Can you give some examples?
3. Do you think English is a passport to a better life? Give your reasons or evidence to support your answer.

Part C More Topics for Oral Practice

Directions: *Based on the news reports, talk on each of the following topics for at least five minutes. Be sure to make your points clear and logical with adequate supporting details.*

News Report 1:

It is inevitable for a speaker to make a mistake during his or her speech and one of the best ways to deal with it is to learn to laugh at your mistake. Stand-up comedians are excellent examples. When they make a mistake, they would just incorporate the mistake into their performance as if it were also one of their prepared jokes (or part of their act). And the audience members would laugh not knowing the comedian actually made a mistake.

Topic: *Do you think laughing at your mistakes is the best policy to overcome the feeling of embarrassment? What else can you do to suppress this feeling?*

News Report 2:

China is probably one of the few countries in the world where learning English has almost become a national obsession. However, most people spend much but gain little. Our teaching and testing systems have deviated from the initial purpose of English learning in that it teaches and encourages elite English instead of practical one. Beneficiaries are limited to those who intend to study overseas. Yet, to the millions who have little use of the language, it is a great waste of time, energy and resources.

Topic: *Is it necessary for the whole nation to be crazy about English?*

News Report 3:

Suggestions for ways to put the brake on the capital's rapid population expansion were put forward by members of the public at a forum sponsored by the Beijing municipal government last month. One of the proposals was making it harder for non-Beijingers to settle in the city. Barring migrants that do not have *hukou*, or permanent residence registration, would naturally slow population growth. This seemingly effective and direct method has provoked fresh heated discussions among sociologists and demographers.

Topic: *Should we put the brake on the rapid expansion of urban population and what should be done to control this quick expansion, stop the waves of migrants, set up certain restrictions, or build more satellite towns?*

Part D Useful Expressions

1. All the great speakers were bad speakers at first.
2. The best way to conquer stage fright is to know what you're talking about.
3. Talking without thinking is like shooting without taking aim.
4. You can speak well if your tongue can deliver the message of your heart.

5. Once you get people laughing, you know they're listening and you can tell them almost anything.

6. Only the prepared speaker deserves to be confident.

7. Grasp the subject, the words will follow.

8. Say not always what you know, but always know what you say.

9. Don't talk unless you can improve the silence.

10. Talk to a woman as if you loved her, and to a man as if he bored you.

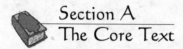

Section A
The Core Text

From Competence to Commitment

Today's students have ambiguous feelings about their role in the world. They are devoting their energies to what seems most real to them: the pursuit of security, the accumulation of material goods. They are struggling to establish themselves, but they also admit to confusion: Where should they put their faith in this uncertain age? Undergraduates are searching for identity and meaning and, like the rest of us, they are torn by idealism of service on the one hand, and on the other hand, the temptation to retreat into a world that never rises above self-interest.

In the end, the quality of undergraduate education is to be measured by the willingness of graduates to be socially and **civically** engaged. Reinhold Niebuhr once wrote, "Man cannot behold except he be committed. He cannot find himself without finding a center beyond himself." The idealism of the undergraduate experience must reflect itself in loyalties that transcend self. Is it too much to expect that, even in this hard-edged, competitive age, a college graduate will live with integrity, **civility** — even compassion? Is it appropriate to hope that the lessons learned in a liberal education will reveal themselves in the **humaneness** of the graduate's relationship with others?

Clearly, the college graduate has civic obligations to fulfill. There is urgent need in American teaching to help close the dangerous and growing gap between public policy and public understanding. The information required to think constructively about the agendas of government seems increasingly beyond our grasp. It is no longer possible, many argue, to resolve complex public issues through citizen participation. How, they ask, can non-specialists debate policy choices of consequence when they do not even know the language?

For those who care about government by the people, the decline in public understanding cannot go unchallenged. In a world where human survival is at stake, ignorance is not an acceptable alternative. The full control of policy by specialists with limited perspectives is not tolerable. Unless we find better ways to educate ourselves as citizens, unless hard questions are asked and satisfactory answers are offered, we run the risk of making critical decisions, not on the basis of what we know, but on the basis of blind faith in one or another set of professed experts.

What we need today are groups of well-informed, caring individuals who band together in the spirit of community to learn from one another, to participate, as citizens, in the democratic process. We need concerned people who are participants in inquiry, who know how to ask the right questions, who understand the process by which public policy is shaped and are prepared to make informed, discriminating judgments on questions that affect the future. Obviously, no one institution in society can single-handedly provides the leadership we require. But we are convinced that the undergraduate college, perhaps more than any other institutions, is obliged to provide the enlightened leadership our nation urgently requires if government by the people is to endure.

To fulfill this urgent obligation, the perspective needed is not only national, but also global. Today's students must be informed about people and cultures other than their own. Since man has orbited into space, it has become dramatically apparent that we are all **custodians** of a single planet. In the past half century, our planet has become vastly more crowded, more interdependent, and more unstable. If students do not see beyond themselves and better understand their place in our complex world, their capacity to love responsibly will be dangerously diminished.

Throughout our study we were impressed that what today's college is teaching most successfully is competence — competence in meeting schedules, in gathering information, in responding well on tests, in mastering the details of a special field. Today the capacity to deal successfully with **discrete** problems is highly prized. And when we asked students about their education, they, almost without exception, spoke about the credits they had earned or the courses they still needed to complete.

But technical skill, of whatever kind, leaves open essential questions: Education for what purpose? Competence to what end? At a time in life when values should be shaped and personal priorities sharply probed, what a tragedy it would be if the most deeply felt issues, the most haunting questions and the most creative moments were pushed to the **fringes** of our institutional life. What a monumental mistake it would be if students, during the undergraduate years, remained trapped within the organizational grooves and narrow routines to which the academic world sometimes seems excessively devoted.

Students come to campus at a time of high expectancy. And yet, all too often they **become enmeshed in** routines that are deadening and distracting. As we talked with teachers and students, we often had the uncomfortable feeling that the most vital issues of life — the nature of society, the roots of social injustice and indeed the very prospects for human survival — are the ones with which the undergraduate college is least equipped to deal.

The outcomes of collegiate education should be measured by the student's performance in the classroom as he or she becomes proficient in the use of knowledge, acquires a solid basic education, and becomes competent in a specific field. Further, the impact of the undergraduate experience is to be assessed by the performance of the graduate in the workplace and further education.

But in the end, students must be inspired by a larger vision, using the knowledge they have acquired to discover patterns, form values, and advance the common good. The undergraduate experience at its best will move the student from competence to commitment.

Notes to the Text:

civically	公民地,民事地
civility	礼貌,斯文
humaneness	深情,慈悲
custodian	看守人;监护人
discrete	不连续的,离散的
fringe	[常作～s]边缘,界限
become enmeshed in	陷入,卷入

Understanding the Text:

1. What does the author mean by saying "from competence to commitment"?

2. What are students' ambiguous feelings about their roles in the

world?

3. How do you understand the statement that the idealism of the undergraduate experience must reflect itself in loyalties that transcend self?

4. Why does the author say the college graduate has civic obligations to fulfill? What are these obligations?

5. What will happen if students do not see beyond themselves or better understand their place in our complex world?

6. What does the author want students to be?

Section B
Sample Interview

Europe versus America in High Education

News Reporter: You seem to be quite critical towards the American system. Then why do you think many European students want to go to the US to study?

Jamie Merisotis: I think it is because of a non-accurate portrait of the USA higher education system. Some projects are working pretty well, though. What attract people are also a heterogeneous system and the possibility of being part of a society which seems diverse and which actually is in certain places. It used to be that the private meant more quality, but now the situation is changing. Some public universities are doing a better job than the private ones.

News Reporter: Could you name some of them?

Jamie Merisotis: For example, Michigan, Berkley and California are more selective than the private ones. The research universities are doing the best job, also because they get money from the government and also from the private institutions.

News Reporter: What do you think about European's project of creating a Higher Education Area?

Jamie Merisotis: If you actually do it, you are going to kick our asses. We are not prepared for that.

News Reporter: However, now we are facing another menace, the potential inclusion of higher education in the so-called Bolkestein Directive. What is your opinion about that?

Jamie Merisotis: The more modification we do in education, the more democratic values we lose. But I think it is very positive that the students are aware about that. In the USA, at universities, they do not know anything about the GATS.

News Reporter: One of Merisotis's most important commitments is the improvement of access to higher education for low-income, minority, and other underrepresented populations.

Jamie Merisotis: The investment in inclusion pays off in the public and private scales and from the social and economic points of view. But if we fail in inclusion, social and economic disparities will grow and there will be higher mortality and more health problems.

News Reporter: What can we learn in Europe from the American system?

Jamie Merisotis: The US example provides a rich set of experiences and lessons, but we cannot apply it wherever, though. Each nation needs to address its unique context. The diversity of institutions is a plus in terms of inclusion, for example. But for example women are still heavily underrepresented in certain fields like hard science or business. In Medicine they got equality for the first time last year. Also parenthood makes the situation much more difficult for them.

News Reporter: And what can the USA learn from the European system?

Jamie Merisotis: There is a lack of leadership among the students in the States. I will try to steer them towards Europe. They have a lot to learn from you.

News Reporter: The introduction of private funding will change priorities in university priorities?

Jamie Merisotis: Yes. I think it can orientate them to more economical, beneficial purposes.

News Reporter: The possible risks of private funding of universities, will they fall into the rules of the market? Will this harm the independence of higher education?

Jamie Merisotis: The US experience may be useful in the sense that we have long had a diversely funded higher education system. We rely heavily on private funding of universities, and in fact in the last decade the proportion of state support for public universities has declined and the private funding has increased. Much of this private funding has come from tuition fees, which have increased very sharply in a short period of time. Public universities also have become more involved in alumni fundraising, as well as in various types of public/private partnership. There are certainly risks to the independence of institutions that face more and more pressure to raise private funds. There are also opportunities, however, in terms of innovation of programs and services. So the market does have some benefits. I don't think that the "market" and public funding are therefore mutually exclusive terms. What is most important, however, is what impact these market strategies have on student access to higher education. Where is the student in these private funding equations? Absent from any serious consideration of the consequences, you can easily end up in a situation where you have the wealthiest students going to university, and others being left behind.

Section C
Information Input and Group Discussion

Directions: *Read the following passages and discuss the questions with your classmates. You may base your discussion on the information given in the passage or on your own ideas.*

1. New Policies on College Life

Chinese universities stopped disciplining students for dating about two decades ago. Five months ago, the Education Ministry lifted the ban preventing students marrying. And recently, they revised restrictions on students living outside of university dormitories.

The reasons are simple. First, the revisions represent a humanistic approach in administrating students. Despite all the social expectations of them to concentrate on studying to become an educated elite, they are, above all, young adults. If young people outside universities have the right and opportunities to enjoy romance, an earlier family life, or a freewheeling lifestyle, so should those inside the Ivory Tower.

Second, the step away from overprotection and over-regulation opens up many life choices to students. At the same time it enables them to form new social links. These skills are much needed to allow young adults to grow up independently and find their places in society.

In a society where parental and institutional overprotection and supervision has been omnipresent in most young people's upbringings, these steps are all the more necessary.

Higher education certainly opens up new possibilities for the young to explore, but with supervision and safeguarding regulations prevalent, and parental financial support continuing to a large extent, their experiences of life, and chances of learning from mistakes, are limited. Most of a student's activities and relationships are confined to within the campus walls. In recent years, because of this, internships and other ways of brushing up social skills have soared in popularity, as graduates face a tough job market.

To generate enough independent, responsible (not only educated) youth for Chinese society to prosper, higher education regulators must get real. They must understand the challenges profound social changes are presenting to young people. They should adjust their administration to remove the barriers to individuals' social and personal development.

By giving students the right and opportunities to decide whether to live on or off campus, whether or not to marry, and whether or not to have children while still studying, universities are letting them learn their own valuable lessons.

With this in mind, the revisions are positive signals that things are getting better. They should be carried even further — by, for example, lifting all the rules on dorm living and beyond.

Questions for Discussion:
1. Do you agree with the idea "no romance in the classroom"?
2. What do you think of the new policy allowing undergraduates to get married?
3. Why does the authority come up with this new policy?
4. What are the possible advantages and disadvantages of students marrying?
5. What do you think of the revised restrictions on students living outside of university dormitories?
6. Do you think the benefits of living outside campus outweigh its drawbacks or vice versa?
7. If you were a college student, where were you likely to live, on or off campus? And what are the reasons for your choice?

2. The Function of Universities

The justification for a university is that it preserves the connection between knowledge and the zest of life, by uniting the young and the old in the imaginative consideration of learning. The university imparts information, but it imparts it imaginatively. At least, this is the function it should perform for society. A university which fails in this respect has no reason for existence. This atmosphere of excitement, arising from imaginative consideration, transforms knowledge. A fact is no longer a burden on the memory, it is energizing as the poet of our dreams and as the architect of our purposes.

Imagination is not to be divorced from the facts: it is a way of illuminating the facts. It works by eliciting the general principles which apply to the facts, as they exist, and then by an intellectual survey of alternative possibilities which are consistent with those principles. It enables men to construct an intellectual vision of a new world, and it preserves the zest of life by the suggestion of satisfying purposes.

Youth is imaginative, and if the imagination be strengthened by discipline, this energy of imagination can in great measure be preserved through life. The tragedy of the world is that those who are imaginative have but slight experience, and those who are experienced have feeble imagination. Fools act on imagination without knowledge; pedants act on knowledge without imagination. The task of universities is to weld together imagination and experience.

Questions for Discussion:
1. What do you think is the primary goal of a university?
2. What does imagination mean to you?
3. Did any of your teachers impart his/her knowledge in an imaginative way in the classroom?
4. In your opinion, what is the best way to teach students?
5. Do you believe that there are too many people in the world who are either fools or pedants?

3. Education Equality Calls for Fair Enrolment

Rising tuition fees, the chances of poverty-stricken students entering colleges, enrolment corruption, regional inequality of enrolment, curriculum reforms — all are themes of vigorous public debate.

A topic of hot debate is the regional inequality of the country's college enrolment.

China's colleges are mostly publicly invested, with some key national universities, such as Peking University and Tsinghua University, financed by the central government, and others mainly funded by local governments.

The Ministry of Education sets quotas for these key colleges and universities concerning how many students they should enroll from different regions. They are entitled to make small adjustments to the quota plan.

The issue of regional inequality arises from the fact that many of the high-quality national universities financed by the central government admit a large proportion of students from where they are located, putting applicants from other regions at a "disadvantage."

At Peking University, for example, students from Beijing will account for about 18 per cent of the total this year, according to its main campus enrolment plan.

One result of this enrolment imbalance is that candidates in Beijing can be admitted into Peking University with marks relatively lower than those of students from other regions.

Some people argue that since these national universities are financed by central government funds, or taxation paid by people from all regions, they should not favor local candidates. By not doing so, they are damaging educational equality.

Proponents of the differentiated enrolment policy argue that these universities have received various policy supports from local governments and it is justifiable for them to offer preferential terms to local applicants.

Both arguments hold water, so this is a complicated question with no easy answer.

It is a practice in many countries to favor, to a varied extent, local candidates in the enrolment programs of colleges and universities. In China's case, these top national universities are mostly located in economically prosperous regions, where local taxpayers contribute relatively more to the central government's revenues.

On the other hand, since the country's college enrolment is mainly based on the marks applicants achieve in the national examinations, the region-based selective enrolment policy would lead to the scenario that some students with lesser marks can enter the top universities while others who get higher marks cannot.

Admittedly, given China's unbalanced educational levels among different regions, the student enrolment of a top national university cannot be equally split among different regions if it is to pick the best students. But an excessively preferential policy does not contribute to equality, either.

A long-term solution would lie in the improvement of China's overall higher education system, in which more colleges and universities can offer quality services and compete with those top national ones.

In this way, students would have more choices and educational equality would be better achieved.

Questions for Discussion:

1. What do you think of the regional inequality of college enrolment

in our country?

2. What are the underlying causes of this inequality in college enrolment?

3. Can you give us an example of this inequality in enrolment?

4. What are the possible effects it may bring on society?

5. Who will benefit most from this policy?

6. What can be done to achieve educational equality? Can you make some suggestions?

 ## Section D
Sample Speech and Oral Practice

| Part A | Sample Speech |

To Learn in an Entertaining Way

There are many ways in the process of learning but generally they can be classified into two, learning in an entertaining, enjoyable way or in a serious and formal way. The two different kinds of learning style, respectively speaking, the serious way and the entertaining way, are assumed to produce different results, which can clearly be discerned by comparing the two different education systems of Europe and of the USA. Personally, I vote for the latter, even though I have been taught in the former system from the very beginning of my education.

The disadvantage of the serious way of learning is found mainly in that students frequently fail to participate in a class actively. The teacher dominates the 45-minute period and the students are refrained from airing their opinions no matter whether they agree or disagree with what the teacher says. In this case, standing up and ringing one's view forward and therefore breaking the quiet atmosphere require a great deal of courage and, sometimes, a long-time premeditation. Even though he does stand up, all these will significantly weaken the effect, and for good reason: the extreme constraint prevents him from expressing his opinion. Furthermore, students are expected to learn only what the teacher tells them. They have little chance to take advantage of others' ideas.

Such defects as mentioned above can be prevented by the other way of classroom learning. A class organized in an enjoyable atmosphere usually provides the students with more than what they expected. A joke may inspire students' interest and enthusiasm and then what they learn gives them a deeper impression. A drastic debate among students will prompt them to learn from the others. In this kind of class they often find that they're motivated by the pleasure of studying. I have an American teacher in whose class I have gained so much. He differs from the image of teachers in my mind enormously in many aspects. What impressed me most was his humor. His satiric remarks were invariably infectious. For the first time I found history is not at all boring. In laughter, not only did I learn the knowledge in the book but I also gained some spiritual things brought about by his characteristics and personality.

A light heart is always helpful.

Part B Presentation Practice

Directions: *Talk on each of the following topics for at least five minutes. Be sure to make your points clear and logical with adequate supporting details.*

Topic 1: College education shifting from competence to commitment

Questions for reference:

1. How do you understand the topic itself?
2. What is the relationship between competence and commitment?
3. Why is it important for us to appeal to commitment?
4. What do you think can be done to achieve this goal?

Topic 2: The greenlight to college students planning to get married

Questions for reference:

1. What do you know about the new marriage regulation?
2. What are the possible advantages and disadvantages of university students getting married?
3. Would you consider getting married if you were an undergraduate? Why or why not?

Topic 3: Revising restrictions on students living outside of university dormitories

Questions for reference:

1. What are the possible advantages and disadvantages of this revision?
2. Do you think the benefits of this change outweigh its drawbacks or vice versa?
3. Would you plan to live outside of campus if you were an undergraduate? Why or why not?

Topic 4: Regional inequality in college enrolment

Questions for reference:

1. Do you think it fair that candidates in one region can be admitted into a key university with marks relatively lower than those from

other regions?

2. What are the possible causes of this inequality in college enrolment?

3. What can be done to deal with this problem?

Part C More Topics for Oral Practice

Directions: *Based on the news reports, talk on each of the following topics for at least five minutes. Be sure to make your points clear and logical with adequate supporting details.*

News Report 1:

The Tsinghua University PhD candidate expressed his equivocal disappointment at the university's education methods and the country's overall educational system in a 10,000-word application to quit from one of the country's most famous universities. His largest dissatisfaction was the school's stipulation that doctoral students can only graduate after publishing at least four papers, some of which must be carried by the country's core academic publications.

Topic: *Is it reasonable that doctoral students can only graduate after publishing at least four papers, some of which must be carried by the country's core academic publications?*

News Report 2:

China has decided to lift from September 2005 a 50-year ban on college students marrying or bearing children but schools continue to confuse students by implementing different new rules. Some universities issued the new school regulation that has caused a stir in public opinion nationwide.

Topic: *Is it necessary for schools to issue different rules to restrain* *students from marrying?*

News Report 3:

Figures from the Ministry of Education indicate that about 2.63 million college students in China suffer from poverty, accounting for 19 per cent of the total of 13.5 million students enrolled. Among them, 1.22 million are categorized as "extremely poor" students. However, there is a solution: The "Green Passage" program, in which poor students may enroll and defer tuition payments, helped 290,000 new students enroll on time last year.

Topic: *Can the "Green Passage" program completely solve the problems of poor students? If not, what else do you think can be done to help those poor students?*

Part D   Useful Expressions

president, Chinese Academy of Sciences	中国科学院院长
academician	院士
president, university	大学校长〈美〉
chancellor	大学名誉校长〈英〉
vice-chancellor	（主持学校日常校务的）大学副校长〈英〉
principal	高等教育机构校长、院长〈英〉
principal, school	中小学校长〈美〉
headmaster, school	中小学校长〈英〉
dean, college	学院院长
trustee, Board of Trustees	校董事会董事〈美〉
governor	公立学校理事会理事、私立学校董事会董事〈英〉

dean, Studies	教务主任
dean, General Affairs	总务长
director, department/dean, the faculty	系主任
visiting professor	客座教授
exchange professor	交换教授
honorary professor	名誉教授
class adviser	班主任
teacher of special grade	特级教师
director, research institute	研究所所长
research professor	研究员
associate professor	副教授〈美、加〉
lecturer	讲师
assistant	助教
senior lecturer/reader	高级讲师〈英〉

（英国还有 reader 也可以译为高级讲师，但地位略高于 senior lecturer/reader。）

$\mathcal{U}$nit $\mathcal{T}$hree

Section A
The Core Text

New Zealand — A Beautiful Country

New Zealand is situated in the South Pacific Ocean, over 1,000 miles southwest of its nearest neighbor, Australia. It consists of two principal islands — the North Island and the South Island — and a number of little islands, some of them hundreds of miles away from the main group. Its population is almost 3,000,000. The land area covers over 260,000 square kilometers. About two-thirds of the land is economically developed or developing, the remainder being mountainous, especially good for tourism.

I. The People

Little is known about the time or manner of the arrival of the first inhabitants, the Maori, except that they came over the sea from the North. The first European that arrived in New Zealand was a Dutch sailor, Abel Janszoon Tasman, who sighted the coast of Westland in December, 1642. Like their Australian neighbors, the New Zealanders are overwhelmingly of British stock. Most of the pioneer white settlers came from Scotland. Quite a large body of assisted Dutch immigrants arrived in the country during the 1950s. Today many of New Zealand's cities still retain a distinct flavor of

Edinburgh and parts of London. There are also groups of Central European architecture built between World War Ⅰ and Ⅱ.

New Zealand is predominantly an English-speaking country. Children of European immigrant families quickly lose their native tongue in favor of English, particularly when their parents are anxious to establish relationships with the existing community. Only Greeks, Chinese and Indians make determined efforts to keep their children bilingual. Many Maori are bilingual, but often unsatisfactorily, speaking neither English nor Maori very well.

II. The Climate

New Zealand's climate is determined by its latitude, its isolation, and its physical characteristics. It has a climate that lets grass grow green the year round. There are no extremes of temperature; it is a sunny land. Many areas, even the cooler areas in the South, enjoy at least 2,000 hours of sunshine a year, much of it occurring in winter. Snow is common only in mountainous regions, but frost is frequent in inland valleys in winter. Rainfall is highest in areas dominated by mountains exposed to the prevailing winds.

III. The Economic Development

Dairy industry is considered to be the most efficient anywhere and the export of dairy products is the largest in the world despite the country's small size and population. Agricultural produce accounts for some 84 per cent of total exports, and forest products for another 6 per cent. Farming in New Zealand is highly mechanized.

Long known as a pastoral country with dairy products leading its economy, New Zealand has begun a diversification of its economy, since World War Ⅱ. Now industry plays a more significant role in its economy than farming. The chief industries are food processing (meat and dairy products), transport equipment, textiles, cement, oil refining, and chemical fertilizers.

IV. The Education

Education in New Zealand is free and compulsory to those between ages of 6 to 15, but almost all children start school at five. Many children attend pre-school classes, which are financially assisted by the government. Nearly all the primary schools are state-owned. State secondary schools offer a broad general academic education with some emphasis on technical training. Students are prepared for an attainment examination (the school certificate) and for tertiary studies, which are provided free to students fulfilling certain academic prerequisites. There are six universities and one agricultural college, as well as several technical institutes. Since the 1960s, the education of the Maori, the native Polynesians who settled in New Zealand about the 13th century, has received great attention. The difficulty of backwardness in education is more social than academic, and its solution may well be within the Maori community itself.

V. The Culture

Since the Second World War there have been great changes in the culture and arts of New Zealand. These changes have much to do with the breaking down of social barriers and the improvement of education. Today, artists, musicians and writers have a much wider public than they had before the war. Far more people now read books and go to the theatres, concerts, picture galleries and fashion shows.

Many of the serious writers of New Zealand were concerned with social and political problems of the present day, among them are: Katherine Mansfield, Ngaio Marsh, and John Mulgan, who are recognized as writers of world fame.

New Zealanders have also been known as great art collectors. Their collections can be seen today in museums, and in picture

46

galleries in many cities which are open to the public. A few artists have been very successful and have had their works accepted by well-known art galleries all over the world, such as Colin McCahon, John Hutton, now having an international reputation.

Because of its rich cultural and natural resources, tourism in New Zealand has been growing rapidly. Now there are about 900 thousand visitors from all parts of the world every year. The Green Precious Stone in the South Pacific has become one of the most attractive places for tourists today.

● Understanding the Text:
1. When did the first European arrive in New Zealand? Who was that person?
2. What nationalities in New Zealand are bilingual?
3. What is the climate like in New Zealand?
4. Can you give a general picture of the culture in New Zealand?
5. Would you like to visit New Zealand some day? Why?

 ## Section B
Sample Interview

Tourism Marketing

Q: You are both an acclaimed tourism marketing practitioner and an award-winning academician. Do you feel tourism marketing is evolving at all as a theory or a practice? Are there any new trends/theories/practices? In turn what parts of past tourism marketing orthodoxy are now considered old-fashioned, or plainly erroneous?

Professor Mann: First of all, it has been suggested that destination marketing is an inappropriate name for what I did during my active career and which I now teach. Marketing, as we all know, consists of the four P's: product, price, place and promotion. Destination marketers, in fact, do not control the first two at all. We are the ultimate middlemen, gathering up information about our destinations and trying to raise awareness and demand. As recently as five years ago, destinations measured their success by the number of inquiries received and brochures mailed out. The Internet has changed all that, thank heavens. Destinations get more sophisticated every day, and are getting smarter about measuring ROI (return on investment) and choosing targeted (and far more effective) promotional techniques.

Q: What is Tourism Marketing for you? Is it just about "meeting the needs of the tourism consumer" or can/should it also try to change/influence the perceived needs of the consumer? Does it annoy you when some people equate "marketing" with "promotion tricks"? And is there any such thing as "ethical marketing" or "fair marketing" as in say, "fair trade," or is there just effective and ineffective marketing?

Professor Mann: Effective and responsible destination marketers tell the truth about their destinations. Travelers today are smart and expect honest descriptions of attributes and activities.

Q: As a managing director of Discover New England you handled the tourism promotion needs of six US states, at the same time, with great success. So, do you believe that government should play a big or even dominant role in tourism promotion, rather than the private sector? Is this view gaining or losing ground around the world?

Professor Mann: The government is the largest beneficiary of tourism dollars in the form of taxes. The government is also the largest stakeholder (parks, national and state). However, the best destination marketing programs are public-private partnerships. Canada and Australia have led the way in these partnership programs, and the rest of the world has been scrambling to catch up over the last ten years or so. I always believed that government's No.1 role in tourism was to serve as the convener, to bring the various members of the tourism industry together to initiative programs, talk about sustainability, etc. Most tourism folks are essentially entrepreneurs, and it's not natural for them to bound out of bed in the morning saying, "Now, what programs can I do in cooperation with the guy next door today?" Turning that competitive spirit into one of cooperation and partnership is, I believe, the No. 1 role for DMOs (destination marketing organizations) today.

Q: You initiated the first US state-level program in cultural tourism. What need was there for such a state-level program, and what would be one main, practical lesson learned for others in the US and around the world wishing to do something similar?

Professor Mann: Partnerships are the key to success in all types of destination marketing. No one institution can do it alone; it takes hotels working with museums working with outdoor sites, etc. to make an effective and appealing destination "offer" to consumers.

Q: What is your evaluation and use of the Internet as a tourism marketing tool? Is it a revolution, a welcome addition, or needle in a haystack?

Professor Mann: The Internet has changed the face of destination marketing forever. However, I've never met anyone who got up in the morning, logged on and did a search for "vacation destinations." The Internet is a powerful information and booking tool, but the customer must already have some awareness of and interest in a destination or they will never visit the destination's site. PR (public relations) remains, virtually without exception, the No. 1 marketing technique in tourism.

Q: One has the feeling that international tourism advertising expenses are spiraling upwards or even out of control, always through a few established channels. Too bad for small tourism businesses? Too bad for small advertisers? How is oligopoly explained in this highly competitive market?

Professor Mann: I'm afraid I don't understand this question. Ninety-five per cent of tourism is small business (under 20 employees). Again, partnerships are the solution to rising promotional costs.

Q: You have extensive experience working for non-profit as well as for-profit sectors in tourism and beyond. With nonprofit sectors becoming more commercial in order to compete for scarce funds, and for-profit sectors showing a more "caring" or corporate social responsibility image, is there really a difference nowadays, beyond tax returns, and are roles as distinct as in the past, when "capitalism was humanized through philanthropy"?

Professor Mann: I've worked in for-profit, government and non-profit sectors. The only difference with the latter is that profits aren't distributed at the end of the year. Smart marketers are caring marketers: telling the truth, preserving destinations, advocating for responsible tourism programs — I don't differentiate between the for- and nonprofit groups doing good work in our field.

Section C
Information Input and Group Discussion

Directions: *Go over the following tables and discuss with your classmates the Benefits and Challenges of Tourism.*

1. Benefits and Challenges of Tourism

Potential Benefits of Tourism

Economic	Social/Cultural	Environmental
Protects and provides a source of income for natural and built heritage		
Enhances the image of an area, attracting commercial investment outside the tourism industry as well, by demonstrating to potential investors that the place is good to locate to		
a. A significant catalyst for economic growth and employment b. Increases demand for other non-tourism businesses	Leads to the creation and maintenance of local amenities	Draws attention to the need to protect the natural environment and encourages a more rigorous analysis of the importance of the local ecosystem
Supports and helps to maintain local services, such as shops and restaurants		
Provides reskilling, training and employment opportunities		
Provides supplementary incomes to those seeking second jobs, part-time hours, unsocial hours		
Encourages residents to stay and spend leisure time		
Encourages the upgrading and reuse of derelict land and buildings		
Brings expenditure from external sources into the local market	Supports a program of events, arts, sports and other cultural activities	

(to be continued)

Economic	Social/Cultural	Environmental
	Helps to build distinctive communities, thus increasing local pride and self-confidence	
	Provides opportunities for social inclusion	
	Encourages cultural diversity	

Potential Challenges with Tourism

Economic	Social/Cultural	Environmental
Tourism is a diverse sector so co-ordination is complex and ongoing		
Tourism spending is dependent on economic, social and other factors. High levels of the dollar can reduce the number and spending power of foreign visitors and discourage citizens to travel overseas		Places strain on transport infrastructure, particularly roads and parking
An economic downturn in source countries can lead to a reduction in visitors, which impacts on businesses in the short or long term depending upon the severity of the downturn	Can be an unattractive sector for people entering the labor market because of unsocial hours, seasonal/part-time work	Can place additional pressure on sensitive local environments and therefore needs effective visitor management
Demand can be seasonal and variable over a weekly cycle, which impacts particularly on employment		
Requires all weather facilities and activities		

(to be continued)

Economic	Social/Cultural	Environmental
It is very competitive and increasingly sophisticated		
Requires ongoing investment from local governments		

Questions for Discussion:
1. How many potential benefits are mentioned in the table?
2. What do you think are the most valuable ones?
3. Do we enjoy all these benefits now? If not, why?
4. In your opinion, how can we make full use of these potential benefits?
5. Do we face the same challenges as listed in the table?
6. What are the most serious challenges we are facing now?
7. What are some of the causes involved?
8. What measures can be taken to deal with these problems?

2. Travelers Need a Dose of Civilization

Despite pressure on the public transport system and overcrowding at tourist attractions, we Chinese still enjoy a week-long holiday.

Hordes of travelers in chic dresses holding dinky digital cameras are a sign of growing material wealth. But media reports during Golden Week serve as a poignant reminder that we lack a different sort of wealth — spiritual wealth, or civilization.

Rampant littering is a common scene at tourist sites during the week. An even more appalling report emerged the day after National Day. A group of tourists from the Republic of Korea picked up rubbish left by Chinese tourists at the scenic spots. I felt humiliated at the news. I do not mean the Koreans humiliated us. We humiliated ourselves. A citizen said: "It's like we invited some guests to our home and they cleaned the house for us."

We have more and more tourists going to other countries. How do they behave in foreign lands? Unfortunately, they carry with them the same uncivilized manners they show domestically.

In March this year, I went to Australia. At Sydney airport, I found a long queue of passengers waiting to pass through customs but saw a group of Chinese thronging around the entrance, making the waiting line swell out of shape. Many new arrivals — sadly, all Chinese — came to join the crowd at the front disregarding the waiting line.

Seeing the situation, Australian customs officers opened another entrance and told Western passengers to queue there. Again I felt insulted, but I knew it was we Chinese who insulted ourselves.

The number of Chinese tourists traveling to other countries has been rising dramatically in recent years. Statistics detailing the number of outbound tourists in the past week is not yet available but it will be huge, for the number has been growing at an average annual rate of 20 per cent over the past ten years, according to official statistics. Last year, 28.85 million Chinese tourists traveled to foreign countries — a rise of 43 per cent over the previous year.

Although it is a small number compared to China's population, the absolute number is still huge. Chinese tourists love shopping. Last year, they spent 127 million pounds in Britain. According to a survey, Chinese tourists spend an average US $987 each when they go abroad — the highest rate in the world.

That explains why so many countries endeavor to be included on the list of China's approved destinations. There are already 76 countries and regions on the list and the number is expected to reach 100 by the end of this year.

It is really embarrassing for a Chinese to see a notice in a toilet in Australia (and in some other Western countries) written only in Chinese that reads: "Please flush after using." There are other similar signs of warning written only in Chinese, for example: "Please don't talk loudly" in hotel lobbies and restaurants.

To be fair, I have to admit that Chinese tourists in foreign countries have abandoned some of their bad habits, such as spitting, littering and crossing streets at will. But there is other behavior that causes foreigners to look shocked that we may not even notice. Talking loudly in public places, for instance, may not be seen as a serious faux pas. But Westerners would think it rude and a breach of public peace.

Respect for privacy is another problem. In a busy airport toilet, for example, we Chinese tend to stand immediately in front of each booth instead of waiting at the entrance.

This may be the result of differences in culture. I do not mean to determine whether the Eastern or Western culture is more advanced in general. I have found that Westerners also commit public offences. Pavements in Sydney are heavily stained with chewing gum residue.

But we Chinese must cast off our bad habits that cause inconvenience to other people or infringe upon their privacy. We need to learn something from other cultures, in terms of ethics, moral standards and social responsibility.

Questions for Discussion:
1. Have you ever seen a scenic spot with rampant littering?
2. How many uncivilized manners are mentioned in the above

56

passage?

3. What are the underlying causes of these bad manners?
4. Why do some foreigners do better than us in these aspects?
5. With the accumulation of material wealth, should we do something to enhance our spiritual wealth, or civilization?
6. What is to be done to improve our civilization? Can you give some suggestions?

Section D
Sample Speech and Oral Practice

Part A Sample Speech

Travel Makes People Wiser

To travel means to go into the nature to enjoy the beauty of mountains, rivers, trees and forests, and also to admire the colorful world beyond the cities. When people travel, they feel refreshed both in mind and body.

With the development of the national economy and the growing prosperity of society, our living conditions have changed greatly. Millions of people begin to travel to understand the outside world. Today people of all walks begin to take advantage of their holidays and travel to other places, and even to foreign countries. To some extent, travel has become part of needs of human beings. From the perspective of individuals, travelers can gain the following benefits from traveling:

First of all, traveling is a sort of relaxation. After working in an office for a long time, people need to go out for smelling fresh flowers. By doing so, people can become refreshed and energetic again.

Secondly, traveling is a part of education. By visiting historic sites and cultural relics, people can obtain a lot of knowledge concerning history, geography, and various social conventions.

Thirdly, traveling can also broaden one's horizons. By visiting scenic spots and meeting various people, travelers will get more social experience.

Fourthly, traveling can enlarge one's social circle. During the trip, people can be exposed to different kinds of people and make a lot of friends.

Besides, Tourism is an industry without pollution. The national treasury can be increased with the influx of foreign currencies, which will become larger and larger with the rapid development of tourism. Thousands of the unemployed can find jobs in the industry, which is always important for a nation.

Furthermore, it leads to the development of transportation, communications and service sectors. China abounds in tourism resources with its beautiful natural scenery, numerous places of historic interest and cultural sites, and its diversified culture.

In general, we all have such experiences. When one returns home from traveling, he is filled with new experiences and knowledge about different languages, customs, food, clothing, architecture, dwellings and ways of life. These enrich our lives and help us realize the greatness of China more and more.

Part B   Presentation Practice

Directions: *Talk on each of the following topics for at least five minutes. Be sure to make your points clear and logical with adequate supporting details.*

Topic 1: The most impressive visit

Questions for reference:

1. How many scenic spots have you ever visited? What are they?
2. Can you describe one of the most impressive visits?
3. Why do you think it is the most unforgettable one?

Topic 2: Travel makes a wise man better, but a fool worse.

Questions for reference:

1. How do you understand this statement?
2. Can you give some specific examples to support your understanding?
3. What benefits and experience can we get from traveling?
4. Why does travel do good to a wise man and harm to a fool?

Topic 3: Travel overseas

Questions for reference:

1. Why do many Chinese like to travel abroad?
2. What are the possible advantages and disadvantage of overseas travel?
3. What preparations can you make before an overseas travel?
4. Do you want to make a trip to a foreign country? If yes, which country do you want to go first? Give your reasons.

Part C More Topics for Oral Practice

Directions: *Based on the news reports, talk on each of the following topics for at least five minutes. Be sure to make your points clear and logical with adequate supporting details.*

News Report 1:

Whether to drive or take a bus is the question. Had policies favored public transport a decade ago, this would not even have to be considered. It is not too late for the State Council to endorse a document from the Ministry of Construction calling for preference to be given to public transport in terms of the development of urban traffic strategy, with the Premier having emphasized the importance of public transport as a means for easing traffic jams.

Topic: *Do you think it vital to make public transport first choice?*

News Report 2:

Trapped in worsening traffic jams, Chinese cities are set to travel the same road as London did: making motorists pay to drive into their city centers. The British capital is said to have moved faster after cutting traffic by 30 per cent with a five-pound-per-car-per-weekday congestion charge launched in 2003. Shanghai is the furthest ahead in taking the inspiration. A feasibility study on introducing its own congestion fees has won a municipal award. Beijing and Nanjing have shown interest in similar schemes. Both have launched studies and consultations.

Topic: *Do you think congestion fees can alleviate urban traffic jams? Do you have any other suggestions to help ease urban traffic crowdedness?*

News Report 3:

The urgency of passing a law to curb blatant job discrimination was never more apparent in one case in Hunan Province. Women from the province applying for government jobs had to demonstrate they had symmetrically shaped breasts. The rule, which had aroused public uproar, was fortunately scrapped in March last year. For years, rigorous requirements for height, gender, age or physique have existed to screen job applicants. Height and weight count, as numerous job advertisements have shown. But the discrimination is a stark violation of human rights. People are born equal. Those who are younger or better looking, hold higher statures, or own a permanent local residence should be in no way considered "more equal" by employers.

Topic: *Job discrimination is prevalent in many places. What do you think can be done to curb this discrimination?*

Part D	Useful Expressions

artificial scenery	人工风景
landscape scenery	山水风光
mountain resort	山区胜地
grotto	洞窟
stalagmite	石笋
idyllic scenery	田园风光
ruins of an ancient city	古城遗址
famous mountains and great rivers	名山大川
natural preserve	自然保护区
natural scenery	自然风景
Buddha scenic spot	佛教圣地
cityscape	城市风景
holiday resort	度假胜地
cemetery	陵园
bathing beach	海滨浴场
seaside resort	海滨胜地
recreational resort	游乐胜地
wilderness	旷野
waterfall	瀑布
jungle	丛林

tropical scenery	热带风光
Tian An Men Square	天安门广场
Palace Museum, the	故宫博物院
Temple of Heaven, the	天坛
Summer Palace, the	颐和园
Beihai Park	北海公园
Fragrant Hill Park	香山公园
Great Wall, the	长城
Ming Tombs, the	十三陵
Museum of Peking Man, the	北京猿人博物馆
People's Square	人民广场
Shanghai's Town God's Temple	上海城隍庙
Shanghai Library	上海图书馆
Shanghai Museum	上海博物馆
Bund, the	外滩
Emperor Qin's Terra-Cotta Warriors and Horses Museum	秦始皇兵马俑博物馆
Mausoleum of Huang Di, the	黄帝陵
Forest of Stone Tablets, the	碑林
Bell Tower, the	钟楼
West Lake	西湖
Guilin mountains and waters	桂林山水
Sun Moon Lake	日月潭

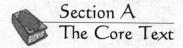

Unit Four

Section A
The Core Text

Culture Shock

The term, culture shock, was introduced for the first time in 1958 to describe the anxiety experienced when a person moves to a completely new environment. This term expresses the lack of direction, the feeling of not knowing what to do or how to do things in a new environment, and not knowing what is appropriate or inappropriate. The feeling of culture shock generally sets in the first few weeks after coming to a new place.

We can describe culture shock as the physical and emotional discomfort one suffers when coming to live in another country or a place different from the place of origin. Often, the way that we lived before is not accepted or considered as normal in the new place. Everything is different, for example, not speaking the language, not knowing how to use banking machines, not knowing how to use the telephone and so forth. Because your views may clash with the different beliefs, norms, values, and traditions that exist in a new place, you may have difficulty adjusting to a new culture and to those parts of the culture not familiar to you. This is culture shock. Evidently, at least four essential stages of culture shock adjustment occur.

The first stage is called "the honeymoon." In this stage, you feel excited about living in a different place, and everything appears marvelous. You like everything, and everybody seems to be so nice to you. Also, the amusement of life in a new culture seems as though it would have no ending.

Eventually, however, the second stage of culture shock appears. This is the "hostility stage." You begin to notice that not everything is as good as you originally thought it was. You become tired of many things about the new culture. Moreover, people don't treat you like a guest anymore, everything that seemed to be so wonderful at first is now awful, and everything makes you feel distressed and tired.

Usually at this point in your adjustment to a new culture, you devise some defense mechanisms to help you cope and to protect yourself against the effects of culture shock. One type of coping mechanism is called "**repression**." This happens when you pretend that everything is acceptable and that nothing bothers you. Another type of defense mechanism is called "**regression**." This occurs when you start to act as if you were younger than you actually are; you act like a child. You forget everything, and sometimes you become careless and irresponsible. The third kind of defense mechanism is called "isolation." You would rather be home alone, and you don't want to communicate with anybody. With isolation, you try to avoid the effects of culture shock, or at least that's what you think. Isolation is one of the worst coping mechanisms you can use because it separates you from those things that could really help you. The last type of defense mechanism is called "rejection." With this coping mechanism, you don't think you need anybody. You feel you are coping fine alone, so you don't try to ask for help.

The defense mechanisms you utilize in the hostility stage are not helpful. If you only occasionally use one of these coping mechanisms to help yourself survive, that is acceptable. You must be cautious, however. These mechanisms can really hurt you because they prevent you from making necessary adjustments to the new culture.

After you deal with your hostile feelings, recognition of the temporary nature of culture shock begins. Then you come to the third stage called "recovery." In this stage, you start feeling more positive, and you try to develop comprehension of everything you don't understand. The whole situation starts to become more favorable; you recover from the symptoms of the first two stages, and you adjust yourself to the new norms, values, and even beliefs and traditions of the new country. You begin to see that even though the distinctions of the culture are different from your own, it has elements that you can learn to appreciate.

The last stage of culture shock is called "adjustment." In this stage, you have reached a point where you actually feel good because you have learned enough to understand the new culture. The things that initially made you feel uncomfortable or strange are now things that you understand. This acquisition of understanding alleviates much of the stress. Now you feel comfortable; you have adjusted to the new culture.

Evidently, culture shock is something you cannot avoid when living in a foreign country. It does not seem like a very helpful experience when you are going through its four stages. However, when you have completely adjusted to a new culture you can more fully enjoy it. You learn how to interact with other people, and you learn a considerable amount about life in a culture that is not your own. Furthermore, learning about other cultures and how to adjust to the shock of living in them helps you learn more about yourself.

Notes to the Text:

repression   压抑（把本能的欲望，尤其是与一般公认的行为标准
                     相冲突的欲望，压抑于潜意识中）

regression   回归，倒退（指当个人追求的愿望得不到满足或受严
                     重挫折时，即以与其年龄不相称的发展早期的某
                     些原始的幼稚行为来适应当前，由意识状态倒退
                     到无意识状态的一种变态心理现象）

Understanding the Text:

1. What may a person inevitably encounter when living in a new place?

2. According to the passage, how many stages of culture shock adjustment are there when one studies overseas?

3. Why does one feel excited when in the "honeymoon stage"?

4. What is the second stage and how does one feel in this stage?

5. Why must one be cautious even when occasionally using one of the defense mechanisms to prevent himself from being distressed?

6. What does the "recovery stage" mean?

7. How does one adjust himself in the last stage?

8. In the author's eyes, what are the benefits when one is aware of and is trying to adjust to the new culture?

Section B
Sample Interview

Living Abroad — Cultural Experience

Q: Many people feel that living, working or volunteering abroad may be out of their reach and is something that is usually only accessible to students who don't have many responsibilities. What would you say to them?

Troy: The perceived inaccessibility is the primary obstacle to most people who want to travel but don't. I think you have to decide how important your travel goal is to you. There is no perfect time to travel; you will always have financial obligations, personal relationships, and other considerations. I have spoken with many students over the years who have sold their belongings, deferred their loans, said goodbye to their loved ones, and did it. Volunteering and working afford you a less expensive option. You might find that you can spend one year abroad volunteering for the same cost as a month of Euro railing. Working abroad in most cases will not make you rich, but it may offset the costs of your travel.

Q: What are the benefits of volunteering, working or living abroad for a few months versus a short vacation?

Troy: Often, participants are still experiencing culture shock when their short international program is finished. Longer programs allow participants to work through the initial phases of culture shock and begin to appreciate the local culture. In the case of volunteer programs, very brief programs often create more work for the local organizer. For example, volunteers who are brought into an orphanage every two weeks do not necessarily interact with the children in the same way a long-term volunteer might, and the long-term effects vary. I still support volunteering and living abroad for any length of time. The real benefit is the internal change that is experienced by participants and not the impact they have on the local project.

Q: What are the first steps that one needs to take in order to make living, working or volunteering abroad a reality? Is there a lot of financial sacrifice involved?

Troy: Determine your objectives. If your goal is to experience the local culture, then you should make a list of the country(-ies) you want to visit. If your goal is to make money, then you should explore only those destinations where you can obtain full-time work. Develop a budget, you may find that it is expensive to get to Nepal, but you will only be spending $50 a month there. You should also consider your budget here and compare the two. You won't have auto insurance payments, parking fees, electric bills abroad, but you may have other expenses like Internet café fees, etc.

Q: There are a variety of programs out there. How can we tell the difference between the credible and non-credible programs?

Troy: I advise prospective participants to request alumni or past participants' contact information and then speak to a former participant directly. This is not a foolproof screening method however. Neither can you always rely on alumni's testimonials good or bad; everyone's experience is different. The Internet is a good place to find information and bad press.

Q: Is there only a certain type of person that does well abroad or is it something that you would recommend for everyone?

Troy: I recommend travel for everyone. Often the most close-minded individuals are most impacted by international travel. Anyone who travels should consider their ability to be flexible; they should be patient and willing to accept the local culture.

Q: Given the current situation (attack on America) what advice can you give to people who may be scared to venture outside of the US?

Troy: Recent events sadly show the need for international understanding. US travelers should monitor the State Department Pages. Don't cancel your travel plans! Carefully consider your destination, and be sure it is some place that you are comfortable with. Learn about the local culture and current affairs prior to travel. You should make an effort to immerse yourself in the local culture.

Q: Could you tell us a little about your experiences abroad and what you learned?

Troy: I have studied, volunteered and worked abroad from Latin America to Asia and a few places in between. My experiences have changed my life. I have changed my long-term goals and objectives. I learned a lot about myself through volunteering and working abroad. I learned that I was capable of adapting, capable of opening my mind, and giving of myself. I also learned to be patient and flexible. I now understand that my impact on the local projects was limited but the interactions with the local culture and people I will have forever.

Section C
Information Input and Group Discussion

1. Symptoms of Culture Shock

The symptoms of culture shock can appear at different times. Although one can experience real pain from culture shock, it is an opportunity for redefining one's life objectives. It is a great opportunity for learning and acquiring new perspectives. Culture shock can help one develop a better understanding of oneself and stimulate personal creativity. Generally speaking, culture shock can have the following symptoms:

Symptoms of Culture Shock

- Sadness, loneliness, melancholy
- Preoccupation with health
- Aches, pains, and allergies
- Insomnia, desire to sleep too much or too little
- Changes in temperament, depression, feeling vulnerable, feeling powerless
- Anger, irritability, resentment, unwillingness to interact with others
- Identifying with the old culture or idealizing the old country
- Loss of identity
- Trying too hard to absorb everything in the new culture or country
- Unable to solve simple problems
- Lack of confidence
- Feelings of inadequacy or insecurity
- Developing stereotypes about the new culture
- Developing obsessions such as over-cleanliness
- Longing for family life
- Feelings of being lost, overlooked, exploited or abused

Stages of Culture Shock

Culture shock has many stages. Each stage can be ongoing or appear only at certain times. The first stage is the incubation stage.

In this first stage, the new arrival may feel euphoric and be pleased by all of the new things encountered. This period of time is called the "honeymoon" stage, as everything encountered is new and exciting.

Afterwards, the second stage presents itself. A person may encounter some difficult times and crises in daily life. For example, communication difficulties may occur such as not being understood. In this stage, there may be feelings of discontent, impatience, anger, sadness, and the feeling of incompetence. This happens when a person is trying to adapt to a new culture that is very different from the culture of origin. Transition between the old methods and those of the new country is a difficult process and takes time to complete. During the transition, there can be strong feelings of dissatisfaction.

The third stage is characterized by gaining some understanding of the new culture. A new feeling of pleasure and sense of humor may be experienced. One may start to feel a certain psychological balance. The new arrival may not feel as lost as he/she once did and starts to have a feeling of direction. The individual is more familiar with the environment and wants to belong. This initiates an evaluation of the old ways versus those of the new.

In the fourth stage, the person realizes that the new culture has good and bad things to offer. This stage can be one of double integration or triple integration depending on the number of cultures that the person has to process. This integration is accompanied by a more solid feeling of belonging. The person starts to define him/herself and establish goals for living.

The fifth stage is called the "re-entry shock" stage. This occurs when a return to the country of origin is made. One may find that things are no longer the same. For example, some of the newly acquired customs are not in use in the old culture.

These stages are present at different times and each person has their own way of reacting in the stages of culture shock. As a consequence, some stages will be longer and more difficult than others. Many factors contribute to the duration and effects of culture shock. For example, the individual's state of mental health, type of personality, previous experiences, socio-economic conditions, familiarity with the language, family and/or social support systems, and level of education.

Questions for Discussion:

1. What is culture shock and when does it usually happen?
2. Can you mention some symptoms of culture shock?
3. In your opinion, what is the main cause of this shock?
4. How many stages of culture shock are mentioned in the above passage and what are they?
5. Suppose you travel to a new place or a foreign country. Which stage will be the most difficult for you to overcome?
6. Is culture shock inevitable?
7. What are some of the coping methods that people can use to combat culture shock?
8. If you meet with culture shock, how do you cope with it?

2. When in China, Do As the Chinese Do

As American companies expand their operations in China, the demand for Chinese-speaking managers who understand Chinese culture is surging. Business schools across the United States are adding practical classes about China's economy and tailoring workshops for executives to be sent to China. Consultants with knowledge about

China are also cashing in. Frank Lee, who moved to California from China in the 1980s, opened Global Intelligence Consultation in San Diego in February. Catering to American firms that want help managing their businesses in China, he already has a handful of clients, including two *Fortune* 500 companies. "A lot of companies are realizing they need to be in China," he said. "There is an incredible demand." The surging US trade with China is driving that demand. According to Commerce Department figures, the United States imported \$210 billion worth of goods from China in 2004, nearly twice as much as in 2001.

Rules are different

China is a difficult market for American managers. Not only do executives have to deal with their business, cultural norms are also confusing. "The rules of the game in China are not the same," said Ray Friedman, a professor at Vanderbilt University's Owen Graduate School of Management in Nashville. "You have to spend some time to learn how to do business there."

Part of the problem is that few American executives speak Chinese fluently. Managers at manufacturing plants have had a particularly hard time developing relationships with workers, since few Chinese without college degrees speak English.

Cultural misunderstandings are also a problem. When Lee talks to American managers heading to China, he coaches them on everything from how to earn respect from Chinese staff to how to negotiate.

One point Lee makes is that while Americans are usually clear about what they want, the Chinese are indirect. "In negotiations with the Chinese, the first 30 minutes are just warming up," Lee said. If Americans force Chinese negotiators to get down to business too quickly, conflicts can arise.

Business schools are scrambling to teach similar lessons. At Vanderbilt's Owen school, enrolment in Friedman's "Doing Business in China" course has doubled every year since he started teaching it four years ago. Besides giving students an overview of China's history and economy, Friedman takes a group of students to China for firsthand experience. In May, he and his students examined logistical costs at a beer distributor in Shanghai.

"People have realized they are going to deal with China no matter what, so they'd better learn about it," he said. The University of South Carolina's International MBA program, which accepts about 100 students a year, saw the number of students in its Chinese-language track rise from 5 in 2000 to 14 this year. The program involves intensive training in Chinese and requires more than a year of study in East Asia.

Lessons learned

Sandy Springs-based UPS has taken that approach. In the early 1990s, several American managers lived in China. Today all of the company's 400 China-based employees are Chinese. John Flick, spokesman for the company's international operations, said the company has hired locals "because they understand the language and culture." He added, "These folks have taught us more than we realize." UPS bought its former Chinese joint venture partner last year and plans to expand to 3,500 staffers in China by the end of the year. During the expansion, Flick said, the company will send some Americans to China.

To find good candidates, employees and their families will be screened for adaptability to living in China, will have a chance to visit China before taking jobs there, and will get training on everything from how to use a Chinese bank to Chinese tax laws. "The families have to be happy over there, too," Flick said. Dell Inc., based in Round Rock, Texas, is solving part of its management problem by recruiting Chinese nationals studying at American universities.

New hires are then groomed for key positions in China, said Jess Blackburn, a company representative. Those tactics may be expensive, but Tarun Khanna, a professor of corporate strategy at Harvard Business School, argues that the investments are worth it. "My sense is that Americans tend to be less aware of the rest of the world than, say, Europeans," he said. "If American executives don't catch up soon," he added, "they are likely to be disadvantaged in the next ten years."

Questions for Discussion:
1. Can you briefly describe the main differences in culture between China and the United States?
2. Why should we take culture into account while doing business in a new community?
3. Are you familiar with the saying "When in Rome, do as Romans do"? What does it mean?
4. How do you understand the statement that "When in China, do as the Chinese do"?
5. What is your attitude toward foreign cultures?
6. When we travel to a new place, is it necessary for us to adapt ourselves to the local customs or habits? Why or why not?

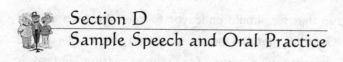

Section D
Sample Speech and Oral Practice

Part A Sample Speech

To Cope with Cultural Diversity

Cultural diversity is a very fascinating phenomenon in every country. People from different countries and cultural backgrounds not only show the charms of their own cultures, but also make the world culture diversified and prosperous. However, cultural differences sometimes cause much trouble for people to get equal career opportunities, and inconvenience to their work and lives.

First of all, as an old saying goes, "When in Rome, do as Romans do." When people go to another country, it is necessary for them to adapt themselves to the local culture. The visitors' compliance with the local culture shows their respect to the host country and people, and maintains a good order in the local society. Take traffic regulations as an example. In some countries like Britain, pedestrians and drivers must walk or drive on the left side of the road. The case is just the opposite in China and some other countries where people must abide by the rule to walk and drive on the right side. If visitors neglect the difference, the traffic will be in chaos. Besides the differences of rules and regulations, the laws in every country are also different. Therefore, visitors should be fully aware of the details of the host country's laws, so as to avoid unnecessary disputes and trouble. All visitors to other countries expect to have an exotic experience of the local cultures, enlarging their knowledge and widening their horizons, and a better understanding of the target cultures can contribute a great deal to the exchange of different cultures.

It is also true that we should endeavor to keep our own culture and customs. On one hand, the host should tolerate cultural differences. Hospitality is a virtue for a great nation and so is tolerance for different cultures. If the host respects different customs and habits, later when they go to other places or countries they will be treated the same way. So to be tolerant of or friendly to other cultures is not only for the good of the guests but also for that of the host themselves. On the other hand, due to the popularity of English, people around the world start to use it in their work or daily lives. Consequently, some cultures in minority regions or underdeveloped countries are disappearing from the earth. Western culture is causing an unprecedented erosion of world cultural diversity as well as languages. Therefore, every government should be on the alert and try to keep its culture flourishing.

In a word, the differences between cultures should be preserved and carefully maintained. Meanwhile, visitors to foreign countries should comply with the local culture and customs, so as to be identified by the host country.

Part B   Presentation Practice

Directions: *Talk on each of the following topics for at least five minutes. Be sure to make your points clear and logical with adequate supporting details.*

Topic 1: Festivals are lifeblood of traditional culture.
Questions for reference:
1. Can you mention some traditional Chinese festivals?
2. What effects can festivals have on traditional culture?
3. What are possible causes of the loss of some traditional Chinese

festivals?

4. What should we do to keep our traditional Chinese festivals going? Can you make some suggestions?

Topic 2: When in Roman, do as Romans do.

Questions for reference:

1. How do you understand this statement?

2. Which do you think is better, for visitors to follow local customs or for the host to welcome cultural differences?

3. What is your attitude towards cultural diversity?

4. What can be done to build bridges between cultures?

Topic 3: Chinese Tea Culture

Questions for reference:

1. What does Tea Culture mean?

2. How many types of tea are there in China and what are they?

3. Do you know something about the process of producing tea?

4. What are possible benefits of tea-drinking?

Part C More Topics for Oral Practice

Directions: *Based on the news reports, talk on each of the following topics for at least five minutes. Be sure to make your points clear and logical with adequate supporting details.*

News Report 1:

Brooks can converge into a mighty torrent, as the saying goes. An important brook is running all the way to Washington, which should contribute to a better understanding between China and the United States. Several US congressmen have tabled a concurrent resolution of the US Senate and House of Representatives, supporting a month-long Festival of China in Washington and calling for more efforts to promote understanding and co-operation between the two countries.

Topic: *Are festivals the best way to bridge cultural gaps? What else can be done to achieve this goal?*

News Report 2:

Anti-dumping investigations, safeguard protection and other means of protectionism taken by worldwide trading partners, by developed countries in particular, are forcing China's policymakers and businesses to quickly adjust their international marketing strategies and shift from "quantity worship" to quality-oriented trade.

Topic: *Do you think the shift from quantity to quality is the best solution to this problem?*

News Report 3:

Recently five auto financing companies run by the world's auto giants including General Motors, Volkswagen AG, Ford Motor Co. and Toyota Motor Corp. have gone into operation in China with the latest one run by DaimlerChrysler operational in Beijing early this month.

Topic: *Can foreign players enliven China's sluggish auto financing market?*

Part D   Useful Expressions

Christmas 圣诞节
Easter 复活节

All Saints' Day	万圣节
Halloween	万圣节前夕
Valentine's Day	情人节
New Year's Day	元旦
Spring Festival	春节
Lantern Festival	元宵节
Arbor Day	植树节
Ching Ming Festival	清明节
Dragon Boat Festival	端午节
Mid-Autumn Festival	中秋节
Double Ninth Day	重阳节
Water-Splashing Day	泼水节
lion dance	舞狮
dragon dance	舞龙
riddles written on lanterns	灯谜
exhibit of lanterns	灯会
Spring Festival couplet	春联
paper-cut	剪纸
New Year painting	年画
family reunion dinner	团圆饭
the dinner on New Year's Eve	年夜饭
jiao-zi	饺子
wonton	馄饨
steamed twisted rolls	花卷
set meal	套餐
rice noodles	米粉
a stick of sugar-coated haws	冰糖葫芦
chafing dish	火锅
eight treasures rice pudding	八宝饭
glass noodles	粉丝

green tea	绿茶
black tea	红茶
Wulong tea	乌龙茶
compressed tea	压制茶，砖茶
scented tea	花茶

$\mathcal{U}$nit $\mathcal{F}$ive

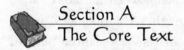

Section A
The Core Text

Harmonious Society — China's Dream

China's per capita value of gross domestic product (GDP) has exceeded US $1,000, but that does not necessarily translate into smooth economic growth and steady social development.

This period is a crucial stage for the economic and social development of a country in the process of modernization, as proven by experiences of many countries in the world.

Some have succeeded in the social and economic transition into prosperity, but many others have suffered from stagnation and social turbulence due to inadequate policy-making.

The problems and contradictions China will face in the next decades may be even more complicated and thorny than others as it is turning from a planned economy to a market economy with its social structure and ideological setup also in major shake-up.

Independent thinking of the general public, their newly developed penchant for independent choices and thus the widening gap of ideas among different social strata will pose further challenges to China's policy makers. Negative and corruptive phenomena and more and more rampant crimes in the society will also jeopardize social stability and harmony.

In view of the international situations, building a harmonious society is also a requisite requirement for the Chinese authorities to clear away challenges and risks in the international relations, including unfair world order, rocky road of multi-polarization of world political framework, pressure from economic globalization, and security concerns.

China now is more than ever embracing social harmony rather than **pinning** the focus on economic growth. A harmonious society should feature democracy, the rule of law, equality, justice, sincerity, **amity** and **vitality**.

Such a society will give full scope to people's talent and creativity, enable all the people to share the social wealth brought by reform and development, and **forge** an even closer relationship between the people and government. These things will thus result in lasting stability and unity. To achieve this goal, we must do the followings:

Strive for sustained, rapid and coordinated economic growth

Sound economic growth and increasing abundance of social wealth are the material foundation for a harmonious society, and the well-being of the country's rural population will play a decisive role. When the farmers can lead a good life and assume a higher overall quality, the vast countryside will be stable and prosperous.

Develop socialist democracy

By developing democracy, the people's opinions may be further let out, their intelligence be fully absorbed, and a democratic policy-making mechanism will help balance different social interests and avoid social conflicts.

Actively enforce the principle of the rule of law

The rule of law is important for the promotion, realization and safeguarding of a harmonious society. This principle should be rigorously implemented in all political, administrative and **judicial** sectors to ensure the powerful be checked and accountable for their misdeeds.

Strengthen ideological and ethical buildup

Without a common ideological aspiration or high moral standard, a harmonious society will be a mansion built on sand. Honesty, unity, fraternity, professional ethics should be advocated to the whole society.

Maintain social equity and justice

Social equity and justice is a key to bringing people's creativity and initiatives to full play, because people will not be happy without it. It is important to balance different interests and strive to ensure equality for all in terms of personal rights, opportunities, game-playing rules and wealth distribution.

Establish a fine-tuned social management system and well handle the people's internal contradictions

Social conflicts are emerging in great numbers and in more varied forms, which are inevitable for China at the present stage. But they must be properly handled in case they pose risks to the overall development of the country.

Beef up environmental protection

The present ecological and environmental situations in China are rather tough and grave in some places. Without a sound natural environment, people will have no clean water to drink, fresh air to breath, or healthy food to eat, which will result in serious social problems.

The government officials should put building a harmonious society on top of their work agenda, do a good job in serving the people, and work on theories relating to the building of a harmonious society.

It will be a long-term, systematic project, and the whole Party and the government must constantly remind themselves of the sense of mission and take up their responsibilities in leading the construction of a harmonious society for the smooth transition of the Chinese society in the next decades.

● Notes to the Text:

pin	钉住；使依附于，使系于
amity	友好，和睦
vitality	活力，生气
forge	铸造；使形成
judicial	司法的

● Understanding the Text:

1. What are the implications of building a harmonious society?

2. What does a harmonious society generally involve?

3. How many steps are mentioned in the passage to embrace a harmonious society and what are they?

4. In your opinion, what can be done to achieve this goal?

5. Being a citizen, what contributions can we make to such a society?

Section B
Sample Interview

On Forgiveness

Q: Dr. Menahem, I want to thank you for taking the time to share your wise and gentle perspective on what I believe is often a very complicated and difficult issue for many people, that of forgiveness.

Dr. Menahem: Thank you, Tammie. It is my pleasure to share my thoughts on this difficult and highly charged topic. It has been my experience that many people have trouble letting go of old grudges, even when they realize it is hurting them more than the other person. Much of my work is centered on helping people to let go and forgive.

Q: What are some of the most common reasons we don't forgive ourselves?

Dr. Menahem: Most people are much too hard on themselves. They think they have to do something great just to be OK. They have brought into our culture madness of competition and success. They feel that they are only as good as what they do and how much money they make from it. If their parents were conditional with their love, critical and controlling, the problem would be even worse. Behavioral perfection is then substituted for spontaneity and conformity replaces individuality.

Q: Why should we forgive our enemies and why is it important?

Dr. Menahem: Most people are sensitive to minor slights or hurts. They feel that they would never be so insensitive and are very critical of others who are insensitive. Sometimes they are upset because the others are getting away with things they couldn't do for either personal or societal reasons. We also dislike people that have qualities we have had to repress. For example, if we have had to repress our anger, we may dislike angry people. We fear that we may be angry like them. When we forgive our enemies, we are accepting a variety of ways of being. We are "letting go" of our fear, anger, guilt and inferiority feelings and promoting love, joy, peace and inter-dependency. This heals us individually by freeing us to be kinder and more loving. It also heals inter-personal strife and creates a more peaceful world.

Q: Can forgiveness actually help in healing physical pains?

Dr. Menahem: Yes, it can heal us physically. When we are being unforgiving we are tense and stressed, creating powerful hormones that are needed for fight or flight reactions. Since there is no need to fight or flee, these hormones build up and create stress in the body, which can result in pain and physical illness. When we forgive, we relax and the body tends to heal itself naturally.

Q: What are the necessary steps we must take in order to forgive?

Dr. Menahem: First, we must accept our angry, fearful or guilty feelings. Second, we must release these feelings willingly. Third, we must affirm our intention to forgive. Fourth, we must take appropriate actions. Finally, we must be thankful for the ability to choose forgiveness and peace.

Q: Is there any way we can skip the grieving process?

Dr. Menahem: No. When we lose someone or something dear to us, it hurts and we must grieve. After a while, we can affirm our spiritual values of faith, love, forgiveness and unity and heal the grief.

Q: How does prayer and meditation fit into your practice as a psychologist?

Dr. Menahem: I pray for and with my patients. I pray that they heal for the highest good of their soul. I suggest they pray for themselves. I teach them how to pray psychologically — to affirm rather than plead for things. I teach them to meditate — harmonizing their consciousness with divine consciousness. I get them in touch with spiritual feelings of love and peace that come up when fear, hate, guilt and inferiority are released.

Q: Could you explain what a self-hypnotic trance is and how this can help your patients?

Dr. Menahem: Self-hypnosis is a sort of selective awareness that arises when the critical, conscious part of the mind is interfering with functioning. By relaxing and turning the criticism off, we are able to release negativity and turn toward peaceful, loving feelings for oneself and others.

Q: What is spiritual psychology?

Dr. Menahem: I see people as primarily spiritual beings, temporarily living in a body. The problems usually seen as psychological like fear, hate, guilt and inferiority are actually solved by developing spiritual qualities — faith, love, forgiveness and unity. Spiritual psychology gives people tools to heal their psychological problems by interacting with the endless source of love and peace — God — or as some people prefer the "Higher Power."

Q:　　　　　　　　What are some of the common myths and misunderstandings about spiritual psychology?

Dr. Menahem:　First, some people think it forces religion on people. Actually spiritual psychology is non-denominational and non-dogmatic. Second, some people feel that it is of no use to agnostics or atheists. Actually, it helps by releasing toxic feelings, leaving spiritual feelings like love and peace to arise naturally. Third, some people think it rejects non-spiritual forms of therapy. Actually, it embraces most traditional forms of psychotherapy, while adding metaphysical and mystical methods — like prayer and meditation.

Q:　　　　　　　　How does one grow spiritually? Is there a step-by-step process for this?

Dr. Menahem:　There is no set formula but the general guidelines call for awareness of problems with thoughts, feelings and behavior, followed by release of these problems and replacement of fear, hate, guilt and inferiority with faith, love, forgiveness and unity with the Spirit.

Section C
Information Input and Group Discussion

1. New Concepts Adopted for Further Development

The 16th Central Committee of the Communist Party of China (CPC) concluded its fifth plenary session with a call for a scientific approach to the development of the nation's economy.

Putting people first and adopting a scientific approach to development is the essence of the proposal for the 11th Five-Year Plan approved by the plenary session. The proposal put forward six "key" principles which are to maintain stable and fast economic growth, speed up changes to the mode of economic development, enhance the capacity for independent innovation, reinforce the building of a harmonious society and ensure further reform and opening up.

China is moving from the blind pursuit of gross domestic product to a focus on prosperity for all the people.

The new concept is a shift from unbalanced growth to comprehensive development, from unfair to fair development, from unsustainable to sustainable development.

The proposal made two goals for the 11th Five-Year Plan, saying that the gross domestic product per capita figure will double between 2000 and 2010 and that energy consumption per GDP unit would go down by 20 per cent.

The former goal mirrored the central government's insistence on targeting economic development while the new goal reflects a scientific approach to development with a different mode.

Compared with previous concepts, the new proposal places more emphasis on environmental protection and on the sustainable use of natural resources.

One of the most vital issues on China's road to modernization is rural development. The new socialist countryside concept outlined in the proposal provides new ideas for solving the problem.

The "new socialist countryside" meant that rural problems will no longer be considered merely in terms of the transfer of rural laborers and urbanization; more attention had to be paid to improving rural development.

In 2004, the central government earmarked more than 200 billion yuan (US $24.75 billion) for rural support. The proposal said that in the 11th Five-Year Plan period more investment would go to rural areas.

The future plan must focus on independent innovation to quicken the construction of a national innovation system.

Innovation is a key engine of national development. China must rely on its own approach to development and innovate across the board in order to enter the new age of reform and opening up.

Questions for Discussion:

1. What is the essence of the proposal for the 11th Five-Year Plan?
2. How many key principles are mentioned in the proposal and what are they?
3. Of these principles, which one do you think is the most critical or are they indispensable to each other?
4. What are the implications of the newly adopted concepts for further development?
5. Do you have any ideas or suggestions for the further development of our country?
6. Being a young man, what can we do to contribute to this development?

2. To Embrace Social Harmony

With the per capita gross domestic product reaching more than US $1,000 in 2004, China is more than ever embracing social harmony rather than pinning the focus on economic growth. A harmonious society should feature democracy, the rule of law, equality, justice, sincerity, amity and vitality.

This focus shift is timely, as many observers point out, as China is confronted with increasingly acute potential social unrest caused by disparity in development and distribution, inequality, injustice, and corruption despite rapid economic progress.

The "harmonious society" initiative has stemmed out of awareness of the social problems cropping up in the process of development, which might hold back the country's sustainable progress and brew up into a real social crisis if they are not dealt with properly. The idea of social harmony demonstrates the central government's determination to overcome thorny social problems caused by inadequate policy decisions and overheated economic development.

Social conflicts as such clearly indicate that Chinese society has entered an unstable period. Containing social inequity and injustice has become crucial. These are not just ethic issues any more. They have become a matter of social and political stability.

Currently, conflicts of various economic interests are primary among the people's internal contradictions. Building a harmonious society is a long-term and systematic project. Balancing different interests cannot be delayed any longer. The government should be the coordinator of different interest groups instead of seeking for profit.

Education and healthcare are prominent in the endeavor to build a harmonious society in rural China. A study conducted by the China Students' Federation showed the average cost for education in a full-time four-year university is 38,500 yuan, equivalent to 40 years of income for a poorest farmer in west China. That means many rural children are denied full education.

As for healthcare, according to the Ministry of Health, in some areas, the medical insurance covers less than 10 per cent of 900 million rural population, although 80 to 90 per cent were covered by an organized cooperative medical system before 1979. An official with the ministry says that many people have slipped back into

92

poverty because of huge debts caused by chronic diseases like cancer.

The rural population plays an important role in fostering a harmonious society. Only when the poor farmers live a better life, can the whole society expect to live in harmony and stability.

The idea of building a harmonious society marks the maturity of the Chinese Communist Party as a ruling party with serving the people as its guideline. These policies lay a theoretical framework to boost sound societal development, steady economic growth, and an abundance of social wealth in the years to come. If we abide by them, social harmony is possible.

Questions for Discussion:
1. Why is it important for China to construct a harmonious society?
2. What are the problems our country is confronted with?
3. Of these problems, which one do you think is the most urgent to be handled?
4. Can you make some suggestions to deal with the problems we are facing now?
5. In your opinion, where should we start to build a harmonious society?
6. What can be done to contribute to the construction of a harmonious society?

Section D
Sample Speech and Oral Practice

Part A Sample Speech

How to Improve Conditions for the Physically Disabled?
Disabled people living in our cities daily face challenging and

potentially difficult situations which society must consider. This essay will offer some suggestions as to how conditions may be improved for people with a physical disability.

One of the most important ways in which life can be improved for disabled people is the provision of financial support. Some disabled people may have difficulty paying the cost of special equipment or care which they need. The government could offer assistance through a range of measures including tax deductions for equipment such as wheelchairs, or loan assistance for major purchases. Even such small measures as concession passes for transport or entertainment would assist in improving life for the disabled.

The special needs of people with disabilities must be taken into account by the education system and the services it provides. For example, the visually impaired would benefit from access to computers which convert text to voice. The hearing impaired may need special tutors skilled in sign language. The goal, however, would be the integration of the disabled into the regular school system while maintaining these services.

Employment is a third factor which must be considered. In order that disabled people can be given equal opportunity to work and contribute to society in every possible field, the government could establish quotas for disabled workers in large companies. Moreover, financial incentives such as tax rebates could be offered to smaller companies who hire disabled workers.

Thus, conditions for the physically disabled can be improved in a number of ways including financial support, adequate educational services and equal employment opportunities. Through the pursuit of these goals, society can ensure that life for the disabled is rewarding and fulfilling.

Part B Presentation Practice

Directions: Talk on each of the following topics for at least five minutes. Be sure to make your points clear and logical with adequate supporting details.

Topic 1: Put people first

Questions for reference:

1. How do you understand this statement?
2. What is the practical and historical significance of doing so?
3. What is to be done to meet this goal?

Topic 2: Scientific approach to development

Questions for reference:

1. What is the practical significance of implementing this policy?
2. Can you give some examples which are against this principle?
3. What can be done to fully carry out this new concept?

Topic 3: Does virtue justify corruption?

Questions for reference:

1. Have you heard the story that an official took bribes to help the poor?
2. Do you think his deeds can be justified? Why or why not?
3. If his virtue is not justified, should he be severely punished?
4. What is a proper way to perform a good deed?

Part C More Topics for Oral Practice

Directions: Based on the news reports, talk on each of the following topics for at least five minutes. Be sure to make your *points clear and logical with adequate supporting details.*

News Report 1:

Now that a new concept for developing rural areas has been put forward by the Chinese Communist Party Central Committee for reference in the formulation of the 11th Five-Year Plan, a good opportunity to solve problems involving agriculture, the countryside and farmers has presented itself. These challenges have long been a bottleneck in the country's modernization drive.

Topic: *What formula do you think is the most effective to help address rural problems?*

News Report 2:

As the HIV infection rate continues to rise, the number of AIDS-caused orphans grows as well. According to statistics from the Chinese Ministry of Health, the number of such children stands beyond 80,000, all living under stigma and discrimination.

Topic: *AIDS-caused orphans in China spark concern. What measures should be taken to help those children?*

News Report 3:

Millions of farmers are flocking to China's cities, seeking work in an effort to secure better lives for their families left behind in rural homelands. Over the past decade, millions of rural elderlies, women and children have been separated from the family's breadwinner as sons, husbands and fathers head to the cities in search of a better wage.

Topic: *Left-behind wives or children should not be forgotten. Who should take care of them, the government, husbands or fathers?*

Part D   Useful Expressions

put people first	以人为本
harmonious society	和谐社会
scientific approach to development	科学发展观
maintain an appropriate rapid economic growth	保持经济适度快速增长
financial capacity	财政的承受能力
compensation for demolition	拆迁补偿费
long-term government bonds	长期国债
urban social security system	城镇社会保障体系
medical insurance for urban workers	城镇职工医疗保险
reform of the urban housing system	城镇住房制度改革
low-level redundant development	低水平重复建设
maintain a high sense of responsibility	保持高度负责的态度
tax-for-fees reform	费改税改革
Law on Personal Income Tax, the	个人所得税法
purchasing power	购买力
reform of state-owned enterprises	国有企业改革
blackmarket transaction in foreign exchanges	外汇黑市交易
grass-roots supervision	基层监督
macro-control targets	宏观调控目标
misappropriation or diversion of financial investment	挤占、挪用财政投资
accelerate economic restructuring	加快经济结构调整
lighten the burden on enterprises	减轻企业负担
increase efficiency by downsizing payrolls	减人增效
develop consumer markets in rural areas	开拓农村消费市场
strategy of invigorating China through	科教兴国战略

the development of science and education, the
expand/increase domestic demand and   扩大内需，刺激消费
    stimulate consumption
stimulate economic growth   拉动经济增长
healthcare reform   医疗改革
hidden employment   隐形就业
advance with the times   与时俱进
overall national strength   综合国力

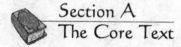

Section A
The Core Text

Economic Implications of Increased Oil Prices

What are the economic implications of the recent increase in oil prices? In the long run, higher oil prices are likely to reduce somewhat the productive capacity of the US economy. That outcome would occur, for example, if high energy costs make businesses less willing to invest in new capital or cause some existing capital to become economically **obsolescent**. Lower productivity in turn implies that wages and profits will be lower than they otherwise would have been. Also, the higher cost of imported oil is likely to adversely affect our terms of trade; that is, Americans will have to sell more goods and services abroad to pay for a given quantity of oil and other imports. The increase in the prices of our imports relative to the prices of our exports will impose a further burden on US households and firms.

Under the assumption that oil prices do not **spike** sharply higher from their already high levels, these long-run effects, though negative, should be manageable. As I have already discussed, conservation and the development of alternative energy sources will, over the long term, take some of the sting out of higher oil prices.

Moreover, productivity gains from diverse sources, including technological improvements and a more highly educated workforce, are likely to exceed by a significant margin the productivity losses created by high oil prices.

In the short run, sharply higher oil prices create a rather different and, in some ways, a more difficult set of economic challenges. Indeed, a significant increase in oil prices can simultaneously slow economic growth while stoking inflation, posing hard choices for monetary policy makers.

An increase in oil prices slows economic growth in the short run primarily through its effects on spending, or aggregate demand. Because the United States imports most of its oil, an increase in oil prices is, as many economists have noted, broadly analogous to the imposition of a tax on US residents, with the revenue from the tax going to oil producers abroad. Since the beginning of the year, the cost of oil imported into the United States has increased by about $75 billion (at an annual rate), or about 3/4 of the gross domestic product. Add to this the effects of the rise in natural gas prices, and the total increase in imported energy costs over a full year — the increase in the "tax" being paid to foreign energy producers — comes to almost $85 billion.

The impact of this decline in net income on the US GDP depends in large part on how the increase in the energy "tax" affects the spending of households and firms. For a number of reasons, an increase of $85 billion in payments to foreign energy producers is likely to reduce domestic spending by something less than that amount. For example, in the short run, people may be reluctant to cut non-energy spending below accustomed levels, leading them to reduce saving rather than spending. Because high energy costs lower firms' profits, they normally reduce the willingness of firms to purchase new capital goods; however, if the increase in energy prices looks to be permanent, firms might decide that it makes sense for them to invest in more energy-efficient buildings and machines, moderating the decline in their capital spending. If higher energy prices reflect in part more rapid economic growth abroad — which seems to be the case in the recent episode — or if foreign energy producers spend part of their increased income on US goods and services, then the demand for US exports may be stronger than it would have been otherwise. With these and many other qualifications taken into account, a reasonable estimate is that the increased cost of imported energy has reduced the growth in US aggregate spending and real output this year by something between half and three-quarters of a percentage point.

At the same time when higher oil prices slow economic growth, they also create inflationary pressures. Higher prices for crude are passed through, with only a very short lag, to increased prices for oil products used by consumers, such as gasoline and heating oil. When oil prices rise, people may try to substitute other forms of energy, such as natural gas, leading to price increases in those alternatives as well. The rise in energy costs faced by households represents, of course, an increase in the cost of living, or inflation. This direct effect of higher energy prices on the cost of living is sometimes called the first-round effect on inflation. In addition, higher energy costs may have indirect effects on the inflation rate — if, for example, firms pass on their increased costs of production in the form of higher consumer prices for non-energy goods or services, or if workers respond to the increase in the cost of living by demanding higher wages. These indirect effects of higher energy prices on the overall rate of inflation are called second-round effects. The overall inflation rate reflects both first-round and second-round effects, of course. Economists and policymakers also pay attention to the so-called core inflation rate, which excludes the direct effects of increases in the price of energy (as well as of food). By stripping out the first-round inflation effects, core inflation provides a useful indicator of the second-round effects of increases in the price of energy.

An important qualification must be added, however. The relatively small effects of higher oil prices on the underlying inflation rate that we have seen in recent years are a consequence of the public's confidence that the Fed will maintain inflation at a low level in the medium term. Moreover, well-anchored inflation expectations have been shown to enhance the stability of output and employment. Maintaining the public's confidence in its policies should thus be among the central bank's highest priorities. For this reason, I would argue that the Fed's response to the inflationary effects of an increase in oil prices should depend to some extent on the economy's starting point. If inflation has recently been on the low side of the desirable range, and the available evidence suggests that inflation expectations are likewise low and firmly anchored, then less urgency is required in responding to the inflation threat posed by higher oil prices. In this case, **monetary** policy need not tighten and could **conceivably** ease in the wake of an oil-price shock. However, if inflation has been near the high end of the acceptable range, and policymakers perceive a significant risk that inflation and inflation expectations may rise further, then stronger action, in the form of a tighter monetary policy, may well prove necessary. In directing its policy toward stabilizing the public's inflation expectations, the Fed would be making an important investment in future economic stability.

102

● Notes to the Text:

obsolescent	荒废的
spike	刺穿
monetary	货币的，金钱的
conceivably	令人信服地

● Understanding the Text:

1. In what way do high oil prices affect economy?

2. Why do high oil prices create a more difficult set of economic challenges?

3. What impacts do high oil prices have on the spending of households and firms?

4. What are the first-round inflation effects of increases in the price of energy and what are the second-round effects?

5. What makes the effects of higher oil prices relatively smaller than expected on the underlying inflation rate that we have seen in recent years?

Section B
Sample Interview

Energy Prices and Policies

Q: Speaker Hastert has called on oil companies to invest in America's energy infrastructure but hasn't Congress kept the hands of energy companies tied to some extent by limiting their ability to develop domestic resources?

Yergin: Yes, the capital is there to invest. It's a question of access and opportunities. You see enormous sums, billions of dollars go into the off-shore Gulf of Mexico because you can drill there. You have seen astonishing improvements in technology. But there is no point drilling where there is no oil and gas resources, and we do also have a lot of resources that are closed off, for instance, off the East Coast. I mean it is a strange situation. We can drill off the Gulf Coast but not off the East Coast and yet there may be very extensive resources as well.

Q: There is a great deal of concern about rising natural gas prices — something that Federal Reserve Chairman Greenspan pointed out in 2003. Are those LNG terminals — liquefied natural gas terminals — going to get built?

Yergin: I think that we have gone from plans and proposals for just a few natural gas re-liquefaction facilities to literally dozens, and we think that at least four, six, something seven like that — maybe eight — will end up being built and that we will have the capacity to import LNG. The big question, of course, is where they are going to be built? Are they going to tend to be built on the Gulf Coast, or will they be spread out? And will at least one or two of them be on the East Coast, which is near the demand centers, near where people are heating their homes with natural gas? And that is a question not of national politics but of local politics.

Q: The statement that Speaker Hastert made just recently was perhaps in response to growing sentiment on the Democratic side for a windfall profit tax on oil companies. This has been tried before. Is it effective at reducing oil prices?

Yergin: What a windfall profit tax does is introducing a lot of distortions. It reduces investment, it increases a sense of political risk and it doesn't achieve the goal that is intended, if it is to facilitate investment in new sources. It obviously responds to a political demand, but it has the opposite effect of increasing supply. It really will lead to decreased supply, not only here, but it will be something that will have an impact around the world. And this is a time when you want to increase and encourage investment, not provide disincentives to investment.

Q: There is a lot of the use of the term "energy independence" in Congress. Is it possible for the United States to stop using foreign oil and turn to domestic resources? What does energy independence mean exactly?

Yergin: You know, that is something I have puzzled over. We are now entering into the era where we have built an enormous amount of new natural gas demand in terms of electric power usage — building lots of gas-fired electric power plants — and we will be importing much more natural gas in the form of LNG. What we need to do is say, well, manage our role in a global economy in terms of energy, making sure we have diversified sources so that the development is going on around the world that we can call upon, and try to reduce unnecessary regulatory barriers or delays, which are so characteristic of the system of development in the US, so we can maintain a vibrant domestic industry. But we should also recognize that we are part of this larger picture and are pursuing all those other things like alternatives and renewals and certainly conservation.

Q: If we were less dependent on foreign sources for oil, let's say, would the price of gasoline drop?

Yergin: Really there are two things that will determine the price of gasoline. One is how much spare production capacity there is in the world. In other words, what is the balance between the ability to produce oil and consumption? Right now it is very tight and that is the number one reason that we see these high prices. The second reason is the lack of what is called a deep conversion capacity in refineries to make the types of product like diesel fuel that the world increasingly wants. So those two things are interacting. If our demand went down, if we became more energy efficient — which I think is a highly desirable goal — that we get more miles to the gallon and then if that took some pressure off the world market, you know, all other things staying constant, then we would see lower prices.

Q: So there is a lot of political pressure building and you have heard about a windfall profit tax or Senator Lieberman is trying to get energy independence from foreign oil and now we have heard about what Speaker Hastert wants to do. I mean, what would you do in response to this political pressure? Is there anything that can be done on the public policy side?

Yergin: I think there are two things we can do. The first thing is that we ought to make sure that people really have the information and knowledge about the minor changes in behavior they can make that will not only save them money but also in a total sense reduce natural gas prices and take the pressure off. The other thing is we should build flexibility into some of these environmental regulations so that for instance, in an area where a utility is only allowed to burn oil four days a month, perhaps in January if there is really pressure on prices they can burn oil eight days a month and reduce their consumption of natural gas. And there is no shortage of residual fuel oil, the type of oil that does get burned in utilities, so it wouldn't add to the price pressure on oil but it would take pressure off natural gas.

Section C
Information Input and Group Discussion

1. Why Do Gasoline Prices Rise and Fall?

Consumers worldwide have watched the cost of gasoline (motor fuels) continue to fluctuate throughout the year. This raises the question, "Why do gasoline prices rise and fall?"

In the long term, the greatest single factor influencing gasoline prices is the cost of crude oil. However, marketplace forces of supply, demand, competition and regulation can have a significant effect on the price of gasoline in the short term.

The Cost of Crude

Crude oil prices have risen dramatically over the last year, driven by strong global demand, limited spare oil production capacity, and continuing political instability in certain oil-producing regions. In late June, the price of West Texas Intermediate (WTI), a benchmark crude oil in the United States, reached an all-time high of $60.95 per barrel. This compares with WTI prices in the $42 to $43 per barrel range at the same time last year.

Surging crude oil demand is being fueled by strong economic growth, particularly in the United States and Asia. The US Energy Information Administration (EIA) estimates that global crude oil demand will grow 2.5 per cent in 2005, reaching 84.7 million barrels per day. Available spare oil production capacity is currently about 1 per cent of total worldwide demand, leaving very little room to compensate for unanticipated supply disruptions or spikes in demand.

Other Factors That Influence Gasoline Prices

Although the cost of crude oil has the most impact on average gasoline prices in the long term, local market conditions, which include the forces of supply, demand, competition, and government regulation, can also have a significant impact on gasoline prices, and explain some of the variations in gasoline prices across different markets.

Supply and Demand

In any market situation, supply and demand imbalances can affect prices in the short term. Supply shortages typically cause upward price pressure, and can result from an unplanned refinery outage, pipeline problems, or an unforeseen increase in demand. Conversely, length of supply, where supply exceeds demand, can result in downward price pressure. For example, last year on the West Coast, average gasoline prices actually dropped while crude oil prices were rising. We believe this occurred because higher gasoline prices attracted more gasoline imports, which resulted in higher inventories and greater supply, while demand was softening with the end of the summer driving season.

Competition

Competition, reflected by the number of choices in the marketplace, can also affect pricing. Almost everyone has experienced the difference in gasoline prices between a lone station on a lengthy interstate and in town, where many intersections may have two or three service stations to choose from.

Generally, price adjustments in the market affect short-term supply-demand imbalances and bring supply and demand back into balance. Whether in a situation of supply tightness or length, price will eventually bring the supply-demand balance into equilibrium by attracting additional supply or influencing demand.

Government Regulation

Government policies can sometimes impede the ability of gasoline markets to react to short-term supply-demand imbalances. For example, environmental regulations adopted by various states and local agencies require refiners to manufacture a wide variety of gasoline types to meet federal and state emission regulations. Gasoline sold in California is not the same as gasoline sold in Phoenix or Las Vegas. Creating these various "boutique" fuels results in "island" markets, and inhibits the ability of refiners and marketers to move supplies from one region to another to meet local or regional demand. The resulting inefficiency created by these regulations can dramatically affect gasoline prices.

Questions for Discussion:
1. In your opinion, what are the main causes of the rise in energy prices?
2. What causes the fall of oil prices?
3. What is the relationship between supply and demand?
4. To what extent does competition give rise to high oil prices?
5. How does the government regulate the price?
6. Can you make some suggestions to deal with this problem?

2. Rising Oil Prices Have Limited
Impact on China's Economy

The oil price increase surely will have impact on China's economy, especially on some sectors, but the impact is limited.

According to the International Monetary Fund, the world oil price will rise by 40 per cent over last year's level. The high price has caused impact on world economy, but China's total oil consumption is not high, accounting for 8 per cent of the world total.

Besides, China has a lot of supplanting energy sources, like coal and natural gas. China's utilization and development of natural gas has great potential. China's natural gas/crude oil consumption proportion stands at 0. 24 ∶ 1, compared with 1 ∶ 1 in some foreign countries.

Coal consumption accounts for 75 per cent of total energy consumption in China. The technology of coal converted to oil has been put into the manufacturing process. Though the impact is limited, China should be cautious and take measures to minimize the impact.

The current oil price couldn't represent the relations between supply and demand and speculation has played a more important role in the increase of oil prices. The speculation of oil prices has caused great attention from all over the world. If the speculation continues, it will do harm not only to China's economy, but also to world economy. The speculators will also be affected when the bubbles break.

The Chinese economy grew a robust 9. 4 per cent in the first nine months. Preliminary estimates show that China's gross domestic product totaled 10. 63 trillion yuan (US $1. 3 trillion), a year-on-year rise of 9.4 per cent, or 0.1 percentage point decline from the growth of a year earlier.

Of this total, the primary industry registered an added value of 1.35 trillion yuan (US $166.5 billion), up 5 per cent. The added value of the secondary industry totaled 6.04 trillion yuan (US $744.8 billion), up 11.1 per cent, and that of the tertiary industry rose 8.1 per cent to 3.23 trillion yuan (US $398.3 billion).

The economy showed a steady growth momentum with GDP growth rates standing at 9.4 per cent, 9.5 per cent and 9.4 per cent for the first, second and third quarter, respectively.

The consumer price index (CPI) rose by 2.0 per cent year-on-year in the first three quarters of this year, a decline of 2.1 percentage points compared with a year earlier. Prices maintained a moderately upward trend with 1.7 per cent rise in cities and 2.5 per cent rise in rural areas.

In terms of commodity categories, slowed increase in food prices, particularly in grain prices was the main reason for the decline in the rise of CPI.

In this period, food prices rose 3.3 per cent, or 7.6 percentage points slower than that of a year earlier. Grain prices rose 1.9 per cent while that of housing climbed 5.6 per cent and prices for recreation, education, culture goods and services rose 2.6 per cent.

Retail sales prices rose 0.8 per cent year-on-year in the first three quarters. Producers' prices of manufactured goods increased 5.4 per cent and purchasing prices of raw material, fuel and power were up 9.2 per cent.

China's currency exchange rate will remain stable for a period of time. China announced its decision on Renminbi (RMB) exchange rate reform, introducing a floating width band of about 2 per cent for the currency against a basket of foreign exchange on July 21 of this year, shortly after the NBS made public figures on the performance of the national economy.

3. Oil Price Hikes Could Hinder China's Growth

Rises in international oil prices can affect China's economy on a grand scale, which manifests itself in the following aspects:

It can hold back economic growth and add to inflation as rising oil prices have a certain adverse impact on the economy and ordinary people's lives. They increase currency outflows, boost corporate and citizens' expenses, and add to the difficulty of managing the economy. According to forecasts, this year's price increases will knock 0.5 - 0.7 percentage point off China's GDP, and bump up 0.8 - 1.2 percentage points for the domestic consumer price index and 3.2 - 4 percentage points for the producer price index.

Then there is an extra outflow of tens of billions of dollars in spending as China's economic growth is more and more closely tied to oil prices. Oil is the single commodity that causes the biggest trade deficit, which amounted to US $35 billion last year and is estimated to reach US $55 billion this year. China's import for the year is expected to total 130 million tons or one billion barrels. If each barrel costs an extra US $15, it means China has to shell out an additional US $15 billion from its foreign currency reserve.

Private citizens will directly bear the increasing cost as their expenditures rise with oil prices. So far, there have been four price hikes of processed oil on the Chinese market, causing some consumers to tighten their purse strings and others to change their spending patterns.

Besides end users, producers also need to bear the burden of additional costs. As the economy expands, growth in oil consumption has been more than 10 per cent for the past two years. Elasticity coefficient of energy consumption goes up and dependency on foreign oil has reached 40 per cent as every domestic industry feels the shocks from price hikes on the international market.

Transportation bears the brunt because it is a big consumer of oil. In terms of the volume of oil consumed, it is next only to manufacturing and it is taking a gradually larger share in the total volume of oil consumption.

Agriculture is also adversely affected as oil price hikes are passed on to chemical fertilizers and vehicles for agricultural use.

Petroleum processing and coking has also seen higher costs. Crude usually takes up 80 per cent of the total cost of a processing and coking plant whereas the industry as a whole soaks up 72 per cent of all crude oil produced. As it is directly below crude production on the food chain, it has incurred an industry-wide deficit this year because its sale price is fixed by the State and therefore cannot pass all the costs on to its own customers.

The automobile industry is also a hit in its growth phase. As higher oil prices affect consumer behaviour, such as their choice of vehicle types, carmakers have to consider gas-conserving cars, which may become popular in the future.

The chemical industry is affected, but it has a higher capability of transferring its costs. The health of the industry is highly correlated with oil prices. In recent years, the industry is in good health and reaping decent profits, but downstream industries such as chemical fiber have to bear the costs.

Questions for Discussion:
1. Do you agree that the rising oil price has a limited impact on China's economy?

2. If yes, in which aspect do you stand by your opinion?

3. If no, can you give reasons or evidence to support your idea?

4. What, do you think, is the most serious impact the high oil price may have on our economy?

5. Do you think the world crude oil price will continue to surge? How high may it rise to?

6. Do you think the high oil price reflects its due value or it is mainly due to an artificial manipulation?

7. Who benefits most and who loses a lot in terms of the high oil price?

8. Can you make some suggestions to reduce the loss to the lowest degree?

Section D
Sample Speech and Oral Practice

Part A Sample Speech

China Is Not to Blame for Rises in Oil Prices

As a matter of fact, big energy-consuming countries such as China, the United States, Japan, Germany, the Republic of Korea (ROK) and India are all contributing to rising oil prices. But in terms of total volume, the rate of increase or the energy sector per se, laying the blame at China's doorstep is not a compelling position.

First, let us look at total volume. According to BP's Statistical Review of World Energy 2005, China consumed 310 million tons of oil in 2004, accounting for 8 per cent of the world total, whereas the United States guzzled 938 million tons — a quarter of the global total and three times China's consumption.

In the same year, China's net imports were less than 149 million tons, accounting for 6 per cent of the world total trade, while the United States took in 590 million tons — four times China's net imports. This shows, as far as volume is concerned, China was not the most crucial factor affecting global oil prices.

Next, China is the world's sixth largest oil producer, and 60 per cent of its oil consumption is domestically produced. Oil makes up only 23 per cent of the country's total energy consumption, far less than coal, which accounts for 68 per cent, and also less than the world average, which is 40 per cent.

By contrast, countries such as Japan and the ROK relied almost completely on the international market for their oil, and the United States, the world's largest oil importer, bought 60 per cent of its oil on the international market. This proves that China, in terms of demand-and-supply structure, is not the major force behind the rising prices.

Rises in oil prices have more complicated explanations. Fundamentally, supply and demand in the global oil market is rather fragile and a primary estimate suggests that, based on supply and demand alone, the price for crude oil should be around US $40 per barrel.

Next is the "terror premium" — the fear of emergencies such as acts of terrorism that bump up oil prices. It is reckoned that this accounts for US $10 – 15 of the current per barrel cost.

The "speculation premium" adds another US $15 – 20.

As for the comparative dependence on oil in China and in the United States, some facts should be clarified. BP's review states that US dependency in 2004 was 63 per cent, and the US Energy Ministry has issued a report that predicts it will reach 72 per cent by 2020.

Let's not envision China's dependency for 2020, but even if it grows to be 60 per cent, it will still be below that of the United

States today or in the future.

It is, therefore, important to study the problem and raise alerts. But inaccurate statements only serve those who want to suppress China.

Part B   Presentation Practice

Directions: Talk on each of the following topics for at least five minutes. Be sure to make your points clear and logical with adequate supporting details.

Topic 1: Oil price and individual's life
Questions for reference:
1. What role does oil play in a nation's economy?
2. To what extent does the fluctuation of oil prices affect an individual's life?
3. What is your speculation of the petrol price? Surging, stable or falling?
4. What can be done to minimize the effects caused by the fluctuation of oil prices?

Topic 2: High rising oil price, a blessing or misfortune to China's economy?
Questions for reference:
1. What role does oil play in the development of a nation's economy?
2. What is the main cause of the rapid increase in oil prices?
3. Do you think the rising oil price is a blessing or misfortune to our country?

Topic 3: Petrol price and car industry

Questions for reference:

1. To what extent does the rising petrol price affect the car industry?

2. With the rising of petrol prices, do you still want to buy or use private cars? Why or why not?

3. What can the car industry do to cope with the problems caused by the high rising petrol price?

Part C   More Topics for Oral Practice

Directions: *Based on the news reports, talk on each of the following topics for at least five minutes. Be sure to make your points clear and logical with adequate supporting details.*

News Report 1:

The credit ratings agency Standard & Poor released a dramatic report, claiming that China's overseas energy strategy is one of the factors destabilizing global oil markets and pushing up prices. Some domestic experts predict that China's dependence on foreign oil will by 2020 surpass that of the United States. This is incorrect and is contributing to the so-called "energy threat from China."

Topic: *Do you think China is to blame for the rise in oil prices?*

News Report 2:

Li Yizhong (director of the State Administration for Safe Production Supervision) was embarrassed when he announced on Monday that fewer than 500 government employees had withdrawn their stakes in coal mining enterprises before the September 22 deadline. The figure was described as "incomplete" based on reports from nine provinces only, which obviously fell far short of public expectations because almost every mining accident investigated has been tainted by corruption.

Topic: *Who should be responsible for serious mining accidents, mine owners or officials who have personal stakes in unlawful coal pits?*

News Report 3:

Despite an average fall in prices of 20 to 30 per cent over the past few months, the Shanghai property market is far from being in a slump as some commentators have suggested. Strong public demand for new and better quality properties has been underlined by solid economic growth, which, in turn, is supported by the rapid development of the city's higher value-added services sector. The present price correction, apparently triggered by government measures to clamp down on excessive speculation, may seem too swift and sharp to those used to the double-digit annual price rises of the past. Indeed, many prospective home buyers are reported to have postponed making a purchase for fear of a further drop in real estate value.

Topic: *Do you think the real estate value in Shanghai will drop, remain stable or be on the up in the longer term?*

Part D   Useful Expressions

energy source	能源
oil extraction	原油开采
petroleum refining	石油提炼
animal dung as fuel	动物粪便作燃料

biogas	沼气
crude oil	原油
petrol	汽油
barrel	桶
energy resources	能源资源
enriched uranium	浓缩铀
fossil fuels	矿物燃料
fuel alcohol	燃料酒精
geothermal energy	地热能
hydroelectric power	水电能
liquefied gas	液化气
methane	甲烷
natural gas	天然气
renewable energy source	可再生能源
nuclear energy	核能
nuclear fuels	核燃料
solar energy	太阳能
thermal sea power	海洋热能
tidal energy	潮汐能
uranium	铀
wave energy	波浪能
coal gasification	煤气化
coal liquefaction	煤液化
electric power	电力
electrical storage device	蓄电装置
energy conservation	能源保护
energy conversion	能源转换
energy efficiency	能源效率
natural gas exploration	天然气勘探

nuclear energy use	核能利用
nuclear power plant	核电站
offshore oil drilling	近海石油钻探
oil exploration	石油勘探
solar heating	日照加热

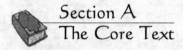

Section A
The Core Text

Future of UN **Hinges** on Effective Reform

In a world increasingly divided along cultural, political and religious lines, would it matter if the United Nations ceased to exist?

The multinational institution, founded 60 years ago in the ashes of World War Ⅱ, remains the only global forum that can meet the **daunting** challenges of a world where poverty and violence are still endemic.

The goals **enshrined** in the UN Charter, particularly those regarding international peace and security, have never been more significant.

The charter's words are as relevant today as they were 60 years ago. The organization is struggling to adapt its high ideals to a world now populated by almost four times as many nation-states as at the time of its creation.

To reach its ambitious targets, the United Nations needs reform and **reinvigoration**. Otherwise, it risks declining credibility.

The future of collective international efforts to deal with the challenges of the new century is at stake.

In September, world leaders accepted a document that

committed them to an **overhaul** of the world body's efforts to fight poverty, terrorism and human rights abuses.

The original thrust of the UN summit was to take action to implement goals set by world leaders at their meeting in 2000. These include cutting poverty by half, ensuring universal primary education and stemming the AIDS **pandemic** by 2015.

Since the United Nations came into being, the possibility of the human race uniting and living in peace and prosperity has remained the pot of gold at the end of the rainbow.

The desire for peace and prosperity transcends every barrier. It is the glue that binds peoples of different religions, political systems and races in pursuit of stability and development.

Global co-operation still remains out of reach in many respects. Yet, the population of the global village has been seeking to make that hope a reality.

The world body has showed its strengths and weaknesses in the past 60 years.

It has largely been delivering on its promise to maintain peace and security, if not in every corner of the world.

The United Nations has made a significant difference in many regions. The good the United Nations does — especially in areas such as refugee aid, development and disease prevention — is essential for billions of poor people around the world.

Rich and poor nations have their own expectations of the world body and what it can do to realize their visions of the world.

Now more than ever, the United Nations is the organization that can address mounting tension between the developed and developing countries, to head off what some analysts have called a clash of civilizations.

The United Nations has fallen far short of attaining some of the goals its founders set. A deeply troubled institution, it is facing an uncertain future, with its effectiveness diminished by a disturbing array of mistakes, power politics, scandals and other shortcomings. These problems could be a recipe for disaster if left unresolved.

The world body should be a channel through which the leading global powers work with the rest of the world rather than a diplomatic **surrogate** for US might.

The future United Nations we would like should be more active and responsive; not waiting until a situation explodes and then rushing in.

The United Nations is a forum where **disparate** members are expected to agree on aspirations and means.

Building a common approach for achieving common objectives is an inherently difficult and **contentious** undertaking.

The world organization must improve its **accountability** and efficiency, and become more responsive to the needs of the world.

◉ Notes to the Text:

hinge	取决于;以……为转移
daunting	使人畏缩的
enshrine	铭记;把……奉为神圣
reinvigoration	重新振作
overhaul	全面检查,全面修订
pandemic	流行性疾病
surrogate	代理,代理人
disparate	不同的
contentious	争论的,有异议的
accountability	有责任

◉ Understanding the Text:

1. When was the United Nations founded?

2. What is the general goal of the United Nations?

3. Why does the United Nations need reform and reinvigoration?

4. What are the strengths and weaknesses of the United Nations?

5. What are the goals set by world leaders at their meeting in 2000?

6. What will the United Nations be like in the next decade?

7. In your opinion, in what aspects does the UN need reform?

Section B
Sample Interview

UN Still Matters in World Affairs

Porter: You mention civil conflict, failed states, terrorism. There is a connection between all of these things.

Annan: Absolutely. The report I've put before the member states makes it quite clear that there is a link between development and security. You cannot have development without security and you cannot have security without development, and all this should be embedded in the respect for human rights and the rule of law. So it all hangs together. And we all need to cooperate to make it happen.

Porter: The United Nations was created to safeguard the world, help the world come together to face those threats you're talking about. But we all know that there is a less than perfect track record and that the UN has been plagued by scandals, not just in the last year but over the course of its history. Is the UN still the best option for the world when it comes to tackling these problems?

Annan: I think the UN is an indispensable organization. We've done a lot for the peoples of the world. Like all organizations, institutions, governments, and corporations, we've had our problems. We've had our share of problems. But we've also had our share of successes. And let's not forget that over the past eight, nine years or so, the UN has done lots of things from the Millennium Development Goals to the elections we've organized around the world, and to our emphasis on human rights and democratization, helping governments to strengthen institutions. A whole range of things, but of course, those... that's not news. That's not news. But I think the UN needs to adapt, it needs to improve. We need to strengthen our management, we need to be much more transparent, and we need to be able to restructure and adapt ourselves to face the challenges of today — and I think the proposals I have put before the members for reform will help us move forward in that direction.

Porter: What is your plan for getting past the events of the first part of this year, and how do you restore confidence both in your leadership and in the institution?

Annan: I think we are moving ahead. That's one of the reasons why I set up a very strong and independent panel, committee, to investigate the accusations that have been leveled against us and to get to the bottom of this, and asked everyone in the organization to cooperate fully. And I, myself, have cooperated very fully with the Volker Committee. And I was happy that on the main issue of insinuation that I may have interfered with the contracting process, there's not an iota of evidence that I did. I think we are moving ahead. We're improving our management. We are taking steps to ensure that peacekeepers do not get involved in sexual exploitation. And we have taken very concrete steps to strengthen the training of peacekeepers, to make sure the governments cooperate with us, and to make sure the governments will allow us to set up a court martial — court martial some of these troops in the country where they are serving. As of today, we have no control over these troops. We borrow them from governments, and if there's wrong doing, we repatriate them back home and the government concerned is supposed to discipline them.

Porter: Is there anything specific that you would like the United States to do between now and September?

Annan: I think the United States has a natural leadership in this organization. And their involvement and cooperation in the reform proposals is extremely important. I have spoken to President Bush since my report came out and also Secretary of State Rice, and they have both indicated to me that they will support and work with me on that reform. Obviously, they don't accept everything in the report, but there are lots of good things in the report that we can all embrace. So I'm looking forward to working with them.

Porter: The high-level panel report said that the erosion of the nuclear nonproliferation process in the world was nearly irreversible or may be irreversible. What can we do to protect this?

Annan: I think we need strengthen the inspection regime. I hope the Additional Protocol would become general and everybody would adhere to it. I hope it would strengthen the NPT (nuclear Non-Proliferation Treaty). We're going to do a non-proliferation treaty regime, which is going to be looked at. And also the countries that have not joined the

Comprehensive Test Ban Treaty, should be encouraged to do it. But I also believe that the nuclear powers should take the lead by demonstrating new energy or seriousness about disarmament, to dissuade others, that it's no use going...it doesn't help you to go in this direction. What's the point of building up weapons, spending lots of money, if you're going to have to dismantle it?

Porter: I'm wondering about your personal motivation in this job. You know, it seems that every time something bad happens in the world that no one wants to deal with, they bring it to the United Nations. What motivates you to get out of bed every morning?

Annan: You're absolutely right that sometimes I go to bed wondering what I'm going to wake up to in the morning, and what we'll have to deal with. And invariably, there's always something that we need to deal with, something that affects the UN agenda when you wake up in the morning. And it's been a tremendous challenge for the past eight, nine years, and also we have lots of problems around the world. But each time I feel that I'm able to make a little difference that affects an individual's life or improves the situation a little bit. And as someone who believes in the ideals of the United Nations, it keeps you going.

Section C
Information Input and Group Discussion

1. UN Is Faced with New Challenges

Over the past 60 years, along with the changed situation on the international stage, the UN has experienced constant development and growth amidst various tests and challenges, growing into a big international family with its membership increasing from 51 in the early period of its founding to 191 at present, and has thus made an important contribution to the world's peaceful development.

Compared with what it was like at the time of the founding of the UN, today's world has undergone tremendous changes. UN activities have gone far beyond maintaining peace and solving conflicts. The UN is not an international organization keeping itself aloof as various UN agencies are engaged in extremely extensive and meticulous work, and they are closely associated with the lives of the people of various countries around the world.

So far, the UN has completed negotiations on solving over 170 regional conflicts and has deployed 60 peacekeeping troops and observation groups in conflicted regions worldwide, thereby restoring tranquility and making it possible for negotiations to be carried on and freeing tens of millions of people from the scourge of conflicts; through the International Atom Energy Agency (IAEA), the UN has adopted security measures for 100 nuclear facilities in 70 countries and has signed 237 security agreements with 152 countries. Through 13 years of efforts by the World Health Organization (WHO), smallpox was thoroughly wiped out from the earth in 1980. This data sheet can be extended. It indicates that with the UN, our planet of today has become more secure.

Sixty years have passed, major changes have taken place in the connotations of international security and peace, and the UN is also faced with new challenges. Poverty, disease, the deteriorating environment and other non-traditional security factors, in particular, are posing enormous threats to the international community and their seriousness is by no means inferior to terrorism and the proliferation of weapons of mass destruction (WMD).

Just as Secretary-General Kofi Annan said at the meeting marking the 60th anniversary of the founding of the UN, this world body must give expression to this new age and should cope with various challenges of the time. As everybody knows, the biggest challenge is that hundreds of millions of helpless people in the world are suffering from the torment of hunger, disease and degeneration of the environment, although the world has no lack of the ability to rescue them.

To better cope with challenges, the UN Millennium Summit put forward the Millennium Development Goals in September 2000. The goals aimed to eliminate poverty, starvation, disease, illiteracy, the worsening environment and the discrimination against women embody humans' longing for a better life as well as their common conviction: Development is an important condition for realizing world peace, stability and prosperity.

To better cope with challenges, the United Nations still needs reform. Only through conducting reasonable and necessary reform is it possible to create a powerful United Nations that can constantly promote common development. Strengthening the ability and authority of the UN through reform is the only way leading to common security and common development of the international community.

As a permanent member of the UN Security Council, China abides by the purposes and principles of the United Nations Charter, actively supports and participates in the UN work in various fields, and has been working unremittingly for the realization of the lofty objective of world peace and human progress.

Questions for Discussion:

1. What new challenges is the United Nations facing now? And what is the biggest one?
2. In what aspect do you think the UN needs reform most urgently today, peace, security, poverty, the environment or terrorism?
3. What do you think of the likely expansion of the permanent membership of the UN Security Council?
4. Do you think only the rich countries should become members of the UN Security Council or there should be a proper proportion between developed countries and underdeveloped countries?
5. In your opinion, how should the United Nations cope with the challenges it faces in the new century?
6. What is your speculation of the reform of the United Nations?

2. Globalization

Globalization of Economy

Advances in communications and transportation technology, combined with free market ideology, have given goods, services, and capital unprecedented mobility. Northern countries want to open world markets to their goods and take advantage of abundant, cheap labor in the South, policies often supported by Southern elites. They use international financial institutions and regional trade agreements to compel poor countries to "integrate" by reducing tariffs, privatizing state enterprises, and relaxing environmental and labor standards. The results have enlarged profits for investors but offered pittances to laborers, provoking a strong backlash from civil society. This page analyzes economic globalization, and examines how it might be resisted or regulated in order to promote sustainable development.

Globalization of Politics

Traditionally politics has been undertaken within national political systems. National governments have been ultimately responsible for maintaining the security and economic welfare of their citizens, as well as the protection of human rights and the environment within their borders. With global ecological changes, an even more integrated global economy, and other global trends, political activity increasingly takes place at the global level.

Under globalization, politics can take place above the state through political integration schemes such as the European Union and through inter-governmental organizations such as the International Monetary Fund, the World Bank and the World Trade Organization. Political activity can also transcend national borders through global movements and NGOs. Civil society organizations act globally by forming alliances with organizations in other countries, using global communications systems, and lobbying international organizations and other actors directly, instead of working through their national governments.

Globalization of Culture

Technology has now created the possibility and even the likelihood of a global culture. The Internet, fax machines, satellites, and cable TV are sweeping away cultural boundaries. Global entertainment companies shape the perceptions and dreams of ordinary citizens, wherever they live. This spread of values, norms, and culture tends to promote Western ideals of capitalism. Will local cultures inevitably fall victim to this global "consumer" culture? Will

English eradicate all other languages? Will consumer values overwhelm peoples' sense of community and social solidarity? Or, on the contrary, will a common culture lead the way to greater shared values and political unity? This section looks at these and other issues of culture and globalization.

Globalization of Law

Law has traditionally been the province of the nation state, whose courts and police enforce legal rules. By contrast, international law has been comparatively weak, with little effective enforcement power. But globalization is changing the contours of law and creating new global legal institutions and norms. The International Criminal Court promises to bring to justice odious public offenders based on a worldwide criminal code, while inter-governmental cooperation increasingly brings to trial some of the most notorious international criminals. Business law is globalizing fastest of all, as nations agree to standard regulations, rules and legal practices. Diplomats and jurists are creating international rules for bankruptcy, intellectual property, banking procedures and many other areas of corporate law. In response to this internationalization, and in order to serve giant, transnational companies, law firms are globalizing their practice. The biggest firms are merging across borders, creating mega practices with several thousand professionals in dozens of countries.

Questions for Discussion:
1. Do you think globalization is a threat or opportunity to the world?
2. Why do some people object to it?
3. Does globalization do good or harm to the development of our economy? Can you give some examples?

4. What does the globalization of politics tend to be?

5. Do you think culture can be globalized? Why or why not?

6. Is it possible for the whole world to have the same law?

Section D
Sample Speech and Oral Practice

Part A　Sample Speech

Does Globalization Increase Poverty and Inequality?

During the 20th century, global average per capita income rose strongly, but with considerable variation among countries. It is clear that the income gap between rich and poor countries has been widening for many decades. The most recent World Economic Outlook studies 42 countries (representing almost 90 per cent of world population) for which data are available for the entire 20th century. It reaches the conclusion that output per capita has risen appreciably but that the distribution of income among countries has become more unequal than at the beginning of the century.

But incomes do not tell the whole story; broader measures of welfare that take account of social conditions show that poorer countries have made considerable progress. For instance, some low-income countries, e. g. Sri Lanka, have quite impressive social indicators. One recent paper finds that if countries are compared using the UN's Human Development Indicators (HDIs), which take education and life expectancy into account, then the picture that emerges is quite different from that suggested by the income data alone.

Indeed the gaps may have narrowed. A striking inference from the study is a contrast between what may be termed an "income gap" and an "HDI gap." The (inflation-adjusted) income levels of today's poor countries are still well below those of the leading countries in 1870. And the gap in incomes has increased. But judged by their HDIs, today's poor countries are well ahead of where the leading countries were in 1870. This is largely because medical advances and improved living standards have brought strong increases in life expectancy.

But even if the HDI gap has narrowed in the long term, far too many people are losing ground. Life expectancy may have increased but the quality of life for many has not improved, with many still in abject poverty. And the spread of AIDS through Africa in the past decade is reducing life expectancy in many countries.

This has brought a new urgency to policies specifically designed to alleviate poverty. Countries with a strong growth record, pursuing the right policies, can expect to see a sustained reduction in poverty, since recent evidence suggests that there exists at least a one-to-one correspondence between growth and poverty reduction. And if strongly pro-poor policies — for instance in well-targeted social expenditure — are pursued then there is a better chance that growth will be amplified into more rapid poverty reduction. This is one compelling reason for all economic policy makers, including the IMF, to pay heed more explicitly to the objective of poverty reduction.

Part B Presentation Practice

Directions: *Talk on each of the following topics for at least five minutes. Be sure to make your points clear and logical with adequate supporting details.*

Topic 1: The reform of the United Nations

Questions for reference:

1. What is the general goal of the reform of the United Nations?
2. Why does the UN need reform?
3. What needs to be improved for this world organization?
4. What role should our country play in this reform? Can you give some comments or suggestions?

Topic 2: Benefits and drawbacks of globalization

Questions for reference:

1. Do you think globalization poses a threat or opportunity to China's development?
2. What are the positive aspects and what are the challenges our country will be faced with?
3. How should we deepen our reform to face up to globalization?

Topic 3: Local protectionism

Questions for reference:

1. What do you think of local protectionism? Does it do good or harm to the development of the local/nation's economy?
2. What are the underlying causes of this protection?
3. Do you think local protectionism is a nation's problem or the world's problem?
4. What do you think is a proper way to deal with this problem?

Part C   More Topics for Oral Practice

Directions: Based on the news reports, talk on each of the following topics for at least five minutes. Be sure to make your points clear and logical with adequate supporting details.

News Report 1:

Leaders from some 150 countries convened in New York on Wednesday to celebrate the 60th anniversary of the founding of the United Nations. The largest-ever world gathering bears witness to the fact that the world pins high hopes on its largest multilateral organization. Participants of the UN's annual gathering are expected to bring with them consensus on UN Secretary-General Kofi Annan's reform proposals to give the world body a much-needed facelift, which will affect the identity and shape of our common future.

Topic: *It is generally believed that UN reform shouldn't change its basic values but what is to be changed for its reform?*

News Report 2:

Despite an obvious advantage in price and quality, made-in-Chinas have to do due homework before doing business with the United Nations (UN), officials of Chinese Ministry of Commerce (MOC) said Sunday. A lack of mutual understanding between Chinese enterprises and the UN's procurement organizations has made China lose a huge overseas market and as for the UN, a good business partner. The UN spent more than US $6 billion for global procurement last year, while only around US $30 million was spent in China and the suppliers were mainly from Beijing and coastal cities like Shanghai and Shenzhen.

Topic: *What are the positive aspects of doing business with the United Nations?*

News Report 3:

The National Administration for the Protection of State Secrets and the Ministry of Civil Affairs declared at a press conference on Monday that starting from August, the death tolls from natural disasters would no longer be a State secret. This appears a step behind practice. Over the years, the public has become accustomed to the media's graphic accounts of human losses to natural disasters. Even the Civil Affairs Ministry itself has been publishing nationwide death tolls from natural disasters in recent years. At local levels, some officials were found to report exaggerated figures of loss to swindle bigger relief packages.

Topic: *What do you think of the statement "Fewer State secrets, better public welfare"? Can you cite some examples to illustrate your opinion?*

Part D   Useful Expressions

Security Council, the	安全理事会
General Assembly	联合国大会
Secretariat	秘书处
Office of the Secretary General	秘书长办公室
Department of Conference Services	会议局
United Nations Conference on Trade and Development Secretariat	联合国贸易与发展会议事务局
United Nations Administrative Tribunal	联合国行政裁判所
International Law Commission	国际法委员会
United Nations Commission on International Trade Law	联合国国际贸易法委员会
Special Committee on Peace-Keeping Operations	维和行动特别委员会
United Nations Trade and Development Board (TDB)	联合国贸易与发展理事会
United Nations Development Program (UNDP)	联合国开发计划署

United Nations Children's Fund 　　　　　联合国儿童基金会
　（UNICEF）

United Nations Industrial Development 　联合国工业发展组织
　Organization（UNIDO）

United Nations Capital Development 　　联合国资本开发基金会
　Fund（UNCDF）

International Labor Organization 　　　　国际劳工组织
　（ILO）

United Nations Food and Agriculture 　联合国粮食农业组织
　Organization（FAO）

United Nations Educational，Scientific 　联合国教科文组织
　and Cultural Organization（UNESCO）

International Civil Aviation 　　　　　　国际民用航空组织
　Organization（ICAO）

World Health Organization（WHO）　　世界卫生组织

International Telecommunications 　　　国际电信联盟
　Union（ITU）

World Meteorological Organization 　　世界气象组织
　（WMO）

Universal Postal Union（UPU）　　　　万国邮政联盟

International Maritime Consultative 　　国际海事协商组织
　Organization（IMCO）

International Finance Corporation 　　　国际金融公司
　（IFC）

International Monetary Fund（IMF）　　国际货币基金组织

International Bank for Reconstruction 　国际复兴开发银行(世界银
　and Development（IBRD）　　　　　　行 World Bank 的主体)

International Development Association 　国际开发协会
　（IDA）

General Agreement on Tariffs and 　　关贸总协定

138

Trade（GATT）

International Atomic Energy Agency　　　国际原子能组织
　（IAEA）

World Federation of Trade Unions　　　世界工联
　（WFTU）

International Confederation of Free　　　国际自由工会联合会
　Trade Unions（ICFTU）

International Chamber of Commerce　　　国际商会
　（ICC）

International Federation of Agricultural　国际农业生产者联盟
　Producers（IFAP）

Unit Eight

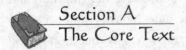

Section A
The Core Text

Is Technology Making Us Smarter?

Today, **terabytes** of easily accessed data, always-on Internet connectivity, and lightning-fast search engines are profoundly changing the way people gather information. But the age-old question remains: Is technology making us smarter? Or are we lazily reliant on computers, and, well, dumber than we used to be?

If there is a good answer to the question, it probably starts with a contradiction: What makes us intelligent — the ability to reason and learn — is staying the same and will never fundamentally change because of technology. On the other hand, technology, from pocket calculators to the Internet, is radically changing the notion of the intelligence necessary to function in the modern world.

Intelligence, as it impacts economist Valderrama, is our capacity to adapt and thrive in our own environment. In a Darwinian sense, it's as true now as it was millions of years ago, when man's aptitude for hearing the way branches broke or smelling a **spore** affected his power to avoid **predators**, eat and survive.

But what makes someone smart can vary in different cultures and situations. A successful Wall Street banker who has dropped into the Australian Outback likely couldn't pull off a great Crocodile Dundee impression. A mathematical genius like Isaac Newton could be — in fact, he was — socially **inept** and a borderline hermit. A master painter? Probably not so good at balancing a checkbook.

What's undeniable is the Internet's democratization of information. It's providing instant access to information and, in a sense, improving the practical application of intelligence for everyone.

Nearly a century ago, Henry Ford didn't have the Internet, but he did have a bunch of smart guys. The auto industry pioneer, as a **parlor** trick, liked to claim he could answer any question in 30 minutes. In fact, he had organized a research staff he could call at any time to get him the answer.

Today, you don't have to be an auto **baron** to **feign** that kind of knowledge. You just have to be able to type G-O-O-G-L-E. People can in a matter of minutes find sources of information like court documents, scientific papers or corporate securities filings.

"The notion that the world's knowledge is literally at your fingertips is very compelling and is very **beguiling**," said Vint Cerf, who co-created the underlying architecture of the Internet and who is widely considered one of its "fathers." What's exciting "is the Internet's ability to absorb such a large amount of information and for it to be accessible to other people, even if they don't know it exists or don't know who you are."

Indeed, Doug Engelbart, one of the pioneers of personal computing technology in the 1960s, **envisioned** in the early 1960s that the PC would augment human intelligence. He believes that society's ability to gain insight from information has evolved with the help of computers.

"The key thing about all the world's big problems is that they have to be dealt with collectively," Engelbart said. "If we don't get collectively smarter, we're doomed."

According to at least one definition, intelligence is the "ability to reason, plan, solve problems, think abstractly, comprehend ideas and language, and learn." Yet intelligence is not just about book learning or test scores; it also reflects a deeper understanding of the world. On average, people with high IQs are thought to live longer, earn more money, process information faster and have larger working memories.

Yet could all this information provided by the Internet and **gadgets dampen** our motivation to remember anything?

Working with the Treo handheld computing device he helped create, Jeff Hawkins can easily recount exactly what he did three years ago on Sept. 8, factor 9,982 and Pi, or describe a weather system over the Pacific Ocean. But without his "smart" phone, he can't recall his daughter's telephone number offhand.

It's a familiar circumstance for people living in the hyper-connected Internet age, when it has become easier to program a cell phone or computer — instead of your brain — to recall facts or other essential information. In some sense, our digital devices do the thinking for us now, helping us with everything from calendar scheduling and local directions to in-depth research and Jeopardy-like **trivia**.

"It's true we don't remember anything anymore, but we don't need to," said Hawkins, the co-founder of Palm Computing and author of a book called *On Intelligence*.

"We might one day sit around and **reminisce** about having to remember phone numbers, but it's not a bad thing. It frees us up to think about other things. The brain has a limited capacity; if you give it high-level tools, it will work on high-level problems," he said.

Only 600 years ago, people relied on memory as a primary means of communication and tradition. Before the printed word, memory was essential to lawyers, doctors, priests and poets, and those with particular talents for memory were revered. Seneca, a famous teacher of rhetoric around A. D. 37, was said to be able to repeat long passages of speeches he had heard years before. "Memory," said Greek playwright Aeschylus, "is the mother of all wisdom."

People feared the invention of the printing press because it would cause people to rely on books for their memory. Today, memory is more irrelevant than ever, argue some academics.

What's important is your ability to use what you know well. There are people who are walking encyclopedias, but they make a mess of their lives. Getting a 100 per cent on a written driving test doesn't mean you can drive.

● Notes to the Text:

terabyte	[计] 兆兆字节(信息量度单位,＝2^{40}字节)
spore	孢子
predator	食肉动物;掠夺者
inept	无能的,笨拙的
parlor	营业室,业务室
baron	巨头,大亨
feign	假装,装作,捏造
beguiling	吸引人的,令人陶醉的
envision	想像,预想
gadget	新发明,小玩意
dampen	使潮湿;使沮丧
trivia	难题答问比赛
reminisce	回忆

Understanding the Text:

1. What does the author mean in the question "Is technology making us smarter?" What is your comment on that?

2. What do you think of the definitions of human intelligence given by Valderrama and Darwin?

3. In what aspects does new technology help us?

4. Why is it important for us to solve the world's problems collectively?

5. How do you understand the statement "The brain has a limited capacity; if you give it high-level tools, it will work on high-level problems"?

6. Do you agree or disagree with the author's opinion?

Section B
Sample Interview

Internal Communications

Q: How did you become involved in internal communications?

Professor Taylor: I came from a background of technical publications, originally as a technical author writing aircraft equipment manuals. As technology has widened the scope of authors and communications, this role took me into general communications and then Intranets. The technical publications side of the business always concerned itself with the maintenance and archive of information and many disciplines I now use stem from this background, including KM (knowledge management).

Q: What is the main role for internal communications within your organization?

Professor Taylor: Internal communications is about change — informing people what is happening in the business and ensuring that they adapt their behavior and so on. It is also about keeping employees up to date so that they feel part of the organization, particularly in a large organization such as Abbey.

Q: How has this evolved over recent years?

Professor Taylor: Communications now has a higher profile as organizations are realizing that people need information to represent the company and to feel a sense of pride in their work. There is a greater expectation that staff will be informed. I think technology such as e-mail and the Intranet has proved a hindrance as much as a help. The communications teams now have to consider the validity of information and police available information. The communication process needs to be slicker than ever before.

Q: How does internal communications relate/interact with other functions within the company, such as HR, marketing, IT, branding?

Professor Taylor: At Abbey we use relationship managers that work directly with the business, and the production areas then work with the relationship managers. In this way, communications becomes an integral part of operations. Communications needs to be seen as a facilitator in the business process: There has to be an outcome or result that benefits the business. Working as part of the specific operating area ensures that this happens.

Q: What tools do you use within internal communications?

Professor Taylor: We use a wide range of activities to suit each need. The Intranet is a key tool and this works in conjunction with our MS-SharePoint sites to facilitate knowledge management and knowledge sharing. Communities of practice and interest are in place and an active measurement and research area feeds information and user opinion back to the business. On the internal communications front, we use talkback sessions, seminars, magazines and business television.

Q: How does knowledge management affect internal communications and what is your role within your company's KM strategy?

Professor Taylor: KM is a result of communication, so there should be no major overlap. Some communication is on the reference side, policy and procedure for instance, and this becomes part of the knowledge set in reality. We try to see reference as part of the company knowledge that is auditable and traceable, while knowledge management concentrates on the task and people information. I have a KM responsibility for company knowledge and HR has a KM responsibility for people knowledge but we work closely together.

Q: From an internal communications perspective,

what are the main benefits/value KM brings?

Professor Taylor: KM can support communications by allowing a user perspective. A greater understanding of the reasons for communications leads to under- standing and retention of information. An informed work force allows a more informed debate, a broader understanding of issues and a wider communications base.

Q: What are the challenges to realizing these benefits?

Professor Taylor: The main challenge is getting buy-in from the user. Some users do not see the value of knowledge sharing or guard their knowledge. The benefits of knowledge sharing must be made clear and systems need to be easy to use.

Q: How are you addressing these challenges?

Professor Taylor: We look closely at the benefits to the user. Allowing the user to have communities that are of interest has worked well and we will continue this method. The systems are also continually under review so that they match the users' needs and operate in as seamless a fashion as possible.

Q: What have been your biggest successes and the main lessons learnt?

Professor Taylor: The rate of take-up has been our biggest success. It took time, but once the systems became "user friendly", the take-up rate was beyond expectations. One of our best groups was focusing on web publishing and the way the group decided on good practice within the interest group was

extraordinary. This method was far more
successful than a standard meeting.

Q: How do you envisage internal communications
and KM developing over the next 18 months?

Professor Taylor: I think it will evolve around the user. Communications, HR and training issues seem to be
coming together and KM seems to be the catalyst
for this. Now KM is under the HR banner, I
believe knowledge will be seen as the key to
personal development. KM may soon be seen as
core to working practice. Communications allows
the day-to-day top-up of knowledge.

Q: What words of advice would you give to your
internal communications peers that are also
involved in KM?

Professor Taylor: Get the user on your side and allow the momentum
to grow through motivation and trust. Patience is
a virtue and cultural change takes time — don't
rush it.

Section C
Information Input and Group Discussion

1. Science and Technology Is a Two-Edged Sword

The 20th century saw more momentous changes than any
previous century: change for better, change for worse; change that
brought enormous benefits to human beings, change that threatened
the very existence of the human species. Many factors contributed to
these changes but — in my opinion — the most important factor was

the progress in science.

Academic research in the physical and biological sciences has vastly broadened our horizons; it has given us a deep insight into the structure of matter and of the universe; it has brought a better understanding of the nature of life and of its continuous evolution. Technology — the application of science — has made fantastic advances that have affected us beneficially in nearly every aspect of life: better health, more wealth, less drudgery, greater access to information.

The continuation of such activities in the 21st century will result in an even greater boon to humanity: in pure science — a wider and deeper knowledge in all spheres of learning; in applied science — a more equitable distribution of material benefits, and a better protection of the environment.

Sadly, however, there is another side to the picture. The creativity of science has been employed to the detriment of mankind. The application of science and technology to the development and manufacture of weapons of mass destruction has created a real threat to the continuing existence of the human race on this planet. We have seen this happen in the case of nuclear weapons. Although their actual use in combat has so far occurred only in 1945 — when two Japanese cities were destroyed — during the four decades of the Cold War, obscenely huge arsenals of nuclear weapons were accumulated and made ready for use. The arsenals were so large that if the weapons had actually been detonated the result could have been the complete extinction of the human species, as well as of many animal species.

To a large extent the nuclear arms race was driven by scientists. They kept on designing new types of weapons, not because of any credible requirement — arsenals 100 times smaller would have sufficed for any conceivable deterrence purpose — but mainly to satisfy their inflated egos, or for the intense exhilaration experienced in exploring new technical concepts.

This is a complete perversion of the lofty ideals of science. It is a severe, but justified, indictment of members of a highly respected group in society. William Shakespeare said: "The web of our life is of a mingled yarn, good and ill together." The above brief review of the application of only one strand of human activities — science — seems to bear out this adage.

Questions for Discussion:

1. Can you mention some benefits science and technology has brought us?
2. What are the possible challenges it may bring us?
3. What do you think of Shakespeare's words, the saying that "The web of our life is of a mingled yarn, good and ill together"?
4. How do you understand the statement that science and technology is a two-edged sword?
5. What is the proper attitude towards science and technology?
6. What will science and technology be like in the next decade?

2. The Power of the Computer

During the last 25 years the computer undoubtedly must be considered one of our greatest inventions. Its rapid development and proliferation of use throughout the world have been remarkable. Certainly, the computer has irreversibly changed the way work is done and brought about progress in written communication, in finance, and in science.

Computers have taken much of the drudgery out of writing.

With the advent of word processors, mistakes can be corrected and editing can be done on the computer without the need to rewrite or retype an entire page. The computer possesses the power to remember all that has been written and can do things that if done manually would be nearly impossible. For example, it can set margins and maintain them — by slightly expanding or compressing the letters in a line, there is no need to hyphenate words and perfectly straight margins on the left and right sides of a page are achieved. Relatively inexpensive machines are now available that are able to generate large, stylized type for headings and illustrations, and it is even possible today to produce a fully ready-to-be-printed book on the computer. The printing press might have been the first invention to have a profound impact on written words, but it was not the last. The computer is changing the way we write today.

The computer has also ushered in remarkable changes in the financial world. Take, for example, the use of the computer in banking and the way banks handle money. Today banks have maintained their traditional working hours of operation, but our money is available to us 24 hours a day, 7 days a week. Why? Because the computer has made possible the automatic teller machines that are placed all over any given city, and as a result, our dollars are closer to us and always available. Banks also keep track of our balances and transactions with the help of computers. In the past this had to be done manually; today the speed of computers can accomplish the same thing in a fraction of the time and at a much lower cost. Computers, additionally, rarely make mathematical errors, and so our chances of being "shortchanged" are fewer today.

The computer has also been a boost to the scientific community, and with its help scientists are making great advances in our knowledge of the world. One small example for this is in the science of weather forecasting. The computer's "number-crunching" power has enabled weather forecasters to do something that is impossible before: store models of the entire atmosphere of the earth in powerful computers. For these models to work, the computer must execute billions of operations per second. Computers today are capable of this, and the models help make forecasts more reliable and long-range trends predictable. The models can also be used today to evaluate the impact of acid rain or the unthinkable aftermath of a nuclear exchange.

The computer's power is so vast and its impact so far-reaching that I have been able to touch on only a few of the ways it is changing our world. The computer is here to stay, and I welcome it. It is truly a giant of our scientific world.

Questions for Discussion:

1. In what ways does computer technology influence our daily lives?
2. If you use a computer at home, work or at leisure, what do you use the computer for?
3. What do you think of online shopping? Have you ever bought anything online? If not, would you consider having a try?
4. Do you think using the Internet for education purposes such as taking classes online is beneficial? Why or why not?
5. Do you think using the Internet for banking purposes is safe and secure?
6. What do you know about hackers? Do you think they pose a threat to national and international security?

Section D
Sample Speech and Oral Practice

Part A Sample Speech

Information Superhighways

What we need is a nationwide network of "information superhighways," linking scientists, business people, educators and students by fiber-optic cable to process and deal with information that is available but unused.

Such a network is the single most cost-effective step America could take to become more competitive in the world economy. It is also the single most important step the United States could take to improve its proficiency in science, technology and research.

Major US corporations spend millions of dollars seeking answers to questions about how to plan for the future and how to gain a competitive edge. In almost every case, all of the information they need to answer those questions is already available. But they have no idea how to find the needle in the haystack, how to distill it and how to make the judgments required to guide those corporations.

Of course, today, scientists, engineers and a few million computer hobbyists know the power of computer networking, and they take the convenience of networking for granted. But imagine that the network could transmit not just text but video and voice. It is easy to imagine uses for such a system because prototypes are already available. But the prototypes are limited because they link only a few computers. Already there's electronic mail, electronic banking, electronic shopping, electronic tax returns and electronic newspapers, but these applications are limited severely by the speed and size of our networks.

The really exciting services are yet to come. Researchers are already developing and demonstrating them. Today they are using supercomputers to organize and distill information for our productive use.

Similarly, the software being developed to allow massively parallel supercomputers to sort through these silos of data will be used to provide network users with access to a quantity of information equal to all the bits of data in the entire Library of Congress.

The interactive features made possible in a network will usher in a second information revolution.

Part B Presentation Practice

Directions: *Talk on each of the following topics for at least five minutes. Be sure to make your points clear and logical with adequate supporting details.*

Topic 1: Online shopping
Questions for reference:
1. Have you ever bought anything online? If not, would you consider having a try?
2. What are the possible benefits and drawbacks of doing shopping on line?
3. Which benefit of online shopping attracts you most, its convenience, economy or efficiency?

Topic 2: Will computers replace teachers in the classroom?
Questions for reference:
1. Do you think it possible for computers to replace teachers in the

classroom in the future? Why or why not?

2. What can computers do for us in the classroom? Can you give some examples?

3. What is the proper attitude towards the use of computer technology in teaching?

Topic 3: Science and technology is a two-edged sword.

Questions for reference:

1. How do you understand this statement? Can you show some examples to support your opinion?

2. Can you explain why science and technology is a mixed blessing?

3. What is a proper attitude towards science and technology? Can we do something for it?

Part C More Topics for Oral Practice

Directions: Based on the news reports, talk on each of the following topics for at least five minutes. Be sure to make your points clear and logical with adequate supporting details.

News Report 1:

On July 21, 2005, China Internet Network Information Centre released a report in which was encouraging news about the development of China's Internet network: By the end of June, the number of people online in China had reached 103 million, second only to the United States. In addition, it was the first time broadband users with a population of 53 million outnumbered dial-up users. These figures marked some epoch-making changes in China's Internet development. They could also be translated into both opportunities and challenges for administrators.

Topic: *Why does the popularity of the Internet hold both opportunities and challenges for administrators?*

News Report 2:

An economist has said China's auto industry is to experience rapid growth in the coming 15 years and the country will become the world's largest automaker by 2020. China's auto output hit 5.07 million units in 2004, ranking fourth among the world's largest automakers following the United States, Japan and Germany.

Topic: *Should China be encouraged to fully develop its car industry?*

News Report 3:

On September 8, the International Literacy Day, China announced it still has 85 million illiterate people. Most of them are clustered in the country's less developed rural areas of the landlocked western regions. Earlier, Liu Xiaoyun, a scholar with China Agricultural University, disclosed that there is the same number of people in China still in the grip of poverty. Again, they are rural residents or migrant "floating" groups from rural areas. The announcements may have been mutually exclusive but the figure of 85 million is more than a coincidence.

Topic: *Illiteracy is believed to be the root of poverty. Do you think education can break the vicious poverty cycle?*

Part D　Useful Expressions

desktop	台式电脑
laptop	便携式电脑；笔记本电脑
analog computer	模拟计算机
computer language	计算机语言

electronics	电子学
integrated circuit	集成电路
magnetic storage	磁存储器
optical scanner	光扫描器
computer crime	电脑犯罪
Internet cafe	网吧
online love affair	网恋
surf the Internet	网上冲浪
cyber friend	网友

$\mathbf{\mathit{U}}$nit Nine

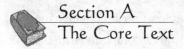
Section A
The Core Text

Environmental Problems and Future Measures in Denmark

The quality of the Danish environment has improved over the last two decades. However, a number of areas remain where the environment is so polluted that it may affect human health or have negative consequences for nature and animals.

One cause of air pollution is suspended particles from diesel vehicles. Recent surveys indicate that suspended particles have an impact on health. The scope of this impact is uncertain. The existing particle level is considered to aggravate conditions, particularly for people with respiratory diseases, and to increase the mortality rate.

Ground-level **ozone** may cause respiratory problems and damage trees and crops. The yield loss due to ozone is estimated at approximately 10 per cent. The greater part of ozone in the air above Denmark is transported here from the south. Ground-level ozone must be limited by reducing NOx emissions in the future.

Many people are exposed to noise nuisance. Traffic is the most important source of noise with road traffic being the largest contributor. According to recent estimates, more than 500,000 dwellings are exposed to noise of more than 55 dB from road traffic, the recommended limit value for new housing areas. For approximately 145,000 of these, exposure exceeds 65 dB.

The ozone layer, high up in the atmosphere, must be preserved. It protects the earth from hazardous ultraviolet radiation from the sun, which in excessive doses increases the risk of skin cancer in humans and impedes plant growth. The greenhouse effect accelerates ozone depletion. In coming years, the thin ozone layer will aggravate the damage.

Industrial waste and air pollution have led to soil contamination — especially in old urban areas. Lead and **tarry** compounds in the soil are a health problem in particular to children living or playing in these areas. Other compounds cause problems because they disperse to groundwater. Pesticide residues, **chlorinated solvents**, MTBE petrol additives and oil and petrol may pose a threat to clean groundwater.

Groundwater and drinking water monitoring shows, however, that in some areas groundwater quality is under threat. In rural areas, groundwater is threatened because of the use of pesticides in agriculture, and nitrogen handling in some parts of Denmark constitutes a major problem. Pesticide use in urban areas also causes the pollution of groundwater. Contaminated soil threatens groundwater because of the inappropriate handling of chemicals in the past.

Discharges to the **aquatic** environment of metals and **xenobiotic** compounds may affect animals and plants in the short as well as the long term. Many compounds accumulate in the food chains and are thus transferred to humans through the food we catch at sea.

Microorganisms are everywhere. Some are vital, and others may be pathogenic. We have knowledge of some microorganisms from, for example, beach water, but risks may also come from waste, sludge and sewage.

The content of suspended particles in the air must be so low as to have no negative impact on the quality of the life and health of the Danish population or the environment. Denmark must focus on reducing the content of suspended particles in the air. First, we must get a precise overview of the extent of the problem in Denmark. At the same time we must increase our knowledge about the effects of various measures and technological solutions as a basis for future measures. In the EU, limit values have been established for emissions of particles from new lorries and buses.

Denmark must reduce acidification, **eutrophication** and ground-level ozone. Effective implementation of international regulations on the emission of SO2, NOx, VOC and NH3 in Denmark by 2010 has top priority. In the long term, it will be necessary to set new goals and launch new initiatives to ensure that these environmental problems are solved completely.

In 2005, the government will present a strategy for reduced noise from road traffic. This strategy will include information regarding the feasibility of achieving a significant reduction in the number of dwellings severely affected by road noise. In addition, the strategy will assess the macro-economic costs. All dwellings exposed to train traffic noise exceeding 65 dB are expected to be offered noise protection by 2010. Noise is an important parameter for environmental approval of heavily polluting enterprises. Companies requiring environmental authorization often draw up action plans for noise reduction.

Ozone **depletion** must be halted to reduce the number of skin cancer cases in humans and improve the growing conditions of plants. Denmark will continue its international efforts to phase out ozone-depleting compounds.

It is important to continue our measures against soil

contamination. We must make sure that soil contamination in urban areas and pollution that may threaten the current or future supply of drinking water do not give rise to health problems.

Clean drinking water remains a high priority. The ban on pesticides endangering groundwater must remain in force. Work has commenced on assessing whether areas especially sensitive to leaching of pesticides can be designated. On this basis, assessments of the need to regulate the application of pesticides in these areas will be carried out. Regional and local authorities and water utility companies must now implement the groundwater mapping framework and groundwater-protecting measures to secure clean groundwater in the long term.

Finally, the Water Framework Directive must be implemented in Danish legislation. The Water Framework Directive implies further protection of the aquatic environment. A new system must be established to define specific environmental objectives for ecological conditions in water districts. Concrete initiatives must be implemented based on the nature of and the human impact on individual aquatic areas. Finally, a water plan must be drawn up which has regard to planning and monitoring results.

Notes to the Text:

ozone	臭氧
tarry	焦油的，沥青的，柏油的
chlorinate	用氯消毒
solvent	溶媒，溶剂
aquatic	水生的，水栖的
xenobiotic	（药物、杀虫剂、致癌物等）异型生物质（的）
eutrophication	海藻污染
depletion	损耗

● Understanding the Text:

1. What may cause respiratory problems?
2. What is the function of the ozone layer in nature?
3. How can xenobiotic compounds affect animals and plants in the short as well as the long term?
4. According to the passage, what may cause skin cancer?
5. What measures should be taken to keep groundwater clean?
6. What is the Water Framework Directive mentioned in the passage?

Section B
Sample Interview

China's Development and Environment

Q: What is the state of China's environment today? For example, it is estimated that China will surpass the US in annual emissions of carbon dioxide within a decade and, in a few decades, in total cumulative emissions of carbon dioxide since the Industrial Revolution. Could you give us a few figures and statistics illustrating the nature of the problem?

Economy: While China's spectacular economic growth over the past two decades or so has provided a significant improvement in the standard of living for hundreds of millions of Chinese people, it has also produced an environmental disaster. There has been a dramatic increase in the demand for natural resources of all kinds, including water, land, and energy. Forest resources have been depleted, triggering a range of devastating secondary impacts, such as desertification, flooding, and species loss. At the same time, the levels of water and air pollution have skyrocketed. Small-scale township and village enterprises, which have been the engine of Chinese growth in the countryside, are very difficult to monitor and regulate and routinely dump their untreated waste directly into streams, rivers, and coastal waters.

Q: What do you think is the primary cause of this alarming state of affairs?

Economy: Much of China's environmental challenge currently stems from its overwhelming reliance on coal as its primary source of energy. China depends on coal to supply almost three-quarters of its energy needs. Burning coal is responsible for 70 per cent of the smoke and dust in the air and 92 per cent of the sulfur dioxide in China. Over the next few decades, China will also likely face significant challenges to its air quality from rapidly increasing automobile use.

Q: If coal is the primary cause of the environmental problems, are there other forms of energy resources that China is planning to draw upon in the future, or do you think the present dependence on coal will continue?

Economy: Certainly, over the past five to ten years, China has made substantial strides in developing alternative sources of energy, including hydropower, natural gas, and to a much lesser extent nuclear, solar, and wind power. The Three Gorges Dam, the West to East Pipeline from Xinjiang to Shanghai, and many other smaller-scale projects will help reshape China's energy mix over the long term. As for the Three Gorges Dam, I must also point out that the Dam will not only produce benefits as an alternative source of energy but also cause problems, such as biodiversity loss, loss of farmland, loss of precious artifacts from ancient Chinese civilizations (because they will be submerged), and a likely dramatic increase of water pollution in the reservoir area — certainly, the ideal would have been to build several smaller dams along the river.

Q: What are the costs to the Chinese economy of China's environmental practices? Recently, Professor Dale Jorgenson of Harvard University was quoted as saying that 5 per cent of China's GDP is lost to the increased health costs and mortality associated with domestic environmental pollution and that this figure will rise to 15 per cent by 2030 if nothing is done.

Economy: One of the factors that may in fact prompt the Chinese leadership to move more quickly on environmental issues is a concern over the economic costs. As you suggest, economists — both in China and in the West — have done studies estimating the economic cost of China's environmental degradation and pollution — including such things as water scarcity, air pollution, and land degradation. In fact, Professor Jorgenson's estimate is on the low side; others, such as the World Bank and the renowned Canadian geographer Vaclav Smil, have estimated annual costs to the economy to be as high as 8 – 12 per cent of GDP. These costs reflect such things as missed days of work or hospital stays from environ- mentally induced health problems, or factories unable to operate because of lack of water. My sense for the trajectory in this regard is that in certain areas such as Shanghai, where city leaders have been quite proactive in investing in environmental protection, we will see such costs decrease. For the majority of the country, where the overwhelming emphasis of local officials continues to be on simply growing the economy as rapidly as possible, such environmental costs will only continue to grow.

Q: In what ways has the Chinese government been addressing these environmental problems? Is there a well-formulated strategy? We know that Beijing appears very desirous of fighting environmental pollution, as seen in its announced intention to play host to the "Green Olympics" in 2008.

Economy: The Chinese leadership essentially has a four-part strategy to address environmental problems. The first is policy guidance from the center. Both China's State Environmental Protection Administration and Environmental Protection and Natural Resources Committee within the National People's Congress are staffed with extremely bright and capable people who are deeply engaged in seeking out new and creative ways to integrate economic development with environmental protection. A second conscious strategy, since about 1989, has been to devolve authority for environmental protection to the local level. Local mayors, in fact, are supposed to be evaluated not only on how well the local economy performs but also on how well they address their environmental challenges. The third part of the country's plan to improve the environment is to tap into the expertise and resources of the international community. China is the largest recipient of environmental aid from the World Bank,

Asian Development Bank, and Global Environmental Facility. Moreover, many multinationals have begun to support China's environmental efforts, introducing the most environmentally sound technologies, undertaking independent and thorough environmental impact assessments, and funding Chinese NGO activities on environmental education projects. Finally, and I think most interestingly, China has opened the door to the involvement of relatively independent non-governmental organizations and the media to work from the ground up on issues of environmental protection.

Section C
Information Input and Group Discussion

1. Environmental Protection in China

As a member of the international community, China has enacted and implemented a series of principles, policies, laws and measures for environmental protection since the 1980s.

Making environmental protection is one of China's basic national policies. The prevention and control of environmental pollution and ecological destruction, and the rational exploitation and utilization of natural resources are of vital importance to the country's overall interests and long-term development. The Chinese government is unswervingly carrying out the basic national policy of environmental protection.

Formulating the guiding principles of simultaneous planning, simultaneous implementation and simultaneous development for economic construction, urban and rural construction and environmental construction, combining the economic returns with social effects and environmental benefits, and carrying out the three major policies of "prevention first and combining prevention with control," "making the causer of pollution responsible for treating it" and "intensifying environmental management."

Promulgating and putting into effect laws and regulations regarding environmental protection, placing environmental protection on a legal footing, continuously improving the statutes concerning the environment, formulating strict law-enforcement procedures and increasing the intensity of law enforcement so as to ensure the effective implementation of the environmental laws and regulations.

Persisting in incorporating environmental protection into the plans for national economic and social development, introducing to it macro regulation and management under state guidance, and gradually increasing environmental protection input so as to give simultaneous consideration to environmental protection and other undertakings and ensure their coordinated development.

Establishing and improving environmental protection organizations under governments at all levels, forming a rather complete environmental control system, and bringing into full play the governments' role in environmental supervision and administration.

Accelerating progress in environmental science and technology, strengthening research into basic theories, organizing the tackling of key scientific and technological problems, developing and popularizing practical technology for environmental pollution prevention and control, fostering the growth of environmental protection industries, and giving initial shape to an environmental protection scientific research system are China's basic principles.

Carrying out environmental publicity and education to enhance the whole nation's awareness of the environment, widely conducting environmental publicity work, gradually popularizing environmental education in secondary and primary schools, developing on-the-job education in environmental protection and vocational education, and training specialized personnel in environmental science and technology as well as environmental administration.

Promoting international cooperation in the field of environmental protection, actively expanding exchanges and cooperation concerning the environment and development with other countries and international organizations, earnestly implementing international environmental conventions, and seeking scope for China's role in global environmental affairs are the tasks to be accomplished.

Questions for Discussion:
1. What causes environmental pollution in modern society?
2. What has resulted from such pollution?
3. What are the chief pollutants? Can you name three of them?
4. What are we going to do about environmental pollution?
5. As a member of the world community, what should we do to protect our earth?
6. What is the relationship between economic development and environmental protection?
7. What do you think of the measures taken by our government? What is the most effective one?
8. Do you have any other ideas to combat pollution or to protect our environment?

2. Hurricane Katrina

Hurricane Katrina, one of the worst natural disasters in US

history, devastated the Gulf Coast of the United States from New Orleans, Louisiana to Mobile, Alabama. Katrina made landfall in the early morning of 29 August 2005. The hurricane is believed to have killed thousands of people, and known to have displaced more than one million — a humanitarian crisis on a scale unseen in the US since the American Civil War.

Death Toll

It is estimated that the hurricane probably has caused thousands of direct and indirect deaths in the city. Direct deaths indicate those caused by the direct effects of the winds, flooding, storm surge or oceanic effects of Katrina. Indirect deaths indicate those caused by hurricane-related accidents (including car accidents), fires or other incidents, as well as clean-up incidents and health issues.

Economic Effects

Most experts anticipate that Katrina will be the costliest natural disaster in US history. Some early predictions in damage exceeded US $100 billion, not accounting for potential catastrophic damage inland due to flooding (which would increase the total even more), or damage to the economy caused by the interruption of oil supply (many of the US energy operations are in the Gulf Coast region), and exports of commodities such as grain. Other predictions placed the minimum insured damage at around US $12. 5 billion (the insured figure is normally doubled to account for uninsured damage in the final cost). There are also effects on ocean shipping, the casino industry and tourism.

International oil prices are rising. In the UK pump prices for unleaded petrol (gas) have in places hit £1 per litre (US $7 per gallon) for the first time (averaging about 95p). That's a rise of about 3 per cent since Katrine hit. Wholesale prices are up 5 per cent as of 6 September, so retailers are trying to keep costs down for consumers (alternatively, they're worried about being the first to pass the £1 per litre mark).

Environmental Issues

Many scientists and critics have stated that global warming was responsible for the rise in ocean surface temperatures that caused Katrina to go from a tropical storm to a devastating hurricane as it crossed the Gulf of Mexico between south Florida and New Orleans. Other scientists acknowledge the possible long-term effects of global warming on cyclonogenesis, but attribute the strength of Hurricane Katrina to a 12-year cycle.

Another direct environmental cause has been the destruction of wetlands in the affected regions, which traditionally have a mitigating effect on hurricane damage acting as a sponge to slow floodwaters.

Sewage, decomposing bodies, and toxic chemicals from the city's many factories, have mixed into the floodwaters, creating a potentially toxic cesspool throughout New Orleans. Experts fear it will pose a serious threat to residents now and into the future with the immediate question of how to safely dispose of the vast quantities of polluted water inside New Orleans being an important environmental issue. If reports from Fox News are correct, the water inside New Orleans will simply be pumped straight back into Lake Pontchartrain, which will be an environmental disaster.

Questions for Discussion:
1. Can you name some other natural disasters?

2. What are the main causes of these disasters?
3. What has resulted from such disasters?
4. Why do some disasters cause terrible losses while others bring about minor ones?
5. Can we predict a disaster and prevent it from occurring?
6. How do you understand "Prevention is better than cure"?

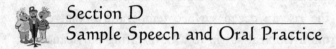

Section D
Sample Speech and Oral Practice

Part A Sample Speech

Promoting "Green" Buildings

Over recent years, governments at all levels have been actively promoting energy-saving buildings in an attempt to reduce energy consumption. However, these efforts have largely been in vain.

Due to a lack of energy-saving consciousness, patchy energy-conservation laws and policies, and the lack of market incentive mechanisms, this promotion of energy-efficient buildings is making only an awkward progress.

With the urbanization process accelerating, the problem of energy waste in the construction sector is becoming acute. A study shows that energy consumption in the construction sector will account for 40 per cent of the country's total energy consumption in the coming years, becoming the most energy-hungry sector.

Obviously, promoting energy-efficient buildings is becoming a pressing task, a task that appears to be hard to accomplish. One major obstacle to the promotion of energy-saving buildings is the lethargic attitude of many developers, put off by the additional 10 per cent construction cost. The incomplete legislation framework concerning energy-saving buildings is another obstacle hampering the wider acceptance of energy-efficient buildings. To make things worse, the current regulations are only loosely enforced.

Energy conservation in the construction sector is a complex issue, which means it should be tackled in a thorough manner. First, the government should do more to increase public awareness of the importance of saving energy. Second, legislation on energy-efficient building construction needs to be enhanced, and properly supervised. Finally, the government should put in place an economic incentive mechanism to encourage the promotion of energy-saving buildings. For example, it could introduce preferential tax reductions on such buildings, and also on energy-saving construction materials.

In short, improved legislation and economic incentive mechanisms are required if progress is to be made in the promotion of energy-saving building construction.

Part B Presentation Practice

Directions: Talk on each of the following topics for at least five minutes. Be sure to make your points clear and logical with adequate supporting details.

Topic 1: To build more "green" buildings
Questions for reference:
1. What do "green" buildings mean and can you mention some in your city?
2. What benefits can these energy-saving buildings bring us?
3. Can you offer some suggestions to popularize such energy-wise

buildings?

Topic 2: The "sand storm reform" and environmental protection
Questions for reference:
1. Do you know anything about the sand storms in Beijing?
2. What are the possible causes and consequences of these storms?
3. What action should be taken to combat sand storms?

Topic 3: The urban greening projects in Shanghai
Questions for reference:
1. What do people in the cities feel when they find green plots in their neighbourhood?
2. What are the benefits of having more trees and flowers in a big city like Shanghai?
3. Is the high cost of urban greening projects worthwhile? Why or why not?

Part C More Topics for Oral Practice

Directions: *Based on the news reports, talk on each of the following topics for at least five minutes. Be sure to make your points clear and logical with adequate supporting details.*

News Report 1:

Many of us in the conservation world are concerned that the natural environment — the fundamental provider of life on this planet — seems to have dropped off the international community's radar screen. This is an alarming realization as natural resources and the environment are being degraded and destroyed at a record pace. Most environmental indicators — from climate change to freshwater and forest habitat loss — have become markedly worse. Despite the multiplicity of international environmental agreements, many have become paralyzed by politics, bogged down in the process, or even worse, ignored.

Topic: *Protecting natural resources and the environment is an urgent mission. What can be done to fulfill this task?*

News Report 2:

The future Nobel laureate in economics had no patience for capitalists who claimed that "business is not concerned 'merely' with profit but also with promoting desirable 'social' ends; that business has a 'social conscience' and takes seriously its responsibilities for providing employment, eliminating discrimination, avoiding pollution and whatever else may be the catchwords of the contemporary crop of reformers."

Topic: *What is social science and how does business take social responsibilities?*

News Report 3:

During its 25 years of reform, China has made an impressive progress in the transition to a market economy. Much of the production and distribution in China is managed through the market, and the efficiency of this mechanism is evident in the country's sustained rapid growth. While the market is good at many things, however, it is not good at everything. One place in particular where the market breaks down concerns the use of natural resources and the environment, particularly where some important resources are freely available. While China's record of production and gross domestic product growth is fantastic, its record of environmental protection is not so good.

Topic：*Should we implement environmental taxes to clean up China's environment?*

Part D   Useful Expressions

air quality	空气质量
carbon dioxide	二氧化碳
greenhouse gas	温室气体
ozone layer，the	臭氧层
indoor air pollution	室内空气污染
global warming	全球变暖
greenhouse effect	温室效应
humidity	湿度
desertification	沙漠化
drought control	抗旱
deforestation	森林砍伐
forest conservation	森林保护
greenbelt	绿化带
biological diversity and protected area	生物多样性和保护区
biological resources	生物资源
biosphere reserve	生物圈保护区
botanical garden	植物园
ecological balance	生态平衡
microorganism	微生物
wildlife conservation	野生生物保护
wildlife habitat	野生生物栖息地
virus	病毒
freshwater resources	淡水资源
conservation of freshwater	淡水保护
subterranean water	地下水

surface water	地表水
water resources conservation	水资源保护
water resources development	水资源开发
environmental accounting	环境核算
environmental auditing	环境审计
environmental health impact assessment	环境健康影响评价
environmental costs	环境成本

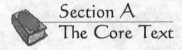

Section A
The Core Text

Why Study Space?

Why study space? The greatest purpose is interest. There are a number of reasons to become interested in outer space. Perhaps the adventure and romance of exploration are enough to **pique** one's interest. Maybe the individual has read a science fiction book about space. Possibly they may have seen one of the many popular space movies such as *Star Wars*. More than likely, they may have seen a television show such as *The Challenger*. Perhaps the interest may have been developed from watching actual launches of the space shuttle or viewing movies of the Apollo Moon Landings. From whichever source the individual's interest came, the idea of humans departing the planet into space is fascinating.

Other than interest, science and technology has made great strides during the years since the advent of the space program. Rocket vehicles have been developed which can withstand great amounts of stress and temperature **variances**. The science of orbital mechanics, for years on the ground because no method of getting into space had been developed, was not only proven true but also advanced as humanity went to the moon and other bodies in our solar system. Planetary geology was strictly earthbound until the Apollo Program and a number of space probes which went to some other planets literally rewrote the entire science. Astronomy books are being rewritten daily as discoveries pour in from the Hubble Space Telescope, the International Ultraviolet Explorer, and the Voyager space probes.

Computer science was zoomed into the future by the space program. President Kennedy was often said to be the true founder of IBM when he challenged the United States within a decade to send a man to the moon and return him safely to earth. This dictated the need to develop smaller and faster computers and led directly to integrated circuits, the microprocessor and our modern computers.

Medicine profited directly from the space program as the remote sensing of an astronaut's bodily functions led to heart pacemakers, CAT scans and the remote sensing monitoring of critical patients in today's Intensive Care Units. The intricate functions of the human body are studied daily by astronaut doctors as humans are establishing a beachhead in the low earth orbits aboard space stations. A serious problem facing the astronauts such as **calcium** loss in the bones has helped study an earthbound **skeletal** disease, **osteoporosis**. Electrophoresis experiments in space have led to a number of new drugs used for earth diseases such as **diabetes** and AIDS. Perhaps a cure for cancer may someday come from experiments run in space.

Earth sensing, the monitoring of our earth from space, obviously came from the space program. What are factories and rainforest burnings doing to our planet? Is the ozone hole a real phenomenon or just scientists' conspiring to bilk millions of dollars from the government for their own pet experiments? Can the remote sensing of the earth be used to find out what's wrong with the planet and if so, how do we fix it? The answer could lie in how we use the space program.

There are a **myriad** of other arguments for exploring space such as increasing knowledge, using applications, developing technology, and advancing economic growth. Because they will inherit the future our young people must be inspired to aspire to greater accomplishments in education. Providing such inspiration is a very important intangible benefit of space exploration.

The space exploration missions have produced basic knowledge about our planet, our environment, the solar system, and the universe which would have been nonexistent if we did not have a space program. This information has given us a deeper awareness of the history of our earth and how we can make better decisions concerning life on our planet and improve it for ourselves and our posterity.

Applications from the space program have made life a totally different experience than it was 40 years ago. Who would have dreamed at that time of picking up a telephone and within 30 seconds speaking to a friend in Australia and hearing them as if they were in the next room? Nightly, we receive live television news reports from such places as Somalia, Beijing, Moscow, and Bosnia as if the reporters were discussing activities taking place in New York, Peoria, Omaha, or Portland. Every night we receive accurate weather forecasts as **meteorologists** intently study the many satellite photographs which show the latest storm systems and how they will affect our future weather. Satellite hurricane prediction has saved many lives. This fact alone has made the space program a worthwhile endeavor.

Space navigation systems have improved safety on both aircraft and shipping by providing extremely accurate information on position, heading, altitude, and speed. With the use of the Global Positioning Satellites aircraft can land within inches of their destinations on any runway without the need of expensive navigation equipment at the airfield. Ships can avoid known icebergs or hazardous shorelines even in the roughest of weather.

Future applications will be possible when scientists are able to use the unique conditions of space such as microgravity, vacuum, and radiation to perform experiments and determine processes which either can't occur on earth due to the laws of physics and chemistry or are too impractical or expensive to recreate on earth. Advanced space technology, created to help people and equipment operate in the forbidding and harsh environment of space, has made life on earth more secure or even possible for all of us. Advances in electronics, medicine, robotics, computers, miniaturization, and remote sensing have occurred quickly because of the space program. If there had not been a space program, these advances would have probably come at a very slow rate if at all.

The space program has contributed greatly to the economic well-being of the entire world's population. The space program is a major part of the aerospace industry upon which is based a US $32 billion trade surplus and around a million jobs. NASA created more than 350,000 new jobs from 1986 to 1992 based on technology transferred to the private sector. As the United States defense budget decreases in the future years, the importance of the space program will increase substantially.

Why study space? The answers are as individual and unique as the person asking the question. Perhaps the reader will develop his or her reason for studying space which could lead to a lifelong career or a hobby.

180

● Notes to the Text:

pique	激起(兴趣、好奇心)
variance	变化
calcium	钙
skeletal	骨骼的
osteoporosis	骨质疏松症
diabetes	糖尿病
myriad	无数,种种
meteorologist	气象学者

● Understanding the Text:

1. How many reasons are mentioned in the passage for man to explore space? What are they?

2. In what aspects does rocket technology contribute to the launching and landing of the manned spaceship?

3. How does medicine profit from the space program?

4. What are the implications of space travel in the development of modern technology?

5. To what extent does space exploration benefit mankind?

6. What is the future development of the space program?

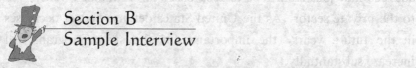

Section B
Sample Interview

An Interview with Ben Bova

Ben Bova is best known for his imaginative science fiction novels, such as *Mars, Jupiter and Saturn*, where humans of the future travel to these planets and sometimes discover new life forms. In his newest book, *Faint Echoes, Distant Stars: The Science and*

Politics of Finding Life beyond Earth, Bova again touches on the possibility of alien life. His book provides an overview of the current science of astrobiology, examining recent discoveries and suggesting what they could mean for the search for life elsewhere. Bova also discusses the politics and personalities that so often influence the direction and future of science. In this exclusive interview with *Astrobiology Magazine*, Bova shares his thoughts about astrobiology, space travel, and the discoveries of the future.

Astrobiology Magazine (AM): Why did you decide to write a book about the scientific field of astrobiology?

Ben Bova (BB): About five years ago, when I was invited to attend the first NASA-sponsored conference on astrobiology, I found the subject so intriguing that I immediately began to plan writing a book about it.

AM: You say that Jupiter may be the most likely place to find extraterrestrial life, since the planet has organisms, water and energy. Yet Jupiter is rarely seen as a likely place for life by most astrobiologists. Do you have any thoughts about what sort of creatures could exist there?

BB: Most scientists ignore Jupiter because of the enormous difficulties of exploring the planet. However, in my novel *Jupiter* I postulated a biosphere that included airborne species below the Jovian cloud deck, and gigantic aquatic species in the planet-wide ocean that girdles Jupiter.

AM: In your book, you say there are interest groups who are afraid of what astrobiologists might find, so they are working to block the search for alien life. Do you think it likely that astrobiologists might open some Pandora's Box that we would later regret, and that is reason enough to NOT look for life elsewhere?

BB: I think such fears are exaggerated. As I pointed out in *Faint Echoes, Distant Stars*, we can use the International Space Station or a dedicated space station as an isolation laboratory in which to study samples returned from other worlds, without the fear of contaminating the earth. We have more to fear, I believe, from fundamentalist religionists who worry that astrobiological research flies in the face of their biblically revealed truths. And, of course, there are the Yahoos in Congress and elsewhere who chopped SETI out of the federal budget.

AM: NASA missions and studies often are at the mercy of politics. As you note in your book, missions must continually fight budget battles in order to survive from inception to launch. Do you think President Bush's call to go back to the moon and then send a man to Mars is likely to survive over time?

BB: I believe it will survive, mainly because President Bush has already allocated funding to the program. The battle will be over how large and how fast the program can be. If President Nixon had proposed such a program in 1972, we could have been conducting this interview on Mars today.

AM: But do you think, given the proper political backing, we would have been able to overcome the technological obstacles and health hazards of establishing a base on Mars within that time frame?

BB: I don't see the technological obstacles and health hazards as being tremendous problems for Mars missions. Humans have lived in space for more than a year aboard the Mir space station. With incremental improvements in existing technology, we could go to Mars in an open-loop life support mode, sending re-supply vehicles ahead of the crewed mission. Radiation shielding will be needed for solar storms, of course. By rotating the spacecraft to give artificial gravity, the problems of long-term weightlessness can be averted. Of course, a closed-loop life support system would be preferable, although the practical answer might be a partially closed, partially open loop.

AM: One of the problems facing long-term space travel is propulsion. NASA's Project Prometheus is studying the possibility of using nuclear fission-based systems for space missions of long duration. As you note, nuclear propulsion is a very controversial topic; where do you stand on this issue?

BB: Nuclear power is the safest method yet devised for generating electricity, by any measure you care to apply. Fossil fuels pollute the atmosphere and contribute to greenhouse warming. Hundreds of coal miners are killed every year. Oil tankers pollute the oceans. Gas lines explode. Even with Chernobyl and Three Mile Island, nuclear energy is far safer. No one was even injured in the Three Mile Island incident. Nuclear propulsion for deep space missions makes sense.

AM: Toward the end of your book, you predict that within a decade, we will discover extraterrestrial life, and we also will create life in the lab from nonliving chemicals. What do you think would be the repercussions of these advances?

BB: Shock and awe, at first, among the general population. Then, as they see that the world is not coming to an end, they will gradually accept the idea that we are not alone in the universe. For scientists, the great question will be to determine if extraterrestrial life comes from the same origin as our own, or has arisen independently.

Section C
Information Input and Group Discussion

1. The Military in Space

Space is very important for the military. First it is global. A military organization can watch possible adversaries anywhere on the earth. If these countries attempt aggression which is not in the interests of the military organization or its country, the aggression can be timely encountered because of the preparation time allowed by the global observation from space. The Iraqi attack against Kuwait is one example. The US government knew the precise minute when the Iraqis invaded. Another case for globalism is the navigation satellite. A soldier, sailor, or airman can be anywhere in the world and can find his/her way by means of the GPS.

Space is economic. Because of the communications, reconnaissance, warning, and navigation capabilities which space affords, a space-faring military no longer needs a large standing army, navy, or air force. The precision and speed which space brings to the battlefield increases the combatants' fighting power.

Space is efficient. Once again, communications, reconnaissance, warning, and navigation can tell a space-faring combatant much about the adversary. This permits "force multipliers" to replace ten soldiers by one. Space allows armies to be smaller and more efficient because speed, precision, and superior intelligence provided by space assets make superior decision-making possible. The correct decision made at a crucial time in a battle is the difference between victory and defeat where seconds can dictate an outcome.

Over the centuries soldiers have fought battles in certain ways using certain principles. Even though they may not have realized that they were following certain ideas, Alexander, Julius Caesar,

Hannibal, Napoleon, Hitler's generals, McArthur, and Schwarzkopf fought battle using the Principles of War. Such principles as objective, mass, security, economy of force, maintaining the offensive, surprise, unity of command, maneuver, and simplicity are as important today as they were during these generals' days, but some of these have changed.

The element of surprise has always been an extremely important principle of war throughout the ages. The Chinese sage Sun Tzu stated that war demands deception and surprise. Surprise was needed to drive the enemy into making erroneous judgments and taking erroneous actions. This principle was classically used in the attack on Pearl Harbor on December 7, 1941 as the Japanese disabled the entire US Pacific fleet. Because of the reconnaissance capabilities of today's spacecraft the principle of surprise for two foes with space assets is considerably reduced. The Soviet Union knew precisely how many ICBMs we had and the US knew exactly how many ICBMs the Soviets had. Both countries knew the exact locations of each other's ICBMs. Both countries had warning systems which would relate quickly the launch of an ICBM. Both countries had eavesdropping spacecraft in the form of ELINT spacecraft; each country could monitor radio and telephone traffic to determine whether the other side had increased its alert status. In short, there was no surprise readily available because of space assets.

If a country with space assets fought a country without space assets, then surprise could be enhanced. A classic example of this is the coalition forces' left hook as the US-led forces totally surrounded the Iraqis in Kuwait and destroyed their armies in less than 100 hours. Of all the principles of war used for centuries, perhaps the element of surprise has changed the most due to the introduction of space assets to warfare.

Questions for Discussion:

1. Why is space important for the military? Can you illustrate your opinion?
2. What role does space play in future military action?
3. What is the present situation in the military use of space?
4. Do you think it possible for mankind to fight in space in the future?
5. If other countries develop their military capabilities in outer space, should we do the same thing?
6. What do you think is a proper use of space?

2. Shenzhou VI — A Leap Forward

Although it was only China's second manned space flight, Shenzhou VI was in many ways a great leap forward compared with the maiden space voyage in 2003.

China became just the third country after the United States and the former Soviet Union to put a man in space in October 2003 with the Shenzhou V mission.

The basic launch module technology of Shenzhou V and VI is identical, but experts have been able to count about 100 novelties.

When China's first man in space Yang Liwei spent 21 hours orbiting the earth 14 times in Shenzhou V, he did not leave his seat, take off his space suit or conduct any experiments.

Fei and Nie conducted a series of experiments.

Astronauts Fei Junlong and Nie Haisheng aboard Shenzhou VI, which blasted off from Jiuquan Satellite Launch Centre in Inner Mongolia last Wednesday, were much busier than Yang.

Fei and Nie conducted a series of experiments and manoeuvres, including leaving the re-entry capsule and entering the orbital capsule, shedding their bulky suits and donning ordinary work clothes so they could move around easily.

Work also included the testing of the environmental control and life support systems inside the craft.

During their time in space, the astronauts successfully fired rockets to adjust the craft's altitude, ensuring it remained in its pre-planned orbit — which was crucial for its return to earth, according to the mission control bureau.

A mission as long as five days meant facilities also needed to cater for basic needs. Shenzhou VI carried enough food, water and oxygen for a seven-day mission, although the planners had expected it to spend just five days in orbit.

The menu was much more extensive than that of the first.

The spacecraft contained a full larder of Chinese specialities including cuttlefish and meat balls, and beef with orange peel.

The menu was much more extensive than that of the first manned mission in 2003, offering 50 varieties of food instead of the previous 20.

Two years ago, Yang ate only cold meals because the last spacecraft did not have a food heater.

But Fei and Nie dined on heated food including rice, dehydrated vegetables and a wide assortment of fruit — strawberries, bananas and the very sweet Chinese Hami melon.

Naturally, Fei and Nie also became the first Chinese to use a toilet in space. Nie was also the first Chinese to spend his birthday in space.

From mission control in Beijing, Nie's daughter sang *Happy Birthday* to her father, who was celebrating his 41st birthday.

Questions for Discussion:

1. Why do we say the success of Shenzhou VI is a leap forward in the development of our space program?

2. What are the implications of the successful launching and landing of Shenzhou VI?

3. In what way does the manned spaceship contribute to the scientific development of our country?

4. In your opinion, is it worthwhile for our country to spend so much money on space exploration?

5. Fei Junlong and Nie Haisheng have become the nation's heroes and what can we learn from them?

6. Would you like to be a spaceman? Why or why not?

Section D
Sample Speech and Oral Practice

Part A Sample Speech

Space Exploration Is Worth the Expense

When the money used for space exploration is totaled up and presented as a single sum, it looks like a lot of money that one is then tempted to apply to other purposes. That is a deception. In the United States, the federal government each year spends less than 1 per cent of its budget on space exploration, and more than 30 per cent of the budget helping the poor in this country. That means that if the space program were completely eliminated, a poor person instead of getting US $1.00 would then get US $1.03. That does not seem like the extra help they really need to save them.

What would we lose for giving the extra three cents to the poor (or some other program)? Well for one thing without the space program you and I could not be having this e-mail conversation because there would be no communications satellites. There would be no weather satellites so there would be little or no warning of hurricanes or typhoons. I'm not sure about Malaysia, but in the United States it is now unusual for a lot of lives to be lost in a hurricane, whereas in the past we could lose thousands of lives to these storms. The difference is satellite surveillance of weather systems. We would certainly know and understand less about our solar system and universe without the space probes and orbiting telescopes provided by space exploration. We would also understand less about the earth, about ecological systems, about efficient ways of growing crops and controlling pollution.

The reality is that the space program has done a lot to save the earth, save lives, feed people, and bring us together through closer communication. The space program has shown us an example of how to solve seemingly impossible problems. We should use this example to help us solve other difficult problems, like world hunger. It is a mistake to say that since we have problems that we haven't solved, we should stop solving other problems as well.

It is also ironic to claim that we want to save the present and forget the future. What do you do tomorrow, when the neglected future has become the present?

Part B   Presentation Practice

Directions: *Talk on each of the following topics for at least five minutes. Be sure to make your points clear and logical with adequate supporting details.*

Topic 1: Space missions foretell a high-tech boom.

Questions for reference:

1. To what extent does the space program benefit mankind in high technology? Can you show some examples?

2. What potential challenges will man encounter in space exploration in terms of high technology?

3. Can you predict the future development of the space program in the next decade?

Topic 2: Spend money exploring outer space, or for basic needs on earth

Questions for reference:

1. Space exploration is a costly project, should underdeveloped countries spend a lot of money on it while there are still many basic needs unfulfilled in their countries?

2. Is it worthwhile for China, a developing country to spend so much money sending a manned spaceship into outer space?

3. What is your attitude towards mankind's exploration of outer space?

Topic 3: Military race in space

Questions for reference:

1. What's the main purpose of mankind exploring space, for peace or military purposes?

2. Why do some countries strive to develop military capabilities in space?

3. Should our country join in this race? Why or why not?

4. What will the space program be like in the future?

Part C More Topics for Oral Practice

Directions: Based on the news reports, talk on each of the following topics for at least five minutes. Be sure to make your points clear and logical with adequate supporting details.

News Report 1:

Although it was only China's second manned space flight, Shenzhou VI was in many ways a great leap forward compared with the maiden space voyage in 2003. China became just the third country after the United States and the former Soviet Union to put a man in space in October 2003 with the Shenzhou V mission. The basic launch module technology of Shenzhou V and VI is identical, but experts have been able to count about 100 novelties.

Topic: *Can you mention some of the novelties of Shenzhou VI and their implications in science and technology?*

News Report 2:

In recent years professional space tourism studies have been conducted in the United Kingdom, Germany and, especially, Japan. In the US, technological progress has been pronounced; we have had nearly a decade's experience in seeing our astronauts travel to and from low earth orbit safely, and we expect to commence the assembly of an LEO space station housing a half dozen people this year. And our space industry now has new and promising space transportation development programs underway.

Topic: *Space tourism is underway, and what do you think of the prospects of space travel?*

News Report 3:

Two Chinese astronauts, aboard a limousine convertible, are marching on the way in Beijing space city where a grand welcome ceremony is holding for them. Fei Junlong and Nie Haisheng are greeted with bouquets of flowers, cheering crowds, and a traditional Chinese drum show. Their colleague astronauts are on the second convertible following them, all waving happily to crowds on both sides.

Topic: *Would you like to be an astronaut? What do these two heroes teach us?*

Part D   Useful Expressions

spacecraft	航天器
manned spaceship/spacecraft	载人飞船
manned space flight	载人航天
manned space program	载人航天计划
space shuttle	航天飞机
unmanned spaceship/spacecraft	无人飞船
experimental spacecraft	试验太空船
multistage rocket	多级火箭
capsule	太空舱
recoverable satellite	返回式卫星
communications satellite	通讯卫星
remote sensing satellite	遥感卫星
carrier rocket/rocket launcher	运载火箭
Long March II F carrier rocket	长征二号 F 运载火箭
low earth orbit	近地轨道
weather satellite/meteorological satellite	气象卫星
satellite in sun-synchronous orbit	太阳同步轨道卫星

geosynchronous satellite	地球同步轨道卫星
orbital module	轨道舱
re-entry module	返回舱
propelling module	推进舱
command module	指令舱
lunar module	登月舱
launch pad	发射台
emergency oxygen apparatus	应急供氧装置
International Space Station, the	国际空间站
solar panel	太阳能电池板
space elevator	太空升降舱
Hubble Space Telescope, the	哈勃太空望远镜
lunar rover	月球车
artificial satellite	人造卫星
antenna	天线
solar cell	太阳电池
LM-maneuvering rocket	登月舱机动火箭
service module	服务舱
directional antenna	定向天线
nozzle of the main engine	主发动机喷嘴
ascent stage	上升段
descent stage	下降段
hatch	舱口
astronaut	航天员
spacesuit	航天服
access flap	接口盖
life-support system	生命维持系统

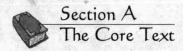

Section A
The Core Text

The True Spirit of the Olympics

The Olympic Games have always brought people together in peace to respect universal moral principles. Over and above sporting exploits, Olympism is a source of multiple passions which unite the worlds of sport, art, culture and collections. Olympism is a state of mind and the Olympic Museum is its symbol. The International Olympic Committee guarantees the promotion of Olympism and the smooth running of the Games in accordance with the Olympic Charter. The Olympic Movement includes the International Olympic Committee (IOC), the Organizing Committees of the Olympic Games (OCOGs), the National Olympic Committees (NOCs), the International Federations (IFs), the national associations, clubs and, of course, the athletes. The upcoming Games will feature athletes from all over the world and help promote the Olympic spirit. Then what is the true spirit of the Games? And what is the hope for us to convey to the next generation?

Baron Pierre de Coubertin (1863 – 1937), a French nobleman, believed that sports and the ideals of the Olympic Games produced the flowering of Greece during "The Golden Age." Almost single handedly, he revived the spirit of the ancient Games to foster brotherhood and friendly competition among athletes of the world. His philosophy, stated in 1903, has been displayed on electronic scoreboards at the opening ceremonies of the Games: "The most important thing in the Olympic Games is not to win but to take part, just as the most important thing in life is not the triumph but the struggle. The essential thing is not to have conquered but to have fought well." In *The Olympic Odyssey*, Renaissance man (author, editor, teacher, adventure travel leader, photographer, and documentary filmmaker) Phil Cousineau starts out with a stirring quotation that matches the Frenchman's to get our attention focused on what really matters in the Games:

"It is in fact the **miraculous** force that **animates** all great art as well as great athletes. Call it spirit, the divine spark, the breath of life — it is the transcendent element that lifts us up when we're down and out, the source of courage, and the soul of inspiration. Strangely, we're not quite sure where it comes from, where it goes when it's crushed, or how to revive it. We just know we need to be in touch with it, which is one reason we turn to art, drama, poetry and sports, especially the Olympic Games, the most watched television event on earth. As the Games unfold every four years, we may be impressed by the skills of the world's greatest young athletes; but what moves us is what novelist and soccer fan Nick Hornsby calls 'the thrilling flash of their spirit.' That mysterious movement of spirit — from an athlete's **aspiration** for a great performance to our inspiration from witnessing it — is at the heart of the age-old fascination with all great games."

In this comprehensive and informative paperback, Cousineau examined the mythic and historical genesis of the Games and the intentions behind these ancient gatherings. He pondered the meaning of excellence, the roots of "the agony and the **ecstasy**," and the celebration of the contest. He laid out the challenges to revive the Games and the passing of the torch from 1896 to 1980. And then, with great flourish, Cousineau commented on the **fiery** pursuit of excellence from 1980 to 2000 with colorful **anecdotes** and **asides** on many of the athletes who hit high stride in their performances. He used a quotation from the wall of an old Philadelphia sports arena to sum up:

To play the game is great.

To win the game is greater.

To love the game is greatest of all.

This is not an easy goal in an age where winning is seen as so important that people are urged to do anything to gain an edge on their opponents, even cheating. It is not easy in a time when commercial interests have taken the joy out of so many games. After a chapter on coaching, Cousineau concluded with his own Olympian vision for the future, and it was well worth the price of the whole book. As you watch the Games, we urge you to ponder it and take to heart. He ended on a note that was as **salutary** as the one he began with on the spirit of sports: "The Olympic Games teach us that life can be a festival, that competitions can enliven the entire community, that the desire to excel makes winners of us all, and that playing at the meaning of life is a noble thing. To convey the spirit of the ancient Games and the soul of the modern Games to the next generation is now our hope; to pass the torch of our passion for a life of excellence is now our task."

Notes to the Text:

miraculous	奇迹的，不可思议的
animate	给予热情，使有活力

aspiration	热望,渴望
ecstasy	入迷,狂喜
fiery	火的,火焰的;炽热的
anecdote	轶事,奇闻
aside	旁白
salutary	有益的

Understanding the Text:

1. What is the spirit of the Olympic Games according to Baron Pierre de Coubertin?

2. What is the most important in the Games?

3. Why do we need the Olympic Games?

4. According to Cousineau, what is the real meaning of excellence?

5. Is it easy to achieve this excellence in an age where winning is so important to a person?

6. What do the Olympic Games teach us?

7. What hope should we convey to the younger generation through the Games?

Section B
Sample Interview

An Interview with Allen Johnson

Q: How would a fifth world 110m hurdles title sound to you?

Allen Johnson: A fifth title would sound great. But this one would be the most difficult one because there are so many people running fast. It's harder as you do things more. I guess it gets more difficult. I'm just looking forward to this one.

Q: Within the last couple of weeks, you've had a little minor injury. You stayed out of a couple of races of late. Could you talk about the injury and how your health is right now?

Allen Johnson: When I was in Lausanne my calves spasmed. If you don't know what a spasm is, that's when the muscle just tightens up. I wouldn't clarify it as an injury *per se*, but if I would have continued to run on it, it probably would have torn some of the muscles on it. I pulled out of Lausanne and I pulled out of Rome, and just went home and trained. I was training the next week at 100 per cent. I'm 100 per cent healthy now just ready to run, waiting for Wednesday so I can start and Friday for the final.

Q: What was your reaction to Ladji Doucoure (of France) running 12.97 seconds?

Allen Johnson: My reaction was "That's pretty quick." I wasn't shocked. He ran 13.02 in Paris. Anytime you run 13.02 or 12.97 that's not a world apart. 12.97 is fast. I probably expect him to run even faster here. I'm expecting anything here.

Q: Being one of the senior members of the team and one with a lot of world experience, what do you tell some of the rookies who are experiencing their first Worlds to expect?

Allen Johnson: I don't know. I tell them to do what they did to get here. I don't believe in experience. I don't think it's experience that makes you win. A lot of people show up first, second time and they win. When you're prepared to win, you win. The fact that it's your first time or your fifth time pretty much has no bearing on whether you win or lose. It's about how you're prepared and what your mind is like. When you're prepared to win, you win. Take Sanya Richards for example. Two years ago at 18, she anchored the 4×400 team to victory. Where was her experience at the Worlds? She didn't have any. I'm a strong believer in the sense of experience being something that you guys always talk about.

Q: What do you think of the Chinese hurdler Liu Xiang? Who do you think is your main rival, Doucoure, or Liu Xiang?

Allen Johnson: Liu Xiang is fast. Who do I think is my main rival? There's no main rival. I don't know how deep a field this is. I guess there are about 40 or 50 of us out there. I guess I have 39 or 49 main rivals. This is the World Championship. Everybody is going to rise to the occasion. If you focus on one person, you're making a mistake, a huge, huge mistake. This is where new stars are made, old stars fade away, while current stars continue to be stars. That's what we are here for. We're going to find out who the main rivals are.

Q: Is this the most competitive field you have known for many years?

Allen Johnson: From my point of view, this is the most competitive in terms of people running fast in the current year. There have been past years where I have competed where Mr. (Colin) Jackson back there, he's the world record holder, you had him and Tony Jarrett. Not everyone was running fast in one particular year. This year, 13.05 is the fifth or sixth fastest time in the world. I've never experienced anything like that. That's what's making this event so exciting. That's why everyone is kind of gearing up, wanting to watch the men's hurdle finals because everyone is so tightly bunched up. They have a .02 seconds separating one from two, from three, from four.

Q: You and Liu are alike in a way. He's the Olympic champion. There're going to be a lot of expectations on him. You had your unfortunate fall last year in the quarters in Athens. What did that do for you? Did it motivate more for these world championships or is that all in the past and is this meet what's happening right now?

Allen Johnson: It's a little bit of both. Anytime you have a failure, you want to come back the next year and try to make up for it. There is no way for me to make up for the fall. But I'd be lying to you if I said that wasn't on my mind. I felt like I had to do something to make up for that. It's a little bit of motivation. But at the same time, this year is different from last year. In this world championship, no matter what happened last year, I would have been geared up and really motivated to try and perform well. The motivation this year is to try and win a fifth title. As far as I know, no one has ever won a fifth title on the track. I know it's happening on the field with Bubka. But on the track, nobody has won more than four titles. That's something that really motivates me to try and accomplish it.

Section C
Information Input and Group Discussion

1. 2008 Beijing Olympics

The 2008 Beijing Olympics is a game with its own special feature. The word "feature" here can be summed up as "Chinese style, that is, human elegance, epochal traits, public participation and high level."

What we call "Chinese style" means the need to fully display the 5,000-year-long history and splendid culture of the Chinese nation, and to give expression to the rich lingering charm of China, so that the 2008 Olympic Games will become the best window through which people worldwide will get a deeper understanding of and experience in Chinese history, culture, populace and natural landscapes.

"Human elegance" here means the need to give prominence to the idea of human Olympics and expression to the Olympic spirit, the need to give full respect to and concentrated show of the excellent ethnic cultures of various countries worldwide and of the diversified brilliant cultures, and to boost cultural exchanges between China and other countries. The Olympics should be made a stage by which to enhance citizens' cultural qualities, raise the level of public morality, and show the harmonious, and perfect, fine tradition of Chinese sons and daughters.

The "epochal traits" here suggests expressing the Chinese people's mental outlook featuring their unremitting efforts to become stronger and accomplish great things, expressing the Chinese people's youthful spirit and vigor featuring their eagerness to aim high and make progress, and their strong desire to jointly pursue peace, friendship and progress together with the world's people, and expressing their respect, welcome and help to the youngsters and athletes from various countries and their all-out assistance to the contestants in difficulties.

"Public participation" here means showing the graceful bearings of the Chinese people who account for one-fifth of world population and the vast number of Hong Kong, Macao and Taiwan compatriots as well as overseas Chinese taking an active part in the Olympic Games. The Beijing Olympics is both an event to take place in a most populous country in the world, and a game with the broadest section of participants.

"High level" means we should reach eight standards.

1. Stadiums, gymnasiums and other facilities and the organizing work of contests should reach a high level. Athletes from various countries should be enabled to give full play to their talents and various sports organizations to feel satisfied.

2. High-level opening ceremony and cultural activities. A good opening ceremony signals a successful beginning, giving expression to the Olympic spirit and realizing the integration of sport and culture through varied and colorful cultural activities.

3. High-level media service and good public opinion appraisal. Making meticulous arrangement of services for the media of various countries, and giving play to the media's positive influence on the Olympic Games.

4. High-level safe defense work. Taking measures against the occurrence of any accidents that endanger safety is the basic requirement for holding large-scale activities.

5. High-level contingents and services of volunteers. Volunteers' smiles will become the "visiting cards" for the 2008 Olympic Games.
6. High-level traffic organization and service for daily life, so that Olympics officials, athletes and spectators can enjoy comfortable, convenient and efficient services.
7. High-level image of a civilized city. This is the foundation work that must be done well with all our strengths, so that athletes can compete in a satisfactory environment and a good impression is left on the spectators.
8. Remarkable achievements gained by Chinese athletes are also an important aspect manifesting a high level of sporting excellence.

Questions for Discussion:
1. What is the special feature of the 2008 Beijing Olympics?
2. Why should we host the Games with a "Chinese style"?
3. What does "human elegance" mean to you?
4. What efforts should be made to hold the Games with "epochal traits"?
5. As citizens of the country, how should we take an active part in the upcoming Games?
6. What do you think of the eight standards which are set to hold a high-level Games?
7. Can you offer some suggestions to make the Games more colorful and unforgettable?

2. Why to Be a Volunteer for the Special Olympics?

I can't think of a better way to give back to your community than to volunteer for Special Olympics. I was lucky enough to spend the weekend coaching bocce, and it had to be one of the greatest times of my life. We had lots of laughs, some tears and experiences we would never forget. I have only been a volunteer for eight months, but have grown so much and spent time with many new friends. I look forward to the time each week I get to spend coaching. When all is said and done, I am so grateful for the opportunity I was given. To be a volunteer contributes to the following:

- Spiritual growth because you feel very good when you help people that need you.
- Satisfaction when you see a smile because of something you have done.
- Power in your own life because athletes show you that nothing is impossible.
- The satisfaction of knowing that what you do counts.
- Pride in knowing that you are contributing to the happiness and achievements of the athletes.

What do volunteers do?

Simply put, volunteers do it all. As a global organization that operates on a grass-roots level, Special Olympics can be successful only with the dedicated and able assistance of its more than 500,000 volunteers around the world. There is no charge to athletes for participation in Special Olympics, and volunteers make that possible.

What are the benefits of volunteering with Special Olympics?

"The Special Olympics athletes and other people I have met along the way have shaped my life in such a dramatic way. I found strength in them that I could not discover in anyone else. As I helped them, they changed me," said one volunteer.

If you're looking for a volunteer opportunity that can make a difference in both your life and the lives of others, Special Olympics is the place for you.

When you volunteer with Special Olympics, you have an opportunity to work with some of the world's most gifted individuals — Special Olympics athletes. Many organizations use volunteers. But only with Special Olympics can you walk out on the athletic field and see how your time and effort has made an immediate impact. All over the world, all year long, it can happen right before your eyes.

Here are just a few of the benefits that Special Olympics athletes say they get out of participating in the movement:

- It gives us the opportunity to develop in an environment of respect and equality.
- It gives us the opportunity to develop as athletes and persons.
- It makes it easier for us to integrate into society.
- It helps us to get to know and participate with other athletes from other schools, other provinces and countries.
- It changes our lives, gives us more independence and helps us to make relationships easier, and to have more friends that are athletes and volunteers.

Question for Discussion:

1. Why does the author choose to be a volunteer as a means to help Special Olympics athletes?
2. What contributions can a volunteer make to Special Olympics?
3. What benefits can Special Olympics athletes get out of participating in the movement?
4. In 2008, our country will host the Olympic Games and do you like to be a volunteer? Why or why not?
5. What are the implications of being a volunteer when you do

something for others without payment?

6. What do you think will benefit you when you are doing volunteering work?

Section D
Sample Speech and Oral Practice

| Part A | Sample Speech |

Martial Arts — Chinese Wushu

Do you know Bruce Lee, Jet Li or Jackie Chan, all famous Chinese film stars adept in Wushu? Wow, how magic and terrific! Anyone who has seen classical Chinese Kung Fu movies will be deeply impressed by the Chinese Wushu, which is called Kung Fu or Chinese martial arts in the West. This year's hottest Kung Fu movie is the Hollywood box office hit, Chow Yun-Fat's *Crouching Tiger*, *Hidden Dragon*, another martial arts epic.

Literally, *wu* means military while *shu* means art, thus Wushu the art of fighting or martial arts. Wushu is an important and unique component of Chinese cultural heritage with centuries of cultural history attached. Wushu not only includes physical exercise but also Chinese philosophy, meditation and aesthetics.

In the past, Wushu was developed for the sake of military prowess and physical well-being. Wushu was seen as crucial to a soldier's survival in the time of hand-to-hand combat. Today, its military function has faded and it has been organized and systematized into a formal branch of study in the performance arts by the Chinese, while its physical welfare and athletic functions become dominant. Hence Wushu is popular among the whole nation of China, practiced by men and women, young and old alike. Today many people practice Wushu to pursue health, defense skills, mental discipline, entertainment and competition.

Wushu can be practiced solo, paired or as a group, barehanded or armed with ancient Chinese weapons. In centuries past, Wushu developed into many systems and styles. The most famous systems include Shaolin Temple system and Mt. Wudang system. Only the Shaolin system has hundreds of styles. Among the many styles are *Chang quan* (long fist), *Nan quan* (southern fist), *Taiji quan* (shadow boxing or supreme ultimate fist), *Xingyi quan* (mind fist), and *Bagua quan* (eight directions fist). The former two belong to the external style which emphasizes physical strength and abilities while the latter three belong to the internal style that depends upon internal power — *qi*. The ancient weaponry of Chinese Wushu consists of many represented by 18 named weapons.

Recently, Chinese Wushu has been modernized. Training and competing standard systems have been set up. Continuing its fighting function, Wushu becomes a more athletic and aesthetic performance and competitive sport. More and more foreigners come to learn the mysterious Wushu.

Part B Presentation Practice

Directions: *Talk on each of the following topics for at least five minutes. Be sure to make your points clear and logical with adequate supporting details.*

Topic 1: 2008 Beijing Olympic Games
Questions for reference:
1. What are the implications of Beijing hosting the 2008 Olympic

Games?

2. What benefits can the Games bring us in the development of our politics, economy and culture?

3. How do we make contributions to this Olympics?

Topic 2: The spirit of Olympics

Questions for reference:

1. Can you briefly describe the history of the Olympic Games?

2. What are the symbol and motto of the Olympic Games?

3. What is the spirit of the Olympics? What does it mean to you?

4. How do you understand the common saying that friendship first and competition second?

Topic 3: Do famous athletes deserve high bonuses?

Questions for reference:

1. What do you think about the common practice that famous athletes often get high bonuses?

2. What do you think might be some proper ways to reward the athletes who have achieved a great success in their profession?

3. Do you think high rewards can contribute to good achievements on the sports ground? If yes, to what extent does it play the role?

Part C   More Topics for Oral Practice

Directions: *Based on the news reports, talk on each of the following topics for at least five minutes. Be sure to make your points clear and logical with adequate supporting details.*

News Report 1:

Liu Xiang became the first Asian in history to win the men's

110m hurdles at the Olympic Games in Athens, clocked a world record-equaling time of 12.91 seconds for the gold. In October 2005, the Olympic champion was awarded a free entry to study for a doctor's degree by Shanghai's East China Normal University, though having not attended a class in a college.

Topic: *Do famous people deserve a free entry into a university for further education?*

News Report 2:

It is very important that schools offer a wide range of subjects to cater to all students in their care. It is also true that students need more than the knowledge of a subject. They need to know how to work in groups to achieve a mutual goal, how to work as a team. Where is better to learn those skills than on the sports field? After all, the school is preparing students for life and for career.

Topic: *Do sports games teach us more about life than learning in the classroom?*

News Report 3:

The most important thing in the Olympic Games is not to win but to take part, just as the most important thing in life is not the triumph but the struggle. The essential thing is not to have conquered but to have fought well. It is in fact the miraculous force that animates all great art as well as great athletes. Call it spirit, the divine spark, the breath of life — it is the transcendent element that lifts us up when we're down and out, the source of courage, and the soul of inspiration.

Topic: *Do you think the most important thing in life is not the product but the process?*

Part D Useful Expressions

professional	职业运动员
amateur	业余运动员，爱好者
champion	冠军
record holder	纪录保持者
ground，field	场地
diving platform	跳台
10-meter platform	10 米跳台
breaststroke	蛙泳
crawl stroke	爬泳
backstroke	仰泳
sidestroke	侧泳
butterfly stroke	蝶泳
rugby	橄榄球
basketball	篮球
volleyball	排球
tennis	网球
baseball	垒球
handball	手球
hockey	曲棍球
cricket	板球
men's singles	男(子)单(打)运动员
mixed doubles	混合双打
gymnastics	体操
horizontal bar	单杠
parallel bars	双杠
rings	吊环
trapeze	秋千
side horse	鞍马

weight-lifting	举重
weights	重量级
judo	柔道
fencing	击剑
sprint	短跑（美作：dash）
100-meter hurdles, the	100 米栏
marathon	马拉松赛跑
decathlon	田径十项全能运动
high jump	跳高
long jump	跳远（美作：broad jump）
triple jump	三级跳
pole vault	撑杆跳
throwing	投掷运动
shot put	推铅球
discus throw	掷铁饼
hammer throw	掷链球
javelin throw	掷标枪

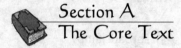

Section A
The Core Text

To Be Media Wise

Most families are concerned about the influence of media violence on their teenagers, but many families don't know what to do about the problem. The good news is that there are effective ways to teach your teenagers to be media wise.

As director of the TV Center at City University of New York, I helped develop some of the first media literacy courses in the late 1970s. Since then, years of research have produced a very clear understanding of how to teach media literacy. There are four pillars of media wisdom.

The first is to understand the influence of the media, which may be titled, "breaking the bonds of denial." As Dale Kunkel, professor at the University of California, Santa Barbara, points out, after thousands of intensive studies in this area, only one significant researcher still denies the influence of the media, and that researcher last did real research in this area in the mid-1980s. In the wake of the Columbine High School massacre, CBS president Leslie Moonves put it quite bluntly, "Anyone who thinks the media has nothing to do with this is an idiot." Thus the American Psychological Association's report on media violence concludes, "There is absolutely no doubt that those who are heavy viewers of violence demonstrate an increased acceptance of aggressive attitudes and behavior."

Of course, the media is not the whole problem, but one part of the equation could be summed up with the **sage biblical** injunction found in one Corinthians, "Do not be misled: 'Bad company corrupts good character.'" This is the message of the Surgeon General's Report released on youth violence; bad company corrupts good character, whether that bad company is gangs, peer pressure, or violent mass media of entertainment.

Breaking the bonds of denial also means noting that there is a lot of good media out there, which we honor every March at the Movieguide ® Annual Awards Gala and Report to the Entertainment Industry in Los Angeles and which will be broadcast on PaxTV on Easter Sunday, April 15. In fact, the number of movies with worthwhile **redemptive** content has doubled in the last four years.

The second step in media wisdom is to understand the **susceptibility** of children at each stage of cognitive development. Not only do children see the media differently at each stage of development, but different children are susceptible to different stimuli. As the research of the National Institute of Mental Health showed many years ago, some children want to copy media violence, some are susceptible to other media influences, some become afraid, and many just become **desensitized**. Just as an alcoholic would be **inordinately** tempted by a beer commercial, so the **propensity** for susceptibility plays an important part in what kind of media will influence your child at each stage of development.

The third part of media wisdom is to understand the grammar of the media so that you can deconstruct and **critique** what you are watching by asking the right questions. Children spend the first 14 years of their lives learning grammar with respect to 16th century technology — the written word. They need to be taught the grammar of the 21st century technology. Thus, they need to know how aspects of different media work and influence them, and how to be able to ask the right questions such as, who is the hero? The villain? Or, the premise?

Finally, your children need to understand your values to be able to use those values to evaluate the answers they get from asking the right questions. If the hero wins by murdering and mutilating, your children need to apply your own values, which may or may not see the hero's actions as heroic or commendable. Families have an easier time with number four, because they can apply their deeply held religious beliefs to evaluate the media. Even so, media literacy and values education are two of the fastest growing areas in the academic community, because educators realize that something is **amiss**. Therefore, I speak all around the world at national education associations and present my deeply held beliefs as the yardstick that I use to evaluate the **ascertainment** questions that need to be asked.

Of course, there is much more to teach media wisdom. Reading to your children five minutes a day is a most effective tool, according to University of Wisconsin research. Having your children prepare their own rating system, and then letting them adhere to it is also helpful, as is having your children review the media they consume by writing up their answers to the right questions. As Theodore Roosevelt said, if we educate a man's mind but not his heart, we have an educated **barbarian**. Media wisdom involves educating the heart so that it will make the right decisions.

Notes to the Text:

sage 贤明的,明智的,审慎的

biblical	圣经的
redemptive	赎回的,挽回的
susceptibility	易感性,敏感性
desensitize	使不敏感
inordinately	过度地,过分地
propensity	倾向
critique	批评
amiss	出差错的
ascertainment	查明,确定
barbarian	粗鲁无礼的人,野蛮人

Understanding the Text:

1. How many pillars of media wisdom are mentioned in the passage? What are they?

2. What does "breaking the bonds of denial" mean?

3. What's your understanding of the susceptibility of children at each stage of cognitive development?

4. Why is it necessary for children to understand the grammar of the media?

5. What role do family values play in teaching children to be media wise?

6. What do you think is the most important to be media wise?

Section B
Sample Interview

Success in Internet Marketing

Q: Corey, as one who has been extremely successful as an online marketer, please tell us how you got started using the

Internet as a marketing tool.

Corey: I started marketing online in the fall of 1994. It was quite a fluke. In my course, I explain that we published my book, *Car Secrets Revealed*, and started selling it offline. The results were pathetic. We thought we had a winning formula and it was barely breaking even. I spent about US $20,000 offline trying to promote it... and it flopped. I took the advice of a friend that was setting up an automotive site on the net and he helped me get a very simple web page online. I saw a few sales trickle in and then took more interest in it, promoting the book online in my spare time.

Q: What are some of the online ventures you are involved in?

Corey: I own four different businesses that now generate over US $2,600,000 in online sales every year. I have interests in many other online projects, as I have done work for clients for a portion of the profits I generate. I also have a clientele base that hires me for online business advice at US $320 per hour.

Q: How long did it take your first online venture to start making a profit?

Corey: The first month the sales trickled in, so I technically made a profit within 30 days... but nothing to live off of. Since I was one of the first group of commercial businesses online... there was a lot of "trying everything," so it took me almost 18 months before I started to see a full-time income. I spent literally 12 - 14 hours a day, 7 days a week trying different techniques and ideas online. Now that I know almost every trick and tip there is, I can literally take almost any business online and make it turn a very healthy profit in a few months. As more and more people got online, many of the standard marketing techniques were getting overused and becoming ineffective... so I developed "twists" to most of them to ensure they still made a profit when everyone was using the "regular" approaches to online marketing. The results: the techniques I use to market online are very unique.

Q: How did you learn about what it takes to succeed?

Corey: At first a lot of trial and error. I took a lot of the concepts and ideas I got from the very expensive seminars I used to attend and material I bought. I took those ideas, and with a little ingenuity and creativity, adapted them to the net (while in the midst of developing my own winning formulas for online success). I came up with formulas that work like wildfire online.

Q: I recognize the names of those other well-known direct marketers that you have learned from. It's apparent that your formulas work. Which avenues are paying off the best for you?

Corey: I have never had an online business that has not made a very healthy profit. My four combined online businesses now generate over US $2,600,000 in sales online per year! And the beauty of it is that I started it myself as a one-man operation. I now have had to hire five employees to take care of the paper work and customer service... but have you ever heard of a retail business that has US $2,600,000 in sales with only a few employees? No! They have at least 15 - 20 employees. That is the beauty of the net: you can automate everything so your overhead is incredibly low.

Q: Do you do all of your business online, or do your online marketing efforts supplement your offline business efforts?

218

Corey: One hundred per cent online. I am a specialist in online sales and marketing. I have become one of the most respected online marketers on the Internet... and for good reason: I can prove my successes. If someone asks me to help them with their magazine advertising, I simply tell them that there are better people than me out there for offline marketing and they should see them instead. I do what I do best... and that is online marketing, so I concentrate all my efforts on that!

Q: What mistakes have you made?

Corey: There are so many, I would fill up your entire newsletter listing them. Let me just say that I have wasted hundreds of thousands of dollars trying techniques that did not work (but from everyone I learned something very important). But that is the "price of education" as I say.

Q: What major mistakes do you see other Internet entrepreneurs make?

Corey: There are a lot of them and I discuss them in great detail in the course, but I will briefly mention a few here. First, I have an ineffective web site that does not turn visitors into sales. This is a very tricky thing to do and I devote a lot of time in my course on how to make a web site profitable. Besides, you should put all your eggs in one basket. Trying one technique and thinking it will make you a fortune. You need to diversify your marketing efforts into different promotions to see which ones pull the most net profit, and then concentrate on those. One more thing is a poor "sales process" in the marketing campaign. That is the manner in which you interest the client into coming to your site, then lead him into a good rapport with yourself, and then — and only then — ask for the order. Most people break the link at some point and lose the sale. That is why most sites only see one sale out of every 200 – 400 visitors and some even worse.

Q: Are there any other tips or suggestions you would like to give others that want to profit from the Internet?

Corey: Research, research, research... Read or study everything you can on online marketing and learn about it before you jump in.

Section C
Information Input and Group Discussion

1. "Super Voice Girls" Wow the Millions

Super Voice Girls makes a grand party for all the participants, who are ordinary people, to sing and experience the charms of TV and it also becomes one of the most widely watched TV programs in the country.

Covering five provinces in China, including Hunan, Sichuan, Guangdong, Henan and Zhejiang, Super Girls has attracted more than 120,000 young women participants to the capital cities of these five provinces for preliminary selections.

Many of them waited in long lines for a whole day before registration and some even skipped school to enter the contest, which promises TV success for the lucky few.

An elimination contest procedure has been adopted for Super Girls and five rounds of regional competitions have been broadcast every week, drawing the sustained attention and exceeding expectations of viewers, since the series started in March.

What makes Super Girls particularly popular is that nearly half of the applicants have the chance to present a 30-second TV spot individually — the TV debut for most of them. By last weekend, eight "super girls" had emerged, out of the ten candidates in the national contest.

According to CVSC-Sofres Media, the audience rating for Super Girls has reached eight per cent in the country, ranking second or third at its broadcast time. This viewing rate is regarded as an unprecedented success for a provincial television station. This record may be reached again when the national final approaches in late August, involving the top three contestants.

In addition, the combination of television and mobile phones has proven to be a winning element of Super Girls. The producer says the final ranking of the singers depends on the text messages sent in by viewers. This has become a common way for audiences to participate in Chinese TV shows.

The show proves the emerging new media age makes instant fame possible, just as Andy Warhol predicted: "In the future, everyone will be world famous for 15 minutes."

More "Super Girls" have emerged since, with their excellent singing skills receiving a wide recognition from the show's young audience. "The long series of contests feels like a TV play that you can't bear to miss, especially when your favorite singer is on," said He, a fan of the show. "Some of them are really cool and brilliant in the show. It is unbelievable that previously they were as ordinary as I."

Liu Zhiyi, a Chinese student now living in Germany, said, "The Chinese people used to put more emphasis on collectivism in the past, but this contest offers young people an opportunity to reveal their personalities and realize their own values."

So far, nearly all the finalists in the national contest have been interviewed by the press, or invited to engage in online chat with their fans. Television has rapidly equipped them with the manner of true stars and driven hundreds of thousands of people crazy for them.

"What's more, the judges in the contest talk more freely and bluntly, quite different from those in formal competitions," said Fan Ning, another viewer. It seems that the "Super Girls" themselves are not the only stars — they are accompanied by a team of judges comprised of pop singers, critics and program designers who have also won fame for their styles of commentary.

Questions for Discussion:

1. Have you ever watched the competition of Super Voice Girls? Are you interested in it?
2. Why can Super Voice Girls wow the millions?
3. Why does the emerging new media age make instant fame possible?
4. If you had the chance, would you like to join in the contest? Why or why not?
5. What are the commercial effects behind the contest?
6. What are the possible benefits and drawbacks for holding such a competition?

2. S. Korean Soap Opera Sparks Boom in China

South Korean movies and television series have been popular in China for years. What is the secret behind this and other shows that have Chinese fans scrambling for the nation's food and fashion?

The formula is not a secret and opinions do not diverge. Both experts and viewers agree, *Dae Jang Geum* grabs, tickles and warms us because it seems exotic. Yet it has such a familiar ring to it that it makes Chinese viewers feel comfortable.

The Chinese culture and the Korean culture overlap in many ways. So Chinese audiences can easily identify with the characters and their behavior, said Jiao Yan, a researcher with the Chinese Academy of Social Sciences. "We see a purer form of Confucianism and are refreshed by it because we feel a sense of belonging."

Wang Li, a Beijing publisher who is on the South Korean bandwagon and has the Chinese rights to several South Korean best-sellers, concurs: "The Confucius tradition reflected in these Korean dramas and books are like dj vu to us because we cannot find it in our own writers and artists.

Besides, a whole family of several generations can enjoy a show together as it is devoid of sex and violence."

Melodrama is a staple to soap opera fans everywhere and this show is no exception. Jang Geum goes through some tough times, such as palace politics, misunderstandings and persecution, but she endures.

On top of everything, in the show, the preparation of Korean food is shown as meticulously presented as in a cooking program. It is so instructive that it has become something like a Martha Stewart episode on how to eat well and eat healthy.

Audiences hardly care for the details. They have been swept off the ground by the exquisite beauty of Lee Young-ae, the actress who plays the title role, and more importantly, by the delicate craft of Korean cuisine and medicine.

It is said that, Bae Yong-joon, the bespectacled star of many popular South Korean movies and TV shows, helped an export boom in 2004 that experts pegged at US$2.3 billion.

Its pop culture has added an aura to anything Korean. This applies not only to cultural or lifestyle products such as books, recordings, food and clothes, but also to home electronics and high-tech.

The penchant of South Korean actresses and actors to have a facelift has also had a palpable effect on the cosmetic surgery business in China. As people marvel at the "before" and "after" photos of Korean beauties, the stigma about surgically changing one's appearance is quickly dissipating.

Others have expressed that the "cultural mecca" of China's Y Generation is now Seoul. It has replaced Europe and the United States as a place of inspiration.

Questions for Discussion:

1. Do you like Korean soap operas? Why or why not?
2. Why do Korean soap operas attract the Chinese viewers?
3. What are the similarities and differences between Chinese and Korean soap operas?
4. Are there any special features among Korean TV series? If yes, would you like to illustrate some?
5. What are the possible advantages and disadvantages of the popularity of foreign TV series?
6. What can be learned from this phenomenon?

Section D
Sample Speech and Oral Practice

Part A Sample Speech

Take Action to Control Negative Influence of Media

It is now well believed that the mass media such as films and TV can be educational and entertaining, but it can also have a bad influence, especially on the young. It is the government's or the public's responsibility to take serious efforts to control harmful information in the media.

The basic reason is that we live in an imperfect world. Right at this moment, wars are being fought and people are being wounded or killed. The media's job is to report such news to the public. It draws public concern to take positive action against violence, but it also affects the minds and thoughts of children, who may be tempted to imitate such crimes. Children are too young to distinguish whether it is harmful or not.

Another reason is that the media often involves a lot of violence. In certain stories, violence may be portrayed as the method to solve problems. Violent characters may also be depicted as heroic figures. Fight scenes can bring pleasure, but they may also encourage violence in society. Children may imitate fight scenes. They may also be misled into believing that violence solves every problem, or thinking that violent people are popular and always win. In fact, we have already tasted the evil fruit. Violence or murders have been heard on campus in recent years.

Of course, films or TV are good to us as a whole. Life, without such media, will be dull or tedious. The key is to remove their disadvantages and make full use of their advantages. As long as the government and the public have realized the serious problems the media may bring to us, we should be confident of a satisfactory solution.

Part B Presentation Practice

Directions: *Talk on each of the following topics for at least five minutes. Be sure to make your points clear and logical* *with adequate supporting details.*

Topic 1: The function of the media

Questions for reference:

1. What is the function of the media?
2. Should we be credulous or dubious about the media? What is the proper attitude towards the media?
3. Based on your personal experience, how do you think one can be media wise?

Topic 2: The government should take measures to control the influence of the Internet.

Questions for reference:

1. Do you think the Internet is a mixed blessing?
2. Why should the government take action to control the influence of the Internet?
3. What measures should be taken to deal with the harmful effects of the Internet?

Topic 3: The commitments of a journalist

Questions for reference:

1. Do you think the journalist has the right to expose any stories to the public no matter what they are?
2. What is the basic quality of a journalist, efficiency, audacity or integrity?
3. In your opinion, what should be the commitments of a journalist?

Part C More Topics for Oral Practice

Directions: Based on the news reports, talk on each of the following topics for at least five minutes. Be sure to make your points clear and logical with adequate supporting details.

News Report 1:

Daily exposure to television provides a centralized mass media production of a coherent set of images and messages produced for total populations, and in its relatively nonselective, almost ritualistic use by most viewers. This total pattern accounts for the historically new and distinct consequence of living with television as a cultivation of shared conceptions of reality among otherwise diverse populations.

Topic: *Compared with other media, do you think television is still the main source of information for most people today? If yes, can you explain the reasons for its popularity?*

News Report 2:

Two recently published studies show that prolonged exposure to gratuitous violence in the media can escalate subsequent hostile behavior and, among some viewers, foster a greater acceptance of violence as a means of conflict resolution.

Topic: *Do you believe that violent movies can increase violent responses in real life?*

News Report 3:

China should make efforts to establish a democratic and scientific policy-making system at different levels within the government. This means important decisions should not be made hastily by an individual big shot. When taking office in March 2003, Premier Wen Jiabao stressed that "the central government must make policies in a scientific and democratic way so as to guarantee the accuracy and effectiveness of policies." He required the State Council and its governmental departments to establish a scientific policy-making system on the basis of democracy.

Topic：*Why is it important for the government to keep the policy-making process transparent?*

Part D Useful Expressions

big news	头条新闻
hot news	最新消息
exclusive news	独家新闻
scoop	特讯；独家新闻
feature	特写，花絮
editorial	社论
review/comment	时评
book review	书评
topicality	时事问题
letters	读者来信
cartoon/comics	漫画
cut	插图；版画
serial story	新闻小说；小说连载
obituary notice	讣闻
public notice	公告
flash-news	大新闻
extra	号外
literary criticism	文艺评论
Sunday features	周日特刊
newsbeat	新闻记者的采访区域
news blackout	新闻管制
press ban	禁止刊行

228

tabloid	小报（通常伴有插图，内容多耸人听闻）
bureau chief/copy chief/editor-in-chief	总编辑
editor	编辑
newsman/newspaperman/journalist	新闻记者
cub reporter	初任记者
war correspondent/campaign badge	随军记者
columnist	专栏记者
star reporter	一流通讯员
news source	新闻来源
informed source	消息灵通人士
newspaper campaign	新闻战
news conference/press conference	记者招待会
International Press Institute，the	国际新闻协会
resident correspondent	常驻记者
special correspondent	特派记者
leading article	报纸上的重要文章；社论
editor's note	编者按

Unit Thirteen

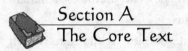

Section A
The Core Text

The Universal Ethic

Policy involves ethics. When we talk about economic and political policy such as tax reform or foreign policy, this involves ethics and values. Human rights imply some moral basis for rights. But people have many different and conflicting ethical beliefs, so whose moral standards should we use for global or even national policy?

If we use the ethic of any particular individuals, cultures, or ideologies, this ethic then becomes arbitrarily imposed by force on those with different ethical views. For universal social justice, we need to use an ethic that applies universally. Such a universal ethic does exist, and we need to understand where it comes from, if we want social justice.

The universal ethic cannot come from any culture, so it must derive from something more universal to humanity: human nature. The two aspects of human nature that the philosopher John Locke used are independence and equality. Locke wrote: "The state of nature has a law of nature to govern it which obliges everyone; and reason, which is that law, teaches all mankind who will but consult it that, being all equal and independent, no one ought to harm another in his life, health, liberty, or possessions."

This "law of nature" or natural moral law is formulated by rules that make up the universal ethic. The ethic **assigns** the moral values of good, evil, and neutral to all human acts. But where do these values come from? The **premise** of independence, that persons think and feel independently, implies that values are ultimately subjective, coming from individual desires and feelings. The premise of human equality gives these values an equal status.

The universal ethic's rule for moral goodness is that acts which are welcomed benefits to others are morally good. Helping another person the way that person wants to be helped is a good act. If you think you are doing something for another's own good, but he does not think it's good for him, then by the universal ethic, it is not good.

The rule for evil is more complicated, because there are two types of acts that individuals feel are personally bad. One is an offense that exists within the subject's mind, and the other is an invasion into the person's body and possessions, thus involving more than just his mind. For example, if someone wears a T-shirt with a message that some find displeasing, that is an offense, since whether one is pleased or displeased depends on one's personal viewpoint. In contrast, if one person shoots a bullet into another person's body, that is an unwelcome invasion. For the universal ethic, only unwelcome invasions are evil, while mere offenses are morally neutral. Also, acts which only affect yourself are either neutral or good, but not evil, since there is no invasion into another's domain.

A society has complete liberty or freedom if its laws prohibit and punish evil as prescribed by the universal ethic, and if any act which is good or neutral is allowed but not required. The universal ethic also tells us what our human or natural rights are: we have the right to do anything that does not **coercively** harm others, and the right to be free from coercive harm.

We have a property right to our own bodies and lives, since if some control others, this violates the premise of equality and becomes an invasion. This self-ownership right implies a property right to our labor and the products of our labor. But self-ownership does not extend to what labor does not produce: natural resources. The premise of equality implies that all persons have an equal property right to the benefits of nature other than our own bodies. These benefits are manifested in the rent that folks bid to use nature. So equality is satisfied only if communities share the rents due to nature and community. The universal ethic therefore prescribes a **fiscal** policy of public and community revenue from rent, along with voluntary user fees. The **taxation** of labor and produced goods is an invasion into what properly belongs to the producers.

For social policy and civil liberties, the universal ethic prescribes that there should be no law where there is no victim of an invasion, thus no victimless crimes. Everyone should be free to do what he or she wants so long as they do not coercively harm others. There should also be no restriction on honest and peaceful enterprise. This implies true free trade: no barriers of any kind.

There are of course many complications in applying the universal ethic to our personal lives and for social policy, such as the rights of children, environmental policy, and the punishment of crimes. The universal ethic provides the general framework that can be applied to particular topics, leaving scope for judgment and circumstances. This framework enables our widely differing cultures to live together in social harmony. The best way to implement the universal ethic for social justice is to make it a permanent part of a country's constitution, along with a decentralized political organization that lets the people rather than **moneyed** elites control the government and policy.

Only when much of humanity recognizes the existence of the universal ethic and applies it to personal and social life will there be universal justice, peace, and harmony.

Notes to the Text:

assign	赋值于
premise	前提
coercively	强制地,压迫地
fiscal	财政的,国库的
taxation	征税,抽税
moneyed	有钱的

Understanding the Text:

1. Where does the universal ethic stem from?
2. What are the two aspects of human nature that the philosopher John Locke used?
3. What assigns moral values to human acts?
4. What is the universal ethic's rule for moral goodness?
5. What is the rule for evil acts?
6. According to the passage, what are our human or natural rights?
7. Why should communities share the rents due to nature and community?
8. What is the best way to implement the universal ethic?

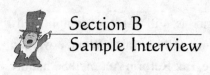

Section B
Sample Interview

How to Make the Tax System Better and Simpler

Q: No one likes to pay taxes. But is the income tax system so broken that it needs a complete overhaul?

McCaffery: Well, yes, and that's a large part of the reason I wrote *Fair Not Flat*. To explain how badly broken it is, why it needs repair, and how we can make that repair happen. The wealthiest people in the United States with property pay little to no tax today, while ordinary wage earners like you and me can't escape from paying high taxes, ranging from a third to half of our earnings! Add to that the tremendous complexity and inefficiency of our system, and you have what I take to be a disaster on your hands.

Q: OK, so the present system isn't fair to everyone. Can't we just reform it or close the loopholes in the tax code to make it more equitable?

McCaffery: If we try minor, ad hoc reforms just to close loopholes here and there, we do nothing about the deep, fundamental, and structural problems in the tax code. These all relate, as I explain in the book, to our obsession with taxing savings directly. Until we rethink that, tax reform is doomed. Take, for example, the Tax Reform Act of 1986. This was a major piece of bipartisan legislation — the centerpiece of Ronald Reagan's second term as president — and it did indeed close a vast array of loopholes and lower tax rates. But less than two decades later, we're right back where we started. The income tax is still far too complicated, inefficient, and fundamentally unfair. Worse, we can see in hindsight that the Tax Reform Act of 1986 mainly shored up the income tax's status as a wage tax — it did nothing about the surprisingly simple ways in which the rich can avoid taxes. Until we fix that, we're stuck with a system that overburdens the working classes while letting the wealthy off scot-free.

Q: There have been a variety of proposals for a flat tax on income — from folks like Congressman Dick Armey, Senator Arlen Specter, and presidential candidates Steve Forbes and Jack Kemp. How does your proposal differ from theirs?

McCaffery: My plan, the Fair Not Flat tax, is progressive. It won't raise tax rates on the middle classes to pay for tax reduction for the rich. You can get almost all of the benefits of these flat tax proposals — in terms of simplicity, economic efficiency, and the fairness of the tax base — without abandoning America's longstanding and sensible commitment to at least moderate progressivity in tax burdens. The wealthy can and should pay a bit more at the margins of their luxurious lifestyles.

Q: But how does it work? What does it mean to have a progressive national sales tax?

McCaffery: A supplemental tax on spending for the wealthiest individuals would make the sales tax progressive. Under the system I propose, a family of four would pay no tax on their first US $20,000 in spending, and 10 per cent on the next US $60,000. Only the few families who spend more than US $80,000 a year would be subject to the supplemental tax. Necessities would be taxed less than ordinary and luxury items. And no one would be taxed directly on savings or investments. It's that simple.

Q: This sounds like the USA Tax plan that was proposed about seven years ago by Senator Pete Domenici and then-Senator Sam Nunn. Is your proposal any different?

McCaffery: Yes and Yes. Yes, it is very similar to the Nunn-Domenici "USA" or "unlimited savings accounts" plan, proposed in Congress in the mid-1990s, and I give credit to that proposal in the book. But the Fair Not Flat plan differs from that proposal in being more technically consistent and in substituting an actual national sales, or value-added tax (VAT) for the lowest brackets of the tax. That latter change poses a huge and welcome simplification for most Americans: They'll no longer have to fill out tax forms or file tax returns.

Q: So this is a national sales tax?

McCaffery: Everyone would pay taxes on the things, or the goods and services that they buy. Then the upper middle and upper classes would fill out a "supplemental spending tax" form every April. As I said, only families of four spending more than US $80, 000 need pay this supplemental tax, and at rates starting at 10 per cent. For these relatively affluent families, this tax adds to the actual sales tax or VAT to get progressivity. Rates keep going up, until families that spend more than US $1,000,000 a year on themselves pay a total tax on their marginal purchases of 50 per cent.

Q: But isn't it dangerous to tax consumption? Spending is

the engine of the economy, isn't it?

McCaffery: Funny, that's the most common question I get, and the one I use to start the Question and Answer section at the back of *Fair Not Flat*. Look, consumption is good. And it is the engine of our economy, especially now that we are in the throes of a recession. But taxing consumption won't slow down our economy further as many fear. Under my plan, tax rates wouldn't increase for any but the wealthiest spenders. For many lower- and middle-class Americans, taxes would actually decrease. And with that money, a vast majority of Americans would be able to spend more if they wanted to. With my proposal, we'd be increasing consumer confidence, and making spending more possible than ever before.

Q: But doesn't taxing the wealthy more amount to class warfare?

McCaffery: Well, there are some who would call my proposal that. But that's not the case at all. What I propose in my new book is class teamwork. Most wealthy people, as books like *The Millionaire Next Door* teach us, want to and, in fact, do save and invest their riches back into the economy. And there's no reason to tax them when they do. Capital helps us all. It keeps interest rates low, and that's good for homebuyers, students, and workers. I'm not proposing that we simply tax the wealthiest people in our country. Simply those who spend the most. I think that's fair, and I think it's in line with classic American values.

Section C
Information Input and Group Discussion

1. Stronger Governance Reflects Public Will

In his maiden "Policy Address" delivered yesterday, Chief Executive Donald Tsang put forward the three main themes of his rule — pursuing excellence in governance, fostering harmony in the community, and helping the economy to power ahead, in the process revealing the characteristics of a people-based and pragmatic government.

It is also an indication that under the current favorable situation, Tsang has not forgotten how the people have placed their trust in him, nor does he want to fall short of the expectations of society and the country. His strengthening of governance is based on public opinion and interests. He is committed to acting out his words, adopting a pragmatic attitude and making himself accountable for his actions.

The most pressing demand of the SAR government under the new chief executive is enhancing its ruling capability. The reason why the administration has been kept in a weak position is complicated — partly because of the hindrance of pan-politicization of society, and partly because of the bottling up of grievances due to economic slowdown. Certainly, the below-par ruling ability of the administration had a lot to do with the problem as well.

Now that the economy is back on the right track and prospects have brightened up again, people are regaining confidence and the social atmosphere has become more harmonious. Such conditions, with the help of the government's rising popularity, help create at a steady pace an environment that is conducive to governance. Under such circumstances, Tsang stressed in his speech the need to rule strictly according to law, to realize executive-led governance, to strengthen the functions of the chief executive office, to empower the chief secretary for administration and the financial secretary to play a bigger role in coordinating government policies, to bolster the number of non-official members of the Executive Council, to invite more talents into the Commission on Strategic Development, and to give more power to district officers, amongst other things.

All these measures to strengthen governance have not been formulated behind closed doors. Instead, they are based on public opinion and interests, with input from a wide spectrum of society. A government with a clear direction, stable policies, strong leadership, resolution and high efficiency that is formed under such conditions is definitely something we should give credit to.

As far as the second theme — fostering harmony in the community — is concerned, Tsang proposed in the "Policy Address", in addition to a series of measures aimed to help the socially vulnerable, ruling under the principle of fairness, and dealing with different interests with impartiality. He is committed to maintaining order and fair competition in the market, making joint efforts to safeguard pluralism and inclusiveness in our community, opposing any form of discrimination, attaching significance to family values, and encouraging the promotion of multiple cultures. Compared with other metropolises in the world, Hong Kong is much more serene and peaceful.

On the other hand, the impact of pan-politicization on society cannot be overlooked. To build a harmonious society, we must depend on the rule of law, and the principles of fairness and righteousness as well as on democracy.

Questions for Discussion:

1. How many themes of rule did Donald Tsang put forward in his talk and what were they?
2. What is crucial in pursuing excellence in governance?
3. Why has the administration been kept in a weak position?
4. In order to foster harmony in the community, what should be done by the government?
5. What do you think of Tsang's ideas or principles?
6. Why is it important for stronger governance to reflect the public will?

2. Make City Life More than Bright Lights

Big does not necessarily mean better. While our cities grow larger, they become less livable.

Last year, Beijing unveiled a grand blueprint for transforming itself into a "modern cosmopolitan city with unique characteristics." The city's planners are eying a place within the ranks of grand global cities such as New York, London and Tokyo. Beijing's desire to build itself into an ultra-modern capital of the future has been followed by a frenzy of copycat metropolises all over the country. The capital has been designed to be totally modernized and have the infrastructure of a world metropolis by 2020.

Once this is achieved, Beijing will be ready to start balancing economic growth with human development. Human factors are fortunately in the minds of the planners, though such considerations have come rather late. In its modernization drive, Beijing has been subjected to extensive urban re-engineering projects.

Similar scenes can be seen in other cities, which are rising with breathtaking speed. All of the cities have been turned into vast construction zones. Cranes peek out from behind skyscrapers wherever you look, turning into a slow-motion ballet as crews work round-the-clock to fill in an already crowded skyline. The monumental signs of progress such as great avenues, massive ring roads, giant steel-and-glass towers and shopping emporiums are hailed as modern.

But the consequences of such a grand development plan are the last thing the city planners are thinking about. The traces of old Beijing such as *hutong* — the city's narrow alleys that crisscross the inner city — have been giving way to re-development. We have more and more cities wearing a supposedly modern face, but growing unfriendly towards their residents. Every city wants to develop, and everyone wants to have an international airport, six-lane highways and export zones, rather than sustainable growth.

That means many provincial officials are trying the same formula — manufacturing and export zones, research parks and self-styled Silicon Valleys. The unchecked development means duplication and waste. The expansion of cities makes motor vehicles must-haves for their residents. More vehicles mean more traffic congestion and more harmful emissions, which now account for nearly two-thirds of China's urban air pollution. As a result, respiratory diseases are on the increase. Many cities growing rapidly will grind to a halt if effective actions are not taken to ease traffic congestion. Congestion means more than just being stuck in traffic. It means more car exhaust and huge economic losses.

It is time for city planners to contemplate what their creations are really for. Cities should be livable. Planners are obliged to provide reliable, affordable and comfortable public infrastructure. They need to consider the future very carefully to make sure our children inherit a city that values its natural assets and preserves its historical and cultural heritage. The planning should be ecologically sound and economically efficient.

Questions for Discussion:

1. What does the title "Make City Life More than Bright Lights" mean to you?

2. What is more important to urban development?

3. Does the city or town you live in have the same problems mentioned in the passage?

4. Which do you think is more significant, the beautiful appearance of a city or the humanity of its citizens?

5. What are the possible causes of cities which focus more on their appearance than on the real improvement of their citizens' living conditions?

6. Can you make some suggestions to the scientific approach to urban development?

Section D
Sample Speech and Oral Practice

Part A Sample Speech

Journalists' Code of Ethics

The duty of the journalist is to further those ends by seeking truth and providing a fair and comprehensive account of events and issues. Conscientious journalists from all media and specialties strive to serve the public with thoroughness and honesty. Professional integrity is the cornerstone of a journalist's credibility. Members of the society share a dedication to ethical behavior and adopt this code to declare the society's principles and standards of practice. Journalists should be honest, fair and courageous in gathering, reporting and interpreting information.

Journalists should test the accuracy of information from all sources and exercise care to avoid inadvertent error. Deliberate distortion is never permissible. To diligently seek out subjects of news stories to give them the opportunity to respond to allegations of wrongdoing is another responsibility for a journalist. It is also important for journalists to identify sources whenever feasible because the public is entitled to as much information as possible on sources' reliability. Besides, journalists should question sources' motives before promising anonymity, clarify conditions attached to any promise made in exchange for information, make certain that headlines, news teases and promotional material, photos, video, audio, graphics, sound bites and quotations do not misrepresent. Moreover, they should support the open exchange of views, even views they find repugnant; give voice to the voiceless — official and unofficial sources of information can be equally valid; distinguish between advocacy and news reporting — analysis and commentary should be labeled and not misrepresent fact or context — and distinguish news from advertising and shun hybrids that blur the lines between the two. It is also necessary for them to recognize a special obligation to ensure that the public's business is conducted in the open and that government records are open to inspection.

In addition to what journalists should do, they should also avoid doing the followings. They should not oversimplify or highlight incidents out of context. Never distort the content of news photos or video. Avoid misleading re-enactments or staged news events. Avoid undercover or other surreptitious methods of gathering information except when traditional open methods will not yield information vital to the public. And never plagiarize. Tell the story of the diversity and magnitude of the human experience boldly, even when it is unpopular to do so. Examine their own cultural values and avoid imposing those values on others. Avoid stereotyping by race, gender, age, religion, ethnicity, geography, sexual orientation, disability, physical appearance or social status.

If journalists can do what they are required to do and avoid doing what they should not do, they are qualified newsmen.

Part B Presentation Practice

Directions: *Talk on each of the following topics for at least five minutes. Be sure to make your points clear and logical with adequate supporting details.*

Topic 1: Is education the answer to ethics?
Questions for reference:
1. Do you think education can solve ethic problems?
2. What should schools do to enhance students' social morality?
3. Are you satisfied with the moral education in your school?
4. Can you make some suggestions to school ethic education?

Topic 2: Should businesses do anything they can to make a profit?
Questions for reference:
1. Do you think the aim of businesses is to get maximum profit?
2. What is the proper attitude towards profits?
3. Besides profits, what else can businessmen do to society?

Topic 3: Tax evasion by the rich
Questions for reference:

244

1. It is reported that the working class makes up the large part of the national tax and that some rich men often defraud the revenue. Is this phenomenon common in your place?
2. What are the possible causes of this phenomenon?
3. What can or should be done to prevent tax evasion of this type?

Part C More Topics for Oral Practice

Directions: *Based on the news reports, talk on each of the following topics for at least five minutes. Be sure to make your points clear and logical with adequate supporting details.*

News Report 1:

The first-ever legislative hearing held by China's top legislature yesterday was a step towards enhancing transparency in the policy-making process. With taxpayers being fully informed of law makers' plans, the public hearing on the adjustment of the personal income tax deduction threshold shed light on a long-overdue taxation update. The reform has aroused interest nationwide as it affects everyone.

Topic: *Is the legislative hearing the best approach to hearing the voice of the public?*

News Report 2:

Tianjin has taken a bold step and broken with tradition by hiring a private attorneys' association to draft a local law concerning public hearings by the city's legislature. It may be the first nationwide and a sign of things to come — letting legal experts, not political figures, draft laws.

Topic: *What are the possible advantages of letting legal experts, not* *political figures, draft laws?*

News Report 3:

In pluralistic Hong Kong, residents never hesitate to take the government to task over real or imagined deficiencies in public services. But this vocal community is rarely heard complaining about the inaccessibility of healthcare services or exorbitant hospital charges. Even the poorest group is assured of good health services, thanks to the government's fundamental philosophy — no one should be denied proper medical care.

Topic: *Do you think that medical reform must ensure healthcare for everyone? If yes, how do we implement this policy?*

Part D　Useful Expressions

generous	大方的；宽宏大量的
genteel	有教养的
gentle	温和的，友善的
hard-working	勤劳的，努力工作的
hearty	衷心的；亲切的
hospitable	殷勤招待的
humble	恭顺的
impartial	公正的
independent	独立的；有主见的
industrious	勤奋的
ingenious	有独创性的
initiative	首创精神
have an inquiring mind	爱动脑筋
intellective	有智力的
intelligent	聪明的，理解力强的

inventive	有发明才能的，有创造力的
kind-hearted	好心的
knowledgeable	有见识的
liberal	自由的；开明的；心胸宽大的
logical	符合逻辑的
loyal	忠心耿耿的
motivated	目的明确的
painstaking	辛苦的；努力的
persevering	不屈不挠的
punctual	严守时刻的
purposeful	有决心的
qualified	合格的
rational	有理性的
realistic	实事求是的
reasonable	讲道理的
reliable	可信赖的
responsible	负责的
self-conscious	自觉的
sensible	明白事理的
spirited	生气勃勃的
sporting	与体育运动有关的；光明正大的
steady	稳定的；踏实的
straightforward	坦率的
strong-willed	意志坚强的
sweet-tempered	性情温和的
temperate	有节制的
tireless	孜孜不倦的

Unit Jourteen

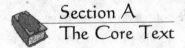

Section A
The Core Text

Beliefs about Wealth and Poverty

The subject of wealth and poverty is certainly not new to our age. Many people down through the centuries have **wrestled** with the apparent inequities of life. The question has often been asked, "Why are some people blessed with wealth, while others cursed with poverty?" The life of the poor is one of hardship and toil. They must rise early and work late simply to earn their daily bread. They do not concern themselves with investments and asset management, but rather with acquiring the necessities of life. They do not see themselves as having unlimited resources of time, talent and opportunity, but often see themselves as being stuck in their poverty. Sometimes they may see this as fate or chance but rarely do they see it as a **divine** blessing. They may feel trapped in their poverty because the wealthy will not allow them to rise above it. As a result there has often been the problem of envy and **strife**, where the poor lust after the wealth and status of the rich and yet hate them for it.

The life of the wealthy on the other hand is quite a different matter. Theirs is a life of apparent ease and luxury. They have all the necessities of life and much more. They do not struggle with earning their daily bread. They worry about how to protect their assets. They do not work for money, they work with money. The often heard cry against the rich is that they have become so by exploiting the poor. As we stand back to observe the conditions of both groups, there seems to be something very wrong, very unjust and very unfair about such a difference in economic levels. A person might be tempted to ask, "How can such inequality be tolerated?"

Through the years, various systems of government have been implemented to try to alleviate these economic problems. In India a **caste** system has been established. In such a system, society is broken down into distinct strata based on differences of wealth, inherited rank or privilege, or profession. It is very difficult to move from one **stratum** to the next, and a person will often remain in the caste into which he was born. Here the poor stay poor and the rich stay rich. Another attempt to try to correct the problem has been socialism. Socialism is an attempt to put everyone on an equal playing field where private enterprise is replaced with the production of goods and services by the state. In this theory of government, there is a collective ownership of property and therefore all people theoretically have an equal say in its allocation. This is an attempt to create a "classless" society where everyone is on an equal footing. While this theory sounds good it does not take into account the human drive toward greed and the desire to get ahead. For socialism to work, all its members must cooperate with its guidelines.

In the United States we have maintained a capitalist economy, but have used government as a means of taking from the majority, through taxes, and redistributing money to the minority through welfare. The problem here is that the criteria for receiving this social welfare may not be as **stringent** as it could be. The result is that there are some who benefit from the program who do not need it. It has also been argued that such a welfare program has **stymied** the incentive for many to provide for their own families. It is much easier to receive from the government, and at times more profitable, than to earn one's own bread.

All of these are systems or facets of government that have been implemented to try to deal with the wealth and poverty of its citizens, but none has succeeded in eliminating the problem. Wherever one goes there are always rich and there are always poor. And so no matter what system of economy is operating where we live, there are some **biblical** truths that speak quite plainly to the subject.

The wealthy are to show consideration to the poor — I have heard of some people who thought that the Golden Rule was, "He who has all the gold makes all the rules." Sometimes it seems that the wealthy make the rules, but the true Golden Rule is found in Matthew. "Whatever you want men to do to you, do also to them." This principle lies at the heart of the way we are to treat others. The wealthy are to put themselves in the shoes of the poor and treat them as they would want to be treated. Deuteronomy states, "If there is among you a poor man of your **brethren**, within any of the gates in your land which the Lord your God is giving you, you shall not harden your heart nor shut your hand from your poor brother, but you shall open your hand wide to him and willingly lend him sufficient for his need, whatever he needs." Job was one who was extremely concerned about the needs of others around him and he did all he could to help them.

Notes to the Text:

wrestle   与(对手)摔跤;挣扎

divine	神圣的,非凡的,超人的
strife	斗争,冲突,竞争
caste	种姓(印度的世袭阶级)
stratum (*pl.* strata)	社会阶层
stringent	严厉的,严格的
stymie	妨碍,阻挠
biblical	圣经的
brethren	弟兄们,同胞

Understanding the Text:

1. What are the author's beliefs about wealth and poverty?

4. What do poor people mainly concern themselves with?

5. What do the rich usually worry about?

6. How many systems of government have been mentioned to deal with the wealth and poverty of its citizens? And what are they?

7. What does the author say about socialism?

8. What is the problem of the system of the United States?

9. According to the author, what is the proper attitude towards this problem?

Section B
Sample Interview

Wealth and Income Inequality

Q: Why is it important to think about wealth, as opposed just to income?

Wolff: Wealth provides another dimension of well-being. Two people who have the same income may not be as well-off if

one person has more wealth. If one person owns his home,
for example, and the other person doesn't, then he is better
off.

Wealth — strictly financial savings — provides security to
individuals in the event of sickness, job loss or marital
separation. Assets provide a kind of safety blanket that
people can rely on in case their income gets interrupted.

Wealth is also more directly related to political power.
People who have large amounts of wealth can make political
contributions. In some cases, they can use that money to run
for office themselves, like New York City Mayor Michael
Bloomberg.

Q: How do economists measure levels of equality and inequality?

Wolff: The most common measure used, and the most understandable
is: What share of total wealth is owned by the richest
households, typically the top 1 per cent? In the United
States, in the last survey year, 1998, the richest 1 per cent
of households owned 38 per cent of all wealth. This is the
most easily understood measure. There is also another
measure called the Gini coefficient. It measures the
concentration of wealth at different per centile levels, and
does an overall computation. It is an index that goes from
zero to one, one being the most unequal. Wealth inequality
in the United States has a Gini coefficient of . 82, which is
pretty close to the maximum level of inequality you can
have.

Q: What have been the trends of wealth inequality over the last
25 years?

Wolff: We have had a fairly sharp increase in wealth inequality
dating back to 1975 or 1976. Prior to that, there was a

protracted period when wealth inequality fell in this country, going back almost to 1929. So you have this fairly continuous downward trend from 1929, which of course was the peak of the stock market before it crashed, until just about the mid-1970s. Since then, things have really turned around, and the level of wealth inequality today is almost double what it was in the mid-1970s. Income inequality has also risen. Most people date this rise to the early 1970s, but it hasn't gone up nearly as dramatically as wealth inequality.

Q: What portion of wealth is owned by the upper groups?

Wolff: The top 5 per cent own more than half of all wealth. In 1998, they owned 59 per cent of all wealth. Or to put it another way, the top 5 per cent had more wealth than the remaining 95 per cent of the population, collectively. The top 20 per cent owns over 80 per cent of all wealth. In 1998, it owned 83 per cent of all wealth. This is a very concentrated distribution.

Q: Where does that leave the bottom tiers?

Wolff: The bottom 20 per cent basically have zero wealth. They either have no assets, or their debt equals or exceeds their assets. The bottom 20 per cent has typically accumulated no savings. A household in the middle — the median household — has a wealth of about US $62,000. US $62,000 is not insignificant, but if you consider that the top 1 per cent of households' average wealth is US $12.5 million, you can see what a difference there is in the distribution.

Q: To what extent is the wealth inequality trend simply reflective of the rising level of income inequality?

Wolff: Part of it reflects underlying increases in income inequality, but the other significant factor is what has happened to the ratio between stock prices and housing prices. The major asset of the middle class is their home. The major assets of the rich are stocks and small business equity. If stock prices increase more quickly than housing prices, then the share of wealth owned by the richest households goes up. This turns out to be almost as important as underlying changes in income inequality. For the last 25 or 30 years, despite the bear market we've had over the last two years, stock prices have gone up quite a bit faster than housing prices.

Q: To what extent is inequality addressed through tax policy?

Wolff: One reason we have such high levels of inequality, compared with other advanced industrial countries, is because of our tax and, I would add, our social expenditure system. We have much lower taxes than almost every Western European country. And we have a less progressive tax system than almost every Western European country. As a result, the rich in this country manage to retain a much higher share of their income than they do in other countries, and this enables them to accumulate a much higher amount of wealth than the rich in other countries. Certainly our tax system has helped to stimulate the rise of inequality in this country. We have a much lower level of income support for poor families than do Western European countries or Canada. Social policy in Europe, Canada and Japan does a lot more to reduce economic disparities created by the marketplace than we do in this country. We have much higher poverty rates than do other advanced industrialized countries.

Q: Do you favor a wealth tax?

Wolff: I've proposed a separate tax on wealth, which actually exists in a dozen European countries. This has helped to lessen inequality in European countries. It is also, I think, a fairer tax. If you think about taxes that reflect a family's ability to pay — a family's ability to pay is a reflection of their income, and also of their wealth holdings — a broader kind of tax of this nature would not only produce more tax revenue, which we desperately need, but it would be a fairer tax, and also help to reduce the level of inequality in this country.

Section C
Information Input and Group Discussion

1. Yellow Light for China's Income Gap

After rapid expansion since 2003, the income gap in China has reached the second most serious "Yellow Light" level.

Unless effective measures are taken, the gap may drift further to the dangerous "Red Light" level in the next five years. The widening income gap in China has become a focal issue in China and aroused the concern of many people.

The United Nations Development Program released statistics that show the Gini coefficient, a statistical measure of inequality in which zero expresses complete equality while one expresses complete inequality, has reached 0.45 in China; 20 per cent of China's population at the poverty end accounts for only 4.7 per cent of the total income or consumption; 20 per cent of China's population at the affluence end accounts for 50 per cent of the total income or consumption.

The income gap has exceeded reasonable limits, exhibiting a further widening trend. If it continues this way for a long time, the phenomenon may give rise to various sorts of social instability. It is worth noting that according to experience in many countries and regions, social contradictions will increase as per capita GDP grows from the US $1,000 level to the US $3,000 level. China is precisely in this period. Decision makers should not turn a blind eye to the big income gap.

The rich population consists of private business owners that got rich due to their talent and diligence as well as people who gained wealth through collusion with officials in power-for-money deals or because they happened to work in monopoly companies or because they stole state assets.

Some experts said "inequality of opportunity" is the root cause of the income gap. Today, our government has begun to take actions to adjust the income gap, as it has formally started the process to amend the individual income tax law. That's a good sign, but the government still has a lot more to do, especially in pushing forward in an orderly way the reform of property rights of state assets, breaking monopolies that have formed on administrative orders and establishing a sound social security net.

Questions for Discussion:
1. What are the possible causes of the income gap?
2. Do you agree "inequality of opportunity" is the root cause of the income gap?
3. What effects can this gap bring to our society?
4. How do the rich help the poor?
5. What can the government do to bridge the gap?
6. Do you have any suggestions to the solution of this problem?

2. Tax Revision Calls for More Reforms

China has decided to set 1,600 yuan per month as the new threshold above which residents must pay personal income tax, raising the cut-off from 800 yuan.

The tax was initiated in 1980, when the country's residents had just started to accumulate personal wealth as China was stepping out of an equal-for-all society. The current cut-off level of 800 yuan was set in 1993, since when the national economic and personal income landscapes have undergone profound changes.

The new cut-off is in line with these changes as average income has been on the rise continually and dramatically.

The expanding rich-poor income gap has aroused widespread concern, and hopes are pinned on personal income taxation playing a larger role in balancing out the disparity.

Researchers agree the bulk of personal income tax revenue is contributed by low- and medium-income earners, which goes against the intentions of legislators — to make use of the law to promote social harmony.

It is hard to determine what the ideal cut-off level for personal income tax should be, although consensus has been reached among the people and legislators that it has to be raised.

At least the democratic procedures (a public hearing was, for the first time, held on the draft amendment to a law) in the legislation process ensure the new threshold is widely accepted by the public.

The new legislative move is a step forward towards a fairer taxation system. But it is only the first step and we still have a long way to go before a mature system is established.

Based on the new threshold, ordinary income earners should be paying less tax. But the same old problem — the rich often taking advantage of loopholes in tax collection to dodge payments — will not be solved simply by raising the cut-off standard.

Legislators and tax officials need to figure out more effective methods to tackle this scourge.

The universal cut-off arrangement does not take into consideration the individual conditions of tax payers. The financial burdens on different earners, in terms of supporting their families, are varied and it is valid to apply differential terms by taking into account housing, education and medical care expenditures, which, in many cases, have to be shouldered by individuals.

Such a detailed taxation arrangement is certainly not possible right now, but it should be the direction in which personal income tax reform proceeds.

Personal income tax is but a part of the overall taxation system. To promote social fairness, other follow-up decisions need to be made to balance out income gaps.

Property tax, gift tax and inheritance tax can play a role in this respect. People remain divided on whether the taxes suit the realities of Chinese society, but preliminary discussions should be encouraged so that a public consensus can be reached earlier rather than later.

China's personal income tax accounts for only 6. 75 per cent of its total tax revenues, but the proportion has been growing quickly in recent years and is set to become a major taxation tool.

Given its increasing weight, more reforms need to follow to keep the tax in line with social changes, and to promote the interests of the majority of the people.

Questions for Discussion:

1. What do you think of the tax revision in 2006?
2. Do you think to set 1,600 yuan per month as the new threshold is

a reasonable choice?

3. Why is the bulk of personal income tax revenue contributed by low- and medium-income earners in our country?

4. Do you think the rich population should contribute more to tax revenues? If yes, how?

5. Why does the new revision call for more reforms?

6. What do you think should follow the tax revision? Can you give some examples to illustrate your opinion?

Section D
Sample Speech and Oral Practice

Part A Sample Speech

Should Citizens Take Out Private Health Insurance by Themselves?

A much debated issue these days is whether citizens should take out private health insurance or not. The cost of providing free medical care for both the wealthy and the poor is far too great for any government, and most people agree that if you can pay for insurance, you should. In this essay, I will argue that all who can afford it should be insured, but free medical care must be made available for those too poor to do so.

The most important reason for encouraging people to take out private health insurance is the cost to the government of healthcare. Free health cover for people who are able to pay for it is a waste of public money. Of course, people will only pay health insurance premiums if they know that they are getting good value for their money. If they get sick, they should pay very little or nothing at all.

In addition, the privately insured are entitled to special benefits such as having the choice of their own doctors, and being able to avoid long waiting lists for hospital beds.

On the other hand, those who really cannot afford to pay private insurance premiums, which are often very high, are still entitled as citizens to the best medical care available — they cannot be expected to pay their own medical bills. However, if they are working, they should still pay a percentage of their wage (say 1 to 2 per cent) as a tax which pays towards the cost of providing real medical services.

In short, most people should privately insure their health, but it is unreasonable to suppose that all citizens can afford it. Therefore, a safety net in the form of a basic free healthcare system must exist for the very poor and the unemployed.

Part B Presentation Practice

Directions: Talk on each of the following topics for at least five minutes. Be sure to make your points clear and logical with adequate supporting details.

Topic 1. To bridge the income gap between the rich and the poor
Questions for reference:
1. It is reported that China's income gap has turned on a yellow light. Can you cite some examples to illustrate the point?
2. What do you think is the main cause of this gap?
3. What action should the government take to prevent the gap from widening? Can you make some suggestions?

Topic 2: What should the government do to create more job opportunities?

Questions for reference:

1. China is facing huge pressures of unemployment. What do you think are the chief causes of unemployment?
2. Who should we blame for the problem of unemployment, the government, society or enterprises?
3. What can be done to ease the unemployment problem?

Topic 3: Is the medical reform in our country basically a failure or success?

Questions for reference:

1. What do you think of the medical reform in our country in the last decade?
2. Why is the cost of medical healthcare increasing all the time?
3. Should citizens be totally responsible for their own health costs?
4. Can you make some suggestions to further reform on medical healthcare?

Part C More Topics for Oral Practice

Directions: Based on the news reports, talk on each of the following topics for at least five minutes. Be sure to make your points clear and logical with adequate supporting details.

News Report 1:

The income divide among Chinese citizens has sharply widened since 2003, and has reached the severe "yellow light" warning level. Statistics show that as of July this year, Chinese rural areas had over 26.1 million denizens in absolute poverty, despite the fact that 27

Chinese provinces and municipalities scrapped agriculture taxation in 2005, resulting in 20 billion yuan (about US $2.5 billion) of subsidies to agriculture and farmers. Some experts hold that China's modernization must give priority to the reform of taxation, social security, and more support for rural areas.

Topic: *What should be done to help the poor in the countryside, the reform of taxation, social security, or more financial support?*

News Report 2:

The Gini coefficient, an international statistical measure of inequality where zero expresses complete equality while one represents complete inequality, has reached 0.45 in China, according to the United Nations Development Program. The UN organization shows 20 per cent of China's population at the poverty end accounts for only 4.7 per cent of the total income or consumption, while 20 per cent of China's affluent population accounts for 50 per cent of the total income or consumption.

Topic: *What should be done to ensure that reforms must not make the income gap any wider?*

News Report 3:

During a time of peace and prosperity, it is fitting to pay tribute to the 90 million or so migrant workers for their contributions to the nation's economic achievements over the past three decades. Their hard work has laid solid foundations for the second stage of economic development, which enables many enterprises to gain confidence to compete with well-established multinational conglomerates in the global marketplace.

Topic: *What efforts should be made to help migrant workers in return for their contributions to the modernization of our country?*

Part D Useful Expressions

insurance industry, the	保险业
ensure funding for priority areas	保证重点支出
clear up pension payments in arrears	补发拖欠的养老金
non-performing loan	不良贷款
multilevel contracting and illegal subcontracting	层层转包和违法分包
credit cooperative in both urban and rural areas	城乡信用社
minimum standard of living for city residents	城镇居民最低生活保障
system of medical insurance for urban workers	城镇职工医疗保障制度
social insurance institution	社会保险机构
unemployment insurance benefits	失业保险金
housing project for low-income urban residents	(针对城镇低收入人群的)安居工程
laid-off worker	下岗职工
repositioning of redundant personnel	富余人员的分流

Unit **Fifteen**

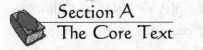

Section A
The Core Text

Principles for International Trade

International trade is an activity mainly conducted by firms or persons led by the principle of **maximizing** their utility function. Nevertheless, there is room for public policy; we can try to define principles that should apply to the rules or the policy-making related to international trade, and particularly to trade negotiations.

In trade negotiations, every country pursues its own interests. It cannot be otherwise because at the end of the day there are different sensitivities, interests and constituencies to answer to. However, a "progressive approach" or "progressive principles" for trade negotiations have to be more sophisticated than just pure and simple individual profit maximization. As a starting point, this would require a vision and a clear political direction to effectively address unbalances, and hence, to achieve a better and fairer environment to negotiate trade rules and to compete.

The following are some of the ideas on principles that should be taken into account if a progressive approach to trade negotiations is to be followed.

The WTO is best.

For a small economy, highly dependent on trade, it is very important to have clear rules in order to provide some degree of certainty to our exporters. They face a rough world and fierce competition. This is true for most small and/or developing countries.

For some people, the role of dispute settlement is enough to justify the existence of the WTO. For others, the WTO has an additional value which is to level the playing field, and allow for more balanced results because small countries create alliances that increase their **leverage**, with the G20 as a remarkable example of this, becoming one of the key players in the agricultural negotiations by playing a constructive role and shifting the decision-making process from the Quad to the FIPs (Five Interested Parties: Australia, Brazil, EU, India, USA).

If the WTO should focus "simply" on ensuring that trade rules are respected, or if it should also pursue trade **liberalization**, these two issues should be discussed. However, in both cases, the WTO has to have **legitimacy** and credibility. And so far, it has both. The WTO is one of the few institutions which show that multilateralism can still work. This is the reason why it should be supported and protected.

Defend your interests, but don't overdo it.

There are currently 148 WTO members with huge differences among them in size, their level of development, and their specific interests. Hence, achieving consensus is a task that is becoming more difficult in each successive round of negotiations.

What to do then? Acknowledge this fact, be realistic and try not to push the line too far. In other words, while we understand that what some developed members will have to do in agriculture will require compensation somewhere else in order to make the round attractive to them, they should bear in mind that the very same arguments they put forth to protect their agricultural sensitivities are valid for most developing countries when it comes to industrial products. Some developed countries argue that, for instance, rice production is sensitive because some farmers depend on it for a living. Fair enough. However, those countries insist that they need to attain "real market access" — actual cuts in the applied tariffs on industrial markets in countries like Brazil and India. Needless to say, Brazil and India do not have safety nets to absorb the negative impacts of trade liberalization, as could be the case with say Japan or Norway. The differences in "social **endowment**" should be considered when " efforts " towards liberalization are discussed in trade negotiations.

If trade is the answer, then what is the question?

In trade negotiations, too often, arguments in favor of trade liberalization are used to argue that this is something good for everybody *per se* and therefore, every country should open their market, regardless of their specific conditions. This argument is not only patronizing; it is also flawed.

In the case of the negotiation of bilateral agreements — where tariffs with the partner are eliminated — it is crucial to have previously undertaken some sort of unilateral or multilateral liberalization, simply because the prospect of moving from an environment in which protection is 30 per cent to one in which it does not exist is likely to create social unrest. There are several examples of countries with a successful story of gradual opening up: China, India and Korea are all good examples. From this viewpoint, a progressive approach to trade liberalization should encourage a gradual and persistent process of opening within a long time frame.

WTO rulings must be respected.

There may be different views on whether or not the Dispute Settlement Understanding (DSU) is the most efficient mechanism to solve disputes, but the most important thing is that their decisions should be respected. When a country simply decides that it will not amend its legislation in accordance to a DSU ruling, the whole Multilateral Trading System (MTS) is being undermined. If a country can get away with a WTO violation, what are the incentives for others to comply?

Some countries have attained a creative way to **incorporate** these issues in the Free Trade Agreements (FTAs) while at the same time not increasing barriers to our trade. Under this approach, parties make a commitment to enforce their own domestic regulations, and if one of the parties fails to do so, a monetary contribution is requested from the **infringing** party which is deposited in a jointly managed fund with the solely purpose of using those resources to improve the enforcement of domestic legislation on the infringing party. Thus, there is no homogenization of standards, no trade sanction, no disruption of trade, and an approach that places emphasis on cooperation based on a system that will provide resources geared towards improving enforcement.

Notes to the Text:

maximize	最大值化,极大值化
leverage	优势,力量
liberalization	自由主义化

legitimacy	合法(性),正统(性),正确(性)
endowment	捐赠的基金(或财物);天资,禀赋
per se	本身,本质上
incorporate	合并,结合
infringe	破坏,侵犯,违反

Understanding the Text:

1. What are the general principles of international trade?

2. What roles does the WTO play in international trade?

3. Why does the author say that you should defend your interests but not overdo it?

4. What does this statement mean, "If trade is the answer, then what is the question?"

5. Why is it critical for businesses or countries to respect WTO rulings?

6. What does it mean to China when she has become a member of the WTO?

Section B
Sample Interview

Enterprise Culture and Business Success

Q: What is meant by a "good enterprise culture"?

Peter Pfluger: A good enterprise culture is simply one that fits the enterprise: the mission of the enterprise, its products and services, and the profile of the staff. So an enterprise culture covers both the behavior patterns and attitudes of staff as a whole towards the external world as well as internally. It should be expressed in relation to all groups that come into contact with the firm, not only between staff but also towards customers and the whole environment of the enterprise such as shareholders, the hometown and the media.

Q: Phonak Group today has 25 companies with 2,500 employees. Of these, only 560 work at the home office in Staffa. How can you obtain such a common ideal worldwide?

Peter Pfluger: We would never acquire a firm whose enterprise culture is the contrary of our own. Naturally, the cultures do not match completely, but if a firm does fit in with ours to some degree, then the executives quickly see that our enterprise culture is an asset and they adapt within two or three years. This is achieved above all by direct contact. The people must be able to discuss things among themselves: "How did you do that? How do you make that change?"

Q: What is special about the Phonak culture?

Peter Pfluger: It is imbued with the spirit of our products. On the one hand we are operating in the high-tech field. On the other, they are medical products which help people to overcome problems with hearing. This positive aspect of our production motivates workers and has a direct impact on their working and behavioral patterns in the firm. From outside — for example from applicants, clients or visitors — we hear that our specific enterprise culture is judged as including openness and energy. We enjoy a higher energy level and commitment among our workers than other firms.

Q: How do you achieve that?

Peter Pfluger: You cannot decide to create a specific enterprise culture in three years. But with the necessary determination you can achieve something over the long term. What is important is to ensure that everything fits together. Every aspect of the enterprise should be an expression of the enterprise culture and contribute to it: personnel policies, product marketing, relations with customers, external relations and publicity.

Q: Phonak House, opened at Staffa in 1987, is famous... What can we do internally?

Peter Pfluger: The enterprise culture can be expressed through architecture and the design of workplaces. It is not insignificant whether workers sit back-to-back or facing each other. If you want openness in the firm, you cannot cut people off in small cells. But you should not cultivate openness only internally but also in your contacts with customers.

Q: Do you have a written guide that contains the principles of your enterprise culture?

Peter Pfluger: No, our enterprise culture is not formalized. Certainly, we have discussed the possibility. It is difficult, however, to write down something that will not sound banal and general. And a nonspecific guide is worthless. Since the emphases and nuances of an enterprise culture change continually, a useful guide would have to be revised every two years if not every year. I prefer it when the culture is "lived" rather than dictated.

Q: What does it mean to "live" an enterprise culture?

Who are those responsible?

Peter Pfluger: Enterprise culture cannot be delegated. It must be a constitutive part of the decision-making process in the company hierarchy. Those responsible can be found at all levels of the enterprise where decisions are taken. The leadership must actively support this attitude and provide an example. Otherwise, nothing can be expected from the other workers. Cultivating an open enterprise culture means speaking openly to staff. In this contacts among staff play a role — for example, whether you can be engaged in conversation in the corridor.

Q: Does that mean that you speak to all workers as if they are close friends and equals?

Peter Pfluger: I would estimate that 80 or 90 per cent of them, at all levels of the hierarchy, say "du" to each other. That is appropriate for a high-tech firm in any case. Many of the staff are highly qualified specialists. People respect each other for their professional competence rather than because of their place in the hierarchy. The friendly relations also come out of the early days of the firm. The founders were young and there were hardly any barriers between them. The friendly, familiar contacts were continued for a long time when the firm climbed to ten and then hundreds of staff. Today informal relations have become one of the cultural values of Phonak.

Q: What are other particularities that form part of the good enterprise culture of Phonak?

Peter Pfluger: For example, there are no checks on hours worked —

exactly as in a university or start-up company. That does not mean people work less. Quite the opposite: the demand for performance generally is much higher. Openness means that there are no protective walls. Everyone is continually on display and thus continually open to criticism. And it is unbelievably demanding to be ready to discuss everything all the time: walking 100 meters through the building and be addressed five times and have to find an answer each time.

Section C
Information Input and Group Discussion

1. The Success of New Products

Why do some new products succeed, bringing millions of dollars to innovative companies, while others fail, often with great losses? The answer is not simple, and certainly we cannot say that "good" products succeed while "bad" products fail. Many products that function well and seem to meet consumer needs have fallen by the wayside. Sometimes, virtually identical products exist in the market at the same time with one emerging as profitable while the other fails. McNeal Laboratories' Tylenol has become successful as an aspirin substitute, yet Bristol-Meyers entered the test market at about the same time with also a substitute for aspirin, which quickly failed.

The nature of the product is a factor in its success or failure, but the important point is the consumer's perception of the product's need-satisfying capability. Any new product conception should be aimed at meeting a customer need, and the introductory promotion should seek to communicate that need-satisfying quality and motivate the customer to try the product. Often, attitude change is involved, and, in the extreme, changes in lifestyle may be sought.

Here the company walks a tightrope. A new product is more likely to be successful if it represents a truly novel way of solving a customer problem, but this very newness, if carried too far, may ask the customer to learn new behavior patterns. The customer will make the change if the perceived benefit is sufficient, but inertia is strong and consumers will often not go to the effort that is required. During the late 1960s and early 1970s Bristol-Meyers met with new product failures that exemplify both of these problems. In 1967 and 1968 the company entered the market with a US $5,000,000 advertising campaign for Fact toothpaste, and a US $11,000,000 campaign to promote Resolve. Both products failed quickly, not because they didn't work or because there was no consumer need, but apparently because consumers just could see no reason to shift from an already satisfactory product to a different one that offers no new benefit.

To introduce a new product and succeed in producing profits in the market is not an easy task. It needs insightful investigation, careful planning and creative promoting. Otherwise one may fail, even if the new product functions well and seems to meet the needs of customers.

Questions for Discussion:

1. Why do some new products succeed, while others fail, though they all seem to meet the needs of customers?
2. What is the secret of introducing a new product successfully?
3. What lessons can we learn from the new product failures met by

Bristol-Meyers?

4. What is the core of marketing?

5. In introducing a new product, besides considering the needs of customers, what else should we take into account?

6. In your opinion, what is the most important factor in promoting a new product?

2. Business Ethics

Business ethics define how a company integrates core values — such as honesty, trust, respect, and fairness — into its policies, practices, and decision making. Business ethics also involve a company's compliance with legal standards and adherence to internal rules and regulations. As recently as a decade ago, business ethics consisted primarily of compliance-based, legally driven codes and training that outlined in detail what employees could or could not do with regard to areas such as conflict of interests or improper use of company assets.

Today, a growing number of companies are designing values-based, globally consistent programs that give employees a level of ethical understanding that allows them to make appropriate decisions, even when faced with new challenges. At the same time, the scope of business ethics has expanded to encompass a company's actions with regard not only to how it treats its employees and obeys the law, but also to the nature and quality of the relationships it wishes to have with stakeholders including shareholders, customers, business partners, suppliers, the community, the environment, indigenous peoples, and even future generations. European companies especially have embraced this expanded definition of ethics. Among the most important business ethics issues faced by companies are:

conflict of interests, financial and accounting integrity, corruption and bribery, consumer and employee privacy, ethical advertising and bioethics.

A series of ethics, governance, and accounting scandals in 2002 rocked the corporate world, damaged stock markets, and caused investors, regulators and others to question the assumption — fairly or unfairly — that most companies do the right thing most of the time. These scandals destroyed major companies and led to fines and prison terms for executives, providing a stark reminder of the importance of ethical business practice. In response, many corporations, especially in the US, took a serious look at strengthening their ethics programs.

Leadership companies have found that ethics policies and programs with some or all of the following elements go a long way toward building an ethical culture, reducing risk, and demonstrating a commitment to integrity: (1) strong, visible support from top management; (2) ensuring that ethical values (e. g. honesty), and not only performance values (e. g. innovation), figure prominently in mission statement and codes of conduct; (3) appointing ethics officers, creating innovative ethics training formats, and setting up ethics help lines; (4) carrying out ongoing evaluations/audits of ethical performance, with rewards and sanctions; (5) creating board ethics and/or corporate responsibility committees. Companies are also making a major push to globalize their ethics initiatives, aligning them with their core values in ways that are meaningful to a diverse workforce spread across dozens of countries.

Questions for Discussion:
1. What do business ethics refer to?
2. Why is it important for companies to design values-based,

globally consistent programs?

3. What effects do scandals in 2002 have on society?

4. Have you heard stories that some dishonest companies succeed, bringing in millions of dollars, while the honest ones fail, often with great losses? If yes, why do you think this happened?

5. What do you think of the business ethics in our country?

6. Why do you think it vital for organizations to conform to business ethics?

Section D
Sample Speech and Oral Practice

Part A Sample Speech

Basic Strategies for Marketing

Marketing is a creative process of meeting the customers' needs profitably. It focuses on the wants of consumers. It begins with first analyzing the preferences and demands of consumers and then producing goods that will satisfy them. There are only three marketing strategies needed to grow a business: (1) increase the number of customers, (2) increase the average transaction amount, and (3) increase the frequency of repurchase. Every marketing strategy should be measured by its ability to directly impact and improve upon each of these three factors. Increasing only one factor will produce linear business growth. Increasing all three factors will produce geometric business growth.

First, you should increase the number of customers. Increasing the total number of customers is the first step most business owners and managers take to grow their business. Losses can occur when inexperienced sales personnel are put in charge of designing and implementing a marketing program — investing corporate resources to find more customers. Executed correctly, basic marketing strategies cost-efficiently produce new prospects who are ready, willing and able to buy products or services. The main purpose of a marketing strategy is to give sales personnel prospects to convert into paying customers. Rewarding existing customers for referring new ones is one easy step business owners can take to increase their total number of customers.

Besides, you should increase the average transaction amount. Owners and managers spend most of their time operating their business and searching for new customers. They often overlook the customers they see regularly. These repeat customers are usually taken for granted and left to conduct entire transactions without ever being asked if they would like to buy more products or services. Complacency, expecting customers to buy a minimum amount of product or service without ever being asked to buy more, can be the undoing of a business. This attitude can eventually cause customers to spend less money. Customers who aren't continuously offered compelling reasons to keep buying more of the same products and services from one business will look for new reasons to buy from another. Cross-selling and upselling, systematically offering customers more value via additional products or services at the point of sale, are two simple steps business owners can take to increase their average transaction amount.

Finally, you should increase the frequency of repurchase. In an established business, an average customer purchasing pattern develops and (like the average transaction amount) is usually taken for granted and rarely improved upon. A customer's repeat business is earned by the business who gives the customer what they want.

Without having basic marketing strategies or processes for consistently offering customers more of what they want, repeat business is earned less frequently. Frequently communicating news and offers to past and present customers via telephone or mail generally increases their frequency of repurchase and is one more step owners can take to grow their business.

Part B Presentation Practice

Directions: *Talk on each of the following topics for at least five minutes. Be sure to make your points clear and logical with adequate supporting details.*

Topic 1: Honesty is the best policy for the success of a business.
Questions for reference:
1. Why do some dishonest businesses gain profits while the honest ones lose money?
2. If you were doing business, what strategies would you take to meet the customers' needs profitably?
3. Do you believe the saying that honesty is the best policy for the success of a business?

Topic 2: What makes a good manager?
Questions for reference:
1. Do you think a good manager is born or cultivated?
2. What qualities should a good manager have in doing business?
3. Do you think a person with an MBA degree is more likely to succeed in business than those who haven't?

Topic 3: The falling prices of electronic products

Questions for reference:

1. What do you think of the falling prices of electronic goods such as TV sets and air conditioners?
2. What are the possible advantages and disadvantages of price reduction for electronic goods and other commodities?
3. Is price reduction an effective means of promotion?

Part C   More Topics for Oral Practice

Directions: Based on the news reports, talk on each of the following topics for at least five minutes. Be sure to make your points clear and logical with adequate supporting details.

News Report 1:

On Thursday, July 21, 2005, the day Yuan was revalued, it closed at 8.11 Yuan per dollar. On that day, the Chinese officials announced that the Yuan will now be allowed to float against the dollar within a band of plus or minus 0.3 per cent of the previous day's closing.

Topic: *Do you think Chinese Yuan will continue to be revalued in the next decade?*

News Report 2:

Prosperity, obstacles and challenges existed side by side in China's foreign trade in the first half of 2005, the fourth year following the country's accession to the World Trade Organization. Already the world's third largest trader, China reported a robust growth in both exports and imports. Now that the three-year post-WTO transition period is ending, however, many domestic businesses have begun to feel the impact of competition and other challenges.

Topic: *Do you think the shift from quantity to quality is the best way to expand our foreign trade?*

News Report 3:

Some foreign countries blamed China for keeping a low exchange rate of Renminbi to boost its export, although China appreciated its currency by more than 2 per cent in July. The expansion of domestic demand is now the most efficient way to reduce trade surplus, Zhou Xiaochuan, China's central bank governor, was quoted by the *China Securities Journal* as saying on Wednesday.

Topic: *Do you think the expansion of domestic demand is the best way to reduce trade surplus? If yes, what strategies should we take to reach this goal?*

Part D Useful Expressions

export credit	出口信贷
export subsidy	出口津贴
dumping	倾销
special trade preference	特别贸易优惠
bonded warehouse	保税仓库
favorable balance of trade	贸易顺差
unfavorable balance of trade	贸易逆差
import quota	进口限额
free trade zone	自由贸易区
value of foreign trade	对外贸易值
value of international trade	国际贸易值

most-favored-nation treatment（MFNT）	最惠国待遇
customs duty	关税
net price	净价
stamp duty	印花税
return commission	回扣
port of shipment	装运港
discount/allowance	折扣
port of discharge	卸货港
wholesale price	批发价
import license	进口许可证
spot price	现货价格
export license	出口许可证
forward price	期货价格
current price/prevailing price	现行价格;时价
world/international market price	国际市场价格
fee on board（FOB）	离岸价;船上交货价
cost，insurance and freight（CIF）	到岸价（成本＋保险费价＋运费）

Unit Sixteen

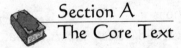

Section A
The Core Text

Shanghai 2010 World Expo

Shanghai to host the World Expo 2010 is the result of China's improved international status and increasing influence, the firm support from the Central Committee of the Communist Party of China (CPC), the State Council and people throughout China, and the wide recognition of the host city of Shanghai in the international community.

The 2010 World Exposition provides China with an important opportunity in the new century, which will greatly promote the building of a well-off society in the country, and **expedite** its socialist modernization drive. The Chinese government will make thorough preparations to provide all participants and their exhibits with complete facilities and satisfactory services, and pledges to give financial support to the World Expo Shanghai 2010. China is fully confident in, and capable of, hosting a most successful, splendid and unforgettable World Expo.

Since the adoption of the reform and opening up policy, China has turned into one of the most dynamic countries in the world with its economy rapidly growing, its comprehensive national strength remarkably **boosted** and people's living standard continuously improved.

Hosting the exposition is also a great event in Shanghai's efforts to build the city into a world center of economy, finance, trade and transportation, which will tremendously help push forward its modernization and internationalization drive, and the economic development of the Yangtze River triangle region and lower reaches. The World Expo Shanghai 2010 will surely become a landmark in the history of world expositions.

Seven companies from around the world have taken part in the international design competition organized by Shanghai for the Expo site. The design model adopted is based on the one submitted by a French company, while incorporating the strengths of other entries.

The Expo site in Shanghai is in the old city proper on one bank of the Huangpu River, covering an area of 5.4 square kilometers. The major exhibition sites with show halls as well as a conference building are planned to be distributed mainly on the east side of the river, which will occupy 240 hectares of land.

The selected site is on the verge of Shanghai's central region, making it possible for the Expo to take full advantage of the convenient transportation facilities as well as surrounding hotels and restaurants.

The Expo site design has **blended** the merits of eight schemes from different countries' celebrated companies. It's quite innovative, with an **elliptic** canal, flower bridge and green corridors. The canal will harmonize the Expo site construction and the development of the Huangpu River's banks.

As ties between nature and urban residents, green plant "corridors" vertical to the river will stretch from the river bank to the city's central region. In addition, a 400-to-500-meter flower bridge crossing the Huangpu River will be set up specially for sight-seeing pedestrians with a **connotation** of linking the past, present and future of Shanghai.

The World Expo can accelerate the city's development, especially the reconstruction of old urban districts. Shanghai will put the World Expo site in the old area of the city, with "Better City, Better Life" as the theme for her bid, which completely meets the IEB's demands and wishes.

The site selection can also help to display the various aspects of the theme, including multicultural integration, economic prosperity, scientific innovation and community construction in urban areas.

The areas on both sides of the Huangpu River are the key places for reconstruction over the next ten years. The World Expo will greatly propel its structural readjustment, old district reconstruction and ecological improvement in the riverbank areas. The site is expected to be a new landmark symbolizing the city's image.

According to the design plan, the canal, green "corridors" and buildings for meetings, exhibitions, entertainment and commerce will all be maintained for further use after the Expo, forming another cultural and commercial center.

Shanghai has spent 700 years developing from an obscure fishing village into the current charming metropolis. She is now yearning for the opportunity of holding the World Expo 2010, which will make her more beautiful and prosperous.

The total investment of Shanghai's "World Expo projects" is estimated at US $3 billion, of which 43 per cent will come from government sources, 36 per cent from companies and 21 per cent from banks. In terms of utilization, 58 per cent is **earmarked** for land acquisition (of existing industrial and residential property) and 42 per cent for construction (of facilities such as World Expo Village and World Expo Park).

   While Shanghai Municipal Financial Administration has
committed to be the guarantor of the 2010 Shanghai World Expo,
China's Ministry of Finance has pledged to provide the financial
guarantees. Financial support will be in the form of paying all kinds
of expenses **incurred** in the run-up to the Expo and before revenues
are realized by the organizer and operator.

Notes to the Text:

expedite	加速
boost	推进
blend	混合
elliptic	椭圆形的
connotation	内涵；寓意
earmark	指定(款项等的)用途
incur	招致

Understanding the Text:

1. What is the significance of Shanghai hosting the World Expo
   2010?
2. Who won the international design competition for the Expo
   site?
3. Where is the Expo site located? Why should we choose this
   place?
4. Where are the major exhibition sites with show halls and a
   conference building planned to be distributed?
5. What is the function of the canal?
6. Where is the flower bridge planned to be built?
7. Can you briefly describe the features of the design?

Section B
Sample Interview

The Theme of Shanghai Expo

Q: My first basic question is, what is the concept of the theme of Shanghai World Expo, "Better City, Better Life", and its sub-themes?

A: There are five sub-themes, urban cultural diversity, urban economic growth and prosperity, innovation of science and technology in urban context, remodeling of urban communities, and interaction between urban and rural areas.

Q: So, is there any stress on programs related to education? For Shanghai at the moment, what is being done in terms of education?

A: Yes, there are many areas that are important in planning urban education; they are not there in the five sub-themes but they are sort of gathered in the five sub-themes. For example, education, we can find it in the urban diversity sub-theme because we have quite a large increase in multicultural cities. We are concerned about how to create a melting pot through a good educational program, and how we can bring children of different nationalities together in a school to be educated on an equal basis so that they can get in touch with other cultures. These are all very challenging issues. Moreover, for the sub-theme of science and technology in urban context, education is the number one important thing. It is the source of innovation, power of the city.

Q: The Expo site is going to be constructed along the Huangpu River and I heard about the relocation of residents in that area, please tell me about this project.

A: In clearing the site for the Expo, we need to show the people that we are really concerned about their living conditions when they are relocated. So they are not just going to be told that they will have to leave and we will give them money, and that's it. We will build residential bases for these people because we need to show them that "Better City, Better Life" is implemented throughout the Expo — not just during the Expo, but also during the preparation stage and its aftermath. We will also make sure that their living standards, their health standards do not deteriorate, but will be improved. That's how we treat this theme at this stage.

A: Is the construction of the Expo site eco-friendly?

Q: The Expo site itself will be more like a showground of eco-friendly technology. Under this theme, it is more enjoyable and of more educational value to show people the most and best of urban living. And this has two aspects, one is the hard aspect and the other is the soft aspect. The hard aspect is about creating an eco-friendly city, i. e. reducing the conflict between man and nature and this is achieved through using all kinds of eco-friendly materials, eco-friendly energies, zero waste, things like that. Just as what people did and are still doing in Aichi, all the buildings on the site are going to disappear after the World Expo. That does not mean they'll go to the dustbin, but that they are going to be reused in a flexible way. Regarding the treatment of garbage in Aichi, they have many dustbins, each of which takes a different kind of waste so that waste can be easily sorted and go into the respective recycle bins. We'll do pretty much the same thing. But in five years' time the technology will be different and as people's concept of eco-friendliness is still changing, we will probably be one step further from Aichi. No one can know for sure what our lives will be like in five years' time.

Q: At Aichi Expo, there are Civic Participation Projects; are there going to be such similar concepts, or such kinds of projects at Shanghai Expo?

A: We are not yet there at this stage because now we are doing site clearance and we are about to design from the organizer's perspective what should be on the site, i. e. the themed pavilions, China Pavilion, and also the whole China area. I think the idea of citizens' participation will likely be incorporated into the agenda in one or two years' time when we are deeper into the design of the event. We have been paying attention to Aichi Expo a lot and we can see that citizens' participation is a very important element to Aichi Expo, so luckily we will try to learn from Aichi. It is also a benefit for a lot more people; they can come and see something while having a good time, not just going home without any deeper contact with the Expo event.

Q: I tried to find information on nonprofit organizations and NGOs (non-governmental organizations) in Shanghai, but I was not able to find many. Please tell me about them in Shanghai, in China.

A: There are very few, or they are not classified as NGOs or nonprofit organizations; they are more like community organizations. There are nonprofit organizations, but they all have a government background. They are not run for profit but are supported by the government. On the community basis there are lots of them, for example job centers, trading centers, women's health centers, and the like. There are actually quite a lot, but they are not very big ones covering the whole city.

Q: As for transportation, what facilities will be set up for access to the Expo?

A: There will be a few subway lines linked to the site. And also the meg-lev train — there is already a section built which will be extended to the Expo site. People can arrive at the airport and go directly into the site. It is a means of transportation and also a show of a future transportation mode, both for entertainment and practical purposes. The meg-lev train is extremely fast; it runs about 400km per hour. Since this is the first meg-lev train line in the world, we want to show people what a great transportation service they can enjoy. There will be shuttle buses as well, or more eco-friendly means of transportation that are battery-operated and can move people to and fro and also within the Expo site. The Expo site will be much bigger than that of Aichi's; it is quite long and therefore needs fast, secure and convenient transportation set up. Also for crossing the river, there will probably be tunnel buses.

Section C
Information Input and Group Discussion

1. Opportunities and Challenges to Shanghai

Shanghai's winning of the bid to host the World Expo 2010 is expected to fuel Shanghai's supersonic growth for at least the next eight years.

Among six billion habitants on the planet, five billion live in the developing world. However, during its 151 years of existence, the World Exposition has never been held in a developing country. Being the largest developing country, China has witnessed the fastest growth in the past 20 years. Shanghai wins the bid and there will be at least 70 million Chinese and foreign visitors to the exposition, which will mark an unprecedented scale in the history of the event.

With the World Expo, Shanghai will continue to be a leading city in China and an international economic, financial, trade and shipping centre in the near future. The Expo means great opportunities to all kinds of businesses, Chinese and foreign. Massive investments in infrastructural projects in the coming years are expected to again turn Shanghai into one of the largest construction sites in the world.

But what should not be like the 1990s is that more old houses and historical sites should be preserved instead of being demolished, so people coming to Shanghai in 2010 will get a sense of the city's rich history, not just a modern and futuristic un-Chinese city with dense high-rises. Concrete jungles built in some local neighborhoods in the past decade are definitely not what we want to present to the rest of the world. Shanghai should be an environmentally friendly city with great mass transport systems, not cramming its streets with highly promoted and polluting family cars.

Average Shanghainese, especially people who have to be relocated because of the Expo, should be able to afford their new apartments, when property prices are driven higher and higher. Senior citizens in this aging city should have a more colorful life. Shanghai residents should behave like citizens from a country with a long civilization. And local residents should have a bigger say in government decision making and in planning the city's future.

Shanghai is characteristic of an all-inclusive city where Eastern civilization and Western civilization meet and converge. Shanghai Expo will add splendor to the dialogue of civilizations and therefore contribute to the peace and prosperity of the world.

Shanghai Expo has an excellent theme — "Better City, Better Life." Urbanism is a common problem faced by all cities in the world. Participants will have much to share during Shanghai Expo. "Better City, Better Life" is definitely an excellent theme for

Shanghai to pursue. The heightened international attention on Shanghai in the years leading to the Expo makes this a great time for Shanghai to tackle its problems and Shanghai will become an even better city for people to live.

Questions for Discussion:

1. Shanghai has become the host of the World Expo 2010 and what does it mean to our country?
2. Being the host of the Expo, Shanghai has its opportunities as well as challenges. What are they respectively?
3. What do you think of the theme "Better City, Better Life" and what does it mean to you?
4. To host the World Expo, there will be a boom in infrastructure construction in Shanghai. Can you make some suggestions to this project?
5. Should we protect the old buildings in the city or just knock them down to make room for new ones?
6. Being a resident in Shanghai, what contributions can you make to this Expo?

2. Urban Traffic Management and Control

Traffic congestion is a growing problem in most urban areas of the world. It threatens the economic well-being of many towns and cities as well as affecting the quality of life of those who live and work there. Car ownership and use continues to grow strongly whilst public transport use continues to decline. A growing pressure on road space underlies an increasing public concern about the impact of road traffic on the environment, particularly in terms of air quality, but also of noise and visual intrusion.

In response to these problems, transport policy is evolving to a network management approach that makes best use of available road space and encompasses the management of all modes of transport and all travelers. Network management objectives can now include, in addition to minimizing vehicle delays and stops:

- giving priority to public transport and other selected vehicles;
- improving conditions for pedestrians, the disabled, cyclists and other vulnerable road users;
- reducing the impact of traffic on air quality;
- improving safety;
- restraining traffic in sensitive areas;
- improved congestion and demand management.

To provide the tools to support an efficient and effective network management and to facilitate competition in the supply of transport services, the Department for Transport (DFT) developed the UTMC (urban traffic management and control) concept. UTMC systems have been specifically developed to:

- create modular systems which are capable of expansion and interoperation with other systems;
- build on and integrate existing systems; increase competition in system supply, expansion and operation;
- maximize the flexibility to meet evolving needs and introduce new technology;
- provide quality information and the means to use this information, particularly to influence travelers;
- provide a means to move from existing systems to UTMC systems.

In short, the UTMC concept is the UK framework for the development and deployment of ITSs (Intelligent Transport Systems) in urban areas. It does not define policy requirements but supports the chosen policy and provides the means to develop systems that can make best use of local opportunities.

Questions for Discussion:

1. What do network management objectives include?
2. What have UTMC systems been developed for?
3. Are there any traffic problems in the city or town where you live? If yes, can you list some of these problems?
4. What are the possible causes of these problems?
5. Are there any steps taken by the local government to deal with the problems? If yes, what are they?
6. Compared with the steps mentioned in the passage, what steps do you think your government has taken are more effective? Less effective?
7. Can you make some suggestions to solve the traffic problems in the place where you live?

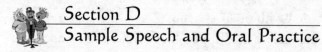

Section D
Sample Speech and Oral Practice

Part A   Sample Speech

Should We Pull Down Old Buildings?

There is always some controversy over whether old buildings in the city should be protected or they should give way to new ones. Though it is impossible and unacceptable to retain all the old architecture, it is important and urgent for us to keep some traditional old buildings.

It is true that old buildings sometimes run into conflict with social advancement. Appealing as it is in the eyes of business people, tearing down old architecture to make room for real estate development is not a wise idea in many ways.

The primary reason is that the old buildings, like our native language, form our cultural identity and keep a unique record of the history of our country. In this sense, the old buildings are considered very valuable as part of our culture. For instance, the traditional Chinese residence in Beijing, *Siheyuan*, was once seen as the remains of the Old World, and therefore was destroyed by the people. Until recently did the people and policy makers realize that it is inexcusable and stupid to have made such a terrible mistake because those old buildings, once gone, are not restorable. Besides, the economic value and aesthetic appeal of the old buildings are also getting people's attention.

Moreover, the old buildings, if planned and preserved properly, could coexist with modern real estate development. In France, the aged buildings have brought millions of dollars of revenue for the government and amazed thousands of tourists. Yet no one thinks the high-rise office and apartment buildings make the old architecture a sore of the eye. On the contrary, the new learn from the old, which makes them both more attractive.

We admit that not all old buildings should be treated the same way and some of them do need to be torn down for various reasons such as safety. However, we should not be too blind to see their value. If only practical factors are being considered, the country will be sorry for its loss in years to come.

As we have discussed, old buildings are part of a country's

history and are valuable in many ways. We should plan well and be wise enough to see their value. At the same time, we should also do our best to find ways to make the old and the new coexist in harmony.

Part B Presentation Practice

Directions: *Talk on each of the following topics for at least five minutes. Be sure to make your points clear and logical with adequate supporting details.*

Topic 1: Better city, better life
Questions for reference:

1. The theme of Shanghai Expo is "Better City, Better Life." How do you understand this theme?
2. In your opinion, what will a better city be like? Does it mean a city with dense high-rises and bright lights, or a city with environmental friendliness?
3. What does a better life mean to you? Can you illustrate it with your own views and examples?

Topic 2: Should we impose high taxes on car owners?
Questions for reference:

1. In order to control the number of cars, some governments impose high taxes on car owners. What do you think of this policy?
2. What are the possible advantages and disadvantages of this policy?
3. Do you have any other ideas to put the number of cars under control and improve urban traffic?
4. Do you have any other ideas to put the number of cars under

control to ease the burden of urban traffic while minimizing its effects on the car industry?

Topic 3: Call for new residence systems
Questions for reference:
1. The present registered permanent residence system has been used for decades and some people call for a new system. Do you think it is time for us to reform it?
2. If there were no such system as registered permanent residence, what would be the result in accordance with the population situation in China?
3. What are the possible benefits and drawbacks of this reform? Do you have any good ideas for the reform of the present residence system?

Part C   More Topics for Oral Practice

Directions: *Based on the news reports, talk on each of the following topics for at least five minutes. Be sure to make your points clear and logical with adequate supporting details.*

News Report 1:
    As the 2005 World Exposition in central Japan's Aichi Prefecture on Sunday staged a glorious finale of its 185-day run, the expo organizer will likely be rejoicing over the larger-than-expected turnout and profits, while also having to reflect upon failures such as long waiting lines at popular pavilions.
Topic: *What strategies can be taken to make Shanghai Expo successful in both profits and services?*

News Report 2:

A week after they were put on the market, not a single apartment has been sold in Shanghai's most expensive new housing project. The failure to shift even one of the flats has been taken as a further sign that Shanghai's once red-hot luxury property sector is continuing to cool off. No deals for Shanghai's costliest houses are a headache to real estate businesses.

Topic: *What is your speculation of Shanghai housing prices, rising, falling or remaining stable?*

News Report 3:

Despite a program of macroeconomic controls launched last year to slow down investment growth in some overheated sectors, China's 180 giant state firms are poised to record profits of more than 500 billion yuan (US $61.7 billion) in the first ten months of this year. Though the current dominance of state firms in some protected industries still guarantees their profit growth, a simple message the authorities need to drive home now is that only efficiency can help them stand on their own feet in a really open market.

Topic: *Why should we say that efficiency matters more than profits and what should be done to give full play to our economy?*

Part D   Useful Expressions

Better City, Better Life	城市让生活更美好
urban cultural diversity	城市多元文化的融合
urban economic growth and prosperity	城市经济的发展和繁荣
innovation of science and technology in urban context	城市科技的创新
remodeling of urban communities	城市社区的重塑
interaction between urban and rural areas	城市与乡村的互动